The Child Stealers

Center Point
Large Print

**This Large Print Book carries the
Seal of Approval of N.A.V.H.**

The Child Stealers

**Center Point
Large Print**

**This Large Print Book carries the
Seal of Approval of N.A.V.H.**

This Center Point Large Print edition
is published in the year 2007 by arrangement with
Golden West Literary Agency.

Copyright © 1973 by Fred Grove.

The text of this Large Print edition is unabridged. In other
aspects, this book may vary from the original edition. Printed in
Thailand. Set in 16-point Times New Roman type.

ISBN: 1-58547-899-7
ISBN 13: 978-1-58547-899-6

Library of Congress Cataloging-in-Publication Data

Grove, Fred.
    The child stealers / Fred Grove.--Center Point large print ed.
        p. cm.
    ISBN-13: 978-1-58547-899-6 (lib. bdg. : alk. paper)
        1. Large type books. I. Title.

PS3557.R7C47 2007
813'.54--dc22

2006028715

The Child Stealers

Fred Grove

CENTER POINT PUBLISHING
THORNDIKE, MAINE

men on the rear seat, one paunchy, booted, broad-hatted, his fleshy face the color of chopped beef, the other lank and dark, his skin stretched like a drumhead across bony features. He wore a seedy black suit and clutched a worn Bible. Across, facing backward, sat the woman, the eager boy by the window. Next to her was an Indian youth dressed like a white man.

A brief pause and the driver's yowl sent the teams trotting toward the river where a ferry nudged the red bank. Presently, as they began drifting across, the enthralled boy stood up to gaze at the broad swell of the Arkansas. When the ferry bumped the far bank and the boatmen slammed down the wooden ramp and tied fast to stumps, the drover shouted his charges up the cut, and shortly Roan felt the stage reach level footing.

Loosening the collar of his uniform, he leaned back on the horsehair cushions and closed his eyes. After the dull routine of Jefferson Barracks, it was good to be going back, though he had no inkling why. *Second Lieutenant Roan H. Kimball, Troop F, 5th Cavalry, will proceed without delay by stage to Fort Washita, Indian Territory. On his arrival, Lieutenant Kimball will report to the commanding officer for further orders.* He felt somewhat amused at all the mystery, a change of station from a section of the country torn by bitterest discord. Missouri newspapers teemed with inflammatory accounts. Proslavery and antislavery hotheads, capable of setting fires but incapable of putting them out, were manifestly in the saddle this uneasy summer

8

CHAPTER 1

Even at this early hour the settlement drowsed in the yellow June sun, shimmering beadlike on the coppery tongue of the sluggish river. Roan Kimball idled another moment within the miserly shade of the Fort Smith Hotel instead of crossing to the stage, flaunting its red, gold, and yellow colors, where hostlers were hitching up three teams of fresh horses. Above the fancifully painted floral design on the door panel, in black, read the coach's destination:

Colbert's Ferry
Indian Territory

He faced toward a sudden commotion. A four-passenger surrey rushing up, wheels dripping dust, a young woman and small boy descending, voicing shrill farewells to an elderly man, while the driver got down to hurry valises to the stage.

Curiously, out of boredom, Roan was watching when she turned to follow, clasping the hand of the coltish boy. He continued to observe her: the fair skin of the oval face beneath the flowered hat, the great arcs of the eyes; green, he thought. The two of them boarded, and then, as if on signal, the hotel disgorged its passengers. Roan, moving with them, tossed his bag in the rear boot.

The last to board, Roan wedged himself between two

7

To Dwain Schmidt,
in appreciation

of 1860, and he was relieved to return to more predictable country.

The coach struck a rock and bounced high and crashed down, swaying on leather thorough braces. Roan, dozing, opened his eyes on the young woman. An Army wife, no doubt. About twenty-six or eight, no older. Army women had a certain calm, a make-do learned from changing circumstances generally harsh, from following their men wherever ordered. Not that she held herself aloof; she did not, yet neither did she encourage familiarity. And he was right the first time: Her eyes were indeed quite green and quite large and luminous, and her mouth full and soft. Her hair, knotted at the back, had tints of brown and red and gold when she turned her head. For a moment he searched his mind, trying to picture the fortunate husband she was going to rejoin.

He was observing her too intently, for she noticed and, giving the slightest movement of her head, looked away at the passing scenery. The fleshy passenger, on Roan's left, was staring at her with bold appreciation. He kept staring until she, aware of his attention, gave him a brief, straight look, no more, and resumed her studious gazing beyond the window.

They were setting out on a rockless stretch now, the teams striding evenly, the leather springs conveying a hammocky swing to the stage. In the distance wooded hills rose like cool green mounds, and the early-summer sun had not yet scorched the lush grass.

"Mighty fetching country," the passenger on Roan's

right said. His voice was hoarse. Momentarily, it evoked for Roan the image of this gaunt, dark man tongue-lashing a scattering of loungers on some dusty street, or promising hell and damnation to the cowed congregation of a little country church.

"I've drove cattle up from Texas all through here plumb to Missouri," said the big man. "Indians always stole us blind. An Indian will steal anything."

The young Indian seemed to lift himself out of deep taciturnity. A keenness ran across his smooth face. "Drovers' herds graze Indian grass. Still, the drovers pay us nothing for passage through our country. It isn't right."

"Plenty grass," replied the drover, his dislike leaping out. "Where'd you learn that folderol? In some fool missionary school?"

"I knew that before I went East."

"Don't tell me that stealin' is right?"

"It is more accurate to state that when Indians take drovers' cattle, they are justly collecting due debts."

"Brothers," said the third man, above the rushing rumble of the coach, "remember our days are but as grass. That we flourish as flowers in the field, which ain't long. An' jest about as soon as the wind passes, we're gone, an' the place there knows us no more."

Grumbling, unappeased, the drover fell silent and hunched his shoulders. Along the young woman's full mouth appeared a faint smile.

The miles fell behind, and when a log stage station grew out of the distance beside the road, the driver drew up to change horses. "Ten minutes, folks," he called. "That don't mean an hour."

With a surprising quickness for a man so large, the drover descended first and prepared to hand the woman down, but she, sending the eager boy ahead, was out before the drover could assist her.

Affront tinged his face. He scrubbed a hand across his bearded mouth and strode for the station.

At boarding time, the men stood back while the woman and the boy took seats. Suddenly the drover, shouldering ahead of the Indian youth, climbed in and planted himself beside the woman. The Indian, unruffled, sat next to Roan. No one spoke, but Roan caught the poised calm rising to her face.

Some miles on where a narrow road snaked out of the woods, an Indian couple and three long-haired children waited beside an ancient mule-drawn wagon. The Indian man waved and the stage halted, and the Indian youth got out and took his one piece of baggage from the boot. Immediately the family surrounded him, all speaking at once. They were still there as the stage pulled out.

"Cherokees," observed the dark white man. "Better educated than most white folks around here."

Onward the coach rolled, rocking gently on the stretches of prairie, iron-rimmed wheels bouncing over the rough slopes. As the afternoon waned and the first purple of evening smeared the hillsides, the driver began to apply his long whip, racing the twilight. Dull lights shone ahead like jaundiced eyes.

Hauling up, the driver called, "Night stop."

Roan, out first on his side, lifted the sleepy boy to the ground, and when the woman took the step, he offered her a hand. Briefly as she brushed against him he caught the vaguely delightful scent of her and felt the lightness of her body; another moment and she was past him, murmuring, "Thank you, Lieutenant." The drover, clambering after her, glared Roan his displeasure and headed, grumbling, toward a long log building where the lights burned.

The driver, standing stiff-legged by the front wheel, growled after him, "If you don't like it, wait for the next stage."

Heavy of brow and gone to tallow, black hair down to his shoulders, the stationmaster emerged from the log house, thick hands pressed against his barrel-shaped middle. "Evening, folks. Supper is waiting. Two-bits apiece. Beds fifty cents. Ma'am, I'll show you and the boy to your room."

Roan's bed was a bunk and a frayed blanket draped over a bedtick supported by stout cords looped to wooden pegs on the sides. He dropped his valise and by candlelight inspected the ticking for bedbugs. To his surprise he found none. On the porch he washed in a tin basin on a bench, dried his hands on a roller towel, passed up the comb suspended from its rawhide string, and went along the porch to go in for supper.

A figure sat hunched there in gaunt caricature, the preacher-looking passenger. He was staring at the twilight-shrouded country. His bony face wore an

12

enduring look, a kind of brooding acceptance. Lost in thought, he was breathing softly into a harmonica, the notes without meaning to Roan. From inside flowed the hum and clatter of the dining room, and the aroma of fried meat and fresh bread and coffee. A sudden understanding went sharply through Roan. He stopped and said, "I'd like to ask you to have supper with me."

The man came erect and pulled on the front of his seedy black coat, hesitating, and Roan saw that he had pride.

"I mean as my guest," Roan said.

"Mighty generous of you."

"Not at all. We'd better get in there. This is a hungry bunch."

The man rose, smiling his acceptance, and thrust out a hand. "I'm obliged to you—uh—Colonel."

"Lieutenant—Second Lieutenant Kimball."

"Noah Loftus. The Reverend Loftus. Bound for Fort Washita and the evils thereof at the settlement of Hatsboro."

"Glad to know you, Reverend. No doubt you'll find plenty of soul-saving work there."

Supper turned out to be plates of hog and hominy and corn bread and bitter coffee, served by Indian girls so shy that they kept their dark eyes lowered as they waited on the long table, lighted by sputtering tallow candles. Flies circled stickily. There was scant talk. The Reverend Loftus filled his plate and fell to, an unbroken wolfishness to his appetite, as did the other men, pausing only to reach or pass when asked.

13

Across from Roan the Army wife, now and then speaking to her son, ate lightly, yet without squeamishness. And he drew a comparison, thinking back to another period in his life, then decided he was being unfair. Some women simply couldn't take the rough frontier and its lack of gentility; it wasn't in them. Valerie was like that. He blocked the thought to eat his supper and discovered that he was hungry. Moments later his eyes returned to the woman passenger, noting her high-necked gray traveling suit of some heavy, quality material, in which, by some feminine alchemy, she managed to look admirably cool and at ease within the banked heat of the dining room. After she and the boy had gone, the men left one by one. Loftus was still eating, and Roan tarried over his coffee. At last, Loftus pushed back. On the porch he spoke his thanks and, casting an eye about and lowering his voice, confided, "Reckon I'll rustle me a bed in the stage."

"A wise choice," Roan agreed. "Better than inside."

A little later, finishing his cigar as he strolled in the yard, Roan Kimball watched twilight vanish from the land, felt the faint coolness rising out of the southwest amid the tinkling of cowbells and the restless milling of the stage horses in the pole corrals.

He swung around at sight of the Army wife outlined against the track of outthrown light from the hotel part of the log building. A bulky figure rose from a bench, and although Roan could catch only the indistinct heaviness of a man's voice, he knew it was the drover. She passed briskly on, walking toward Roan, not

14

seeing him, he realized, because she was looking toward the road. She was almost upon him. To avoid startling her, he spoke a low, "Good evening."

She made an abrupt turn, at the same time drawing away. "Oh, it's you, Lieutenant," she said, relieved. "I thought I would take a walk while the driver entertains my son, Jamie, with blood-and-thunder stories."

"May I accompany you?"

"Is there danger?"

"Hardly, here." It was time that he presented himself. He did so.

"As you wish, *Mr.* Kimball."

She was in motion as she spoke, barely reaching his shoulder, taking even strides, a manner that conveyed an impression: the need of a person who often walked at night for respite, perhaps out of loneliness, or perhaps to assuage concealed unhappiness. He began to feel a curious and unexpected new assessment of her, for she had seemed so poised, so self-sustaining.

They strode in silence along the stage road for a hundred yards or more, the lanes of its hard-beaten trace lying dimly yellow under the climbing moon. It was she who turned to go back, and also to pause, questioning, "You're stationed at Fort Washita?"

"My new station."

"And your family will follow soon?" She was just making small talk, chatting in the pleasant way of an Army woman.

"I have no family."

"Oh—I'm sorry."

15

"Must I have one?"

"Why, yes," she replied positively, strolling slowly on. "Every young officer needs a wife and children."

"Then I've disappointed you. My former wife now lives in Philadelphia, which is her preference, and we have no children. She didn't like the Texas frontier, especially Fort Belknap."

"I'm sorry."

"Don't be. Army wives either choose to follow their husbands from one sun-baked post to another, else go back East. Mine chose the latter."

"You sound somewhat bitter."

"I don't mean to be. I don't blame her. She's happy. I'm happy. By now she's weathered the stigma of divorce. No doubt it has added to her attractiveness and she's considering marriage proposals from several men of means."

"You don't sound happy."

"But I am. I prefer the frontier to the deadening routine of the Eastern posts."

"So does my husband. We're joining him at Fort Washita after visiting relatives in Fort Smith. Possibly you've heard of him, Major Hamilton B. Thayer?"

"No, ma'am, I haven't. Guess I've been buried too long at Jefferson Barracks."

She was maintaining a certain interval between them as she chatted, a distance so marked that he had to smile at her absolute propriety.

"He's just been assigned. I'm Sara Thayer," she explained, continuing in that vein of cheerfulness he

16

liked. "We shall, of course, see you there, Mr. Kimball."

"I'll look forward to that, Mrs. Thayer."

She went on, again taking the night stroller's strides. When the low silhouette of the hotel and its dull squares of fawn light materialized ahead, he said, in apology, "I didn't mean to inflict a confessional upon you."

"You spoke the truth, which is far nobler than subtlety. Thank you for the escort, Mr. Kimball."

"My pleasure. Good night."

Following her with his eyes, he saw her reach the porch and step inside. This time no one rose to speak to her. He watched even after she had disappeared, left contemplative and a little moody, still remembering the pleasant sound of her voice, puzzled by the loneliness he had sensed in her. By chance, he mused, each had partly fulfilled a need of the other, because he was bitter, more than he had realized, and she likewise had sensed that.

"You—soldier," spoke a heavy voice close at his ear.

He jerked in time to see the blur of a man's shape, abruptly too close, and the still closer swiftness of that menace. Pain struck along Roan's jaw and he felt himself reeling sideways and saw the blackness of the ground rushing up. He fell and lay there a breath, stunned, before pushing up on one knee, now recognizing the drover.

"Don't let that purty blue uniform hold you down, soldier."

The tone made Roan furious. Shaking his throbbing

head, he heaved to his feet, swept by a joy that was pure and raw and violent. It hurled him forward, his suddenness catching the man off guard. Roan drove him back, landing a flurry of solid punches to the face; and when the drover recovered, Roan continued to bore in recklessly and they stood toe-to-toe, trading blows, until Roan switched his attack to the other's paunch and found a telltale softness there. Tenaciously the man gave ground. Of a sudden he broke clear, his ragged breathing sawing across to Roan, who charged him again to punish him around the middle.

The drover slumped down; his body thumped when he hit. Roan stared at him a long moment, swaying over him, reaching for wind. When the drover groaned and stirred, Roan turned to the watering trough by the corrals. There he stripped off his jacket and shirt and started scrubbing himself.

Just before dawn the passengers filed out to the stage. The Reverend Loftus stood by the coach's open door. With an awkward bow, he extended a hand to Sara Thayer and the sleep-dulled boy, followed inside, and took the vacant place beside her. Roan sat on the back seat. The drover, who had not taken breakfast, was not yet in sight, and the driver, his voice cranky overhead, called down, "Where's the other man?"

At that, a figure clumped heavily across from the hotel. It was the drover. He climbed aboard without greeting.

For some time they jolted through semidarkness. Roan's body, aching from the night's battering, tensed in protest whenever the stage slammed into ruts and shook itself free. As full daylight came, Roan saw Mrs. Thayer's eyes meet his. He clipped his head to her. Next she glanced at the drover's face, and back to Roan, her gaze lowered to his raw knuckles. A sudden flush prettied her cheeks, after which she found a point of avid interest in the countryside.

Loftus also read the signs, which prompted him to comment on the early heat. When no one replied, he became silent. The day passed with an unbroken sameness, the halts at the lonely stage stations and the changing of teams.

It wasn't dark when the driver, rolling through a rocky gap, drew rein before another station and hotel, this one a two-story affair. Horses lined the hitching rack. There was an air of coming and going. Roan could hear men's voices at the rear on the first floor.

A woman stood on the porch, her cynical eyes appraising as the passengers moved stiffly to the hotel. Curtly, she gestured upstairs to Mrs. Thayer and the boy, "Take the third room down the hall." Her attention shifting to Roan, she touched at her hair and a little sliver of interest roved across her brown face. A remote smile eased the set firmness of her heavy lips.

Roan finished his meal soon after Sara Thayer and her son left the dining room. Entering the hallway, he nearly bumped the woman innkeeper. She said, "There's a game and drinks in the north room," and waited him out, her deep-set eyes darkly gauging him. She had combed her thick hair, rouged her face and changed to a red dress, preparations that relieved the smudges of weariness beneath her eyes and disclosed a trace of prettiness. A discernment told him that she had been waiting there.

He nodded, not realizing until now that he was in a hurry, and that it showed.

"It's that woman." She drove her strident voice at him. "That genteel one that got off the stage with the kid. I saw her look at you. I saw you look at her. Her kind always galls me. Fancy manners an' all. Dressed up like they're goin' to a ten-o'clock ball. Always so damned proper, when behind it all they're just like any other woman."

He grinned down at her. "You're quick at judging people."

"Bein' quick is how I manage to run this hellhole. It's against the law to sell whiskey in Indian Territory. But if I didn't I couldn't stay in business, in which case the stage lines'd have nowhere to stop. But I don't sell to Indians. I got my limits." She moved in a step and he saw invitation and hope mixing behind the dark eyes. "Want that drink, soldier? It's on the house."

"Not now, thanks."

Her shoulders sagged and she leaned back, her heavy red lips turning slack, her animation fading. She said wearily, "It never changes. The kind a woman wants always has his eye on some sweet-smellin' creature that couldn't boil water over a forest fire." She shrugged. "Well, good luck, soldier. Don't walk into any ambushes."

As he started to go past her, a feeling plucked at him

and he swung slowly about. "You're still a pretty woman. Maybe you've forgotten that."

She was still standing there, her eyes turning darkly rich and soft in surprise, when he hurried out into the coolness of the yard, hearing behind him the raucous hum of voices down the hall. On the road a rider came hard to the hotel, flung down, and stomped inside. It was going to be a long and noisy night. Roan ground out his cigar and sensed that he was waiting, posted here by a mounting expectation of something happening again. It seemed unreal. Once more he stood in a moon-washed yard, and once more he saw her pause in the saffron light of a crude log doorway, a small figure but not slight, drifting out to commence her evening walk, taking even steps, her head uplifted to the gauzy webbing of the sky.

A sharpening excitement sent him across. He said, "It's a beautiful night," and she didn't seem startled at his voice.

"Yes—oh yes. Everything is so peaceful this time of evening, so restful."

"I fear the road's too rocky for much walking."

"I'd forgotten."

He hesitated. "There's a meadow beyond the corrals. May I suggest a stroll that way?"

Her reply was to turn slowly in that direction. He fell in alongside her. They reached the edge of the short-grassed meadow. She kept watching the sky.

"Are you happy tonight?" he asked.

"Of course. I'm very happy, Mr. Kimball."

21

"I wish I could believe you."

"Why should you think otherwise?" she asked curiously.

"Just something I feel, I guess. My apologies."

For a while there was only the swish of their feet through grass. "You needn't apologize. For, of course, you are mistaken. My husband has advanced fast. Everyone says he has even a brighter career ahead of him. If he has a fault as an officer, it's being a stickler for detail, for precision. You should see him drill an entire regiment. He's a West Pointer. Everyone—" Rather hastily she placed a hand to her mouth. The gesture, it reached him suddenly, of a woman catching herself unconsciously trying to convince herself of what she was saying, as if by extolling her husband's virtues she removed all her doubts. Already Roan was beginning to feel skeptical about Major Thayer.

"Has the Major served on the frontier before?" he asked.

"No. That's why he asked for Fort Washita. He's second in command. He says promotions are more rapid on the frontier."

"Depends," he said, falling into a reflective tone. "I know men who've been second lieutenants for years—men who will die second lieutenants. Very likely I'm one of them."

"At least a colonel, Mr. Kimball. At least." She was being gay about the slowness of promotions, something Valerie never had.

"I'll settle for that. It's time we turned back, Mrs.

Thayer. We're running out of meadow."

She had been strolling within an arm's length of him. As they retraced their way, she widened the interval between them, a reminder, he saw, of her propriety as a married woman. She said thoughtfully, "You are perceptive, Mr. Kimball. I grant you that." A certain tartness entered her voice. "Do you make a game of delving into the past of every unescorted female you meet and diagnosing her state of mind? Is it that you consider yourself an authority on women?"

"No man's an authority on women," he said. But he saw that he had touched her in a vulnerable spot.

"You are wiser than I thought," she said. Her mood receded, at once natural and unpretentious, like a young girl, he thought. An impulsiveness seemed to come over her. "Would you think me highly improper if I challenged you to a foot race?"

"Not at all. I'm used to racing ladies in the moonlight. How much head start do you want?"

"None." And, holding her skirts, she darted away. Her quickness took him by surprise. Stretching out, he caught up with a burst of speed, running beside her until she let up, uttering breathless, tomboyish cries of delight. Suddenly she stumbled. When he grabbed her arm to steady her, their momentum swung them together.

In a rush, he discovered the faint lavender scent of her hair at the same instant that he saw her upturned face and felt her breathlessness on his face, and the next he knew he was bending his head and kissing her and his arms were around her and he was aware of her smooth body beneath her traveling suit. In the beginning he felt no response whatever, though her lips, quiescent, were sweet and tender. But now he felt her lips part slightly and become giving and needful, as were his, conveying a distinct sensation, and he could feel her fingers lightly drumming his shoulders as he held her. Another instant and she tore herself abruptly back.

He couldn't understand himself, or the odd-sounding voice that he recognized as his own. "I ought to say I'm sorry—but I'm not, though I do apologize. I do indeed. I ask your pardon." He waited for her outburst, which did not come.

"How straightforward you are." She sounded puzzled rather than angry.

"We'd better go in," he said.

She moved carefully to the edge of the meadow, to stand still and thoughtful again, her back turned to him. "You needn't apologize. The fault was mine."

"No one's to blame. It just happened—that's all."

She turned a trifle, speaking over her shoulder. "You are very honest, Mr. Kimball. Therefore, I must be honest too. I'm not sorry."

She hurried toward the hotel. Reaching the porch, she slackened step and looked back. Brief as her movement was, he saw it, and long after she had gone in, that glimpse of her stood framed in his mind as his thinking turned inward and he wondered at himself tonight. Everything had an imaginary yet headlong quality, unfelt before.

CHAPTER 2

Swaying through a wilderness of shaggy hills crowning and dipping like the gentle washings of a serene sea, the coach charged down the widening road and climbed another rounded rise. Below, Roan saw a village of neat buildings along the road, beyond them the high shapes of barracks occupying the south and west sides of a broad rectangle.

"Fort Washita's just ahead," he said, leaning forward.

At once the boy yelled and sprang to the window. In that space of time Sara Thayer stiffened, a kind of acceptance naked behind her eyes, knitting her even brows, quickly controlled as she regained her pleasant composure.

Roan leaned back, his mind steadying on last night: *It didn't happen at all. I just imagined it. It was fantasy. Moonlight and soft wind.* Whatever, he had best forget it.

A small crowd awaited the stage's arrival. The boy, Jamie, watching at the window, shrieked and a man wearing the twin gold leaves of a major waved and stepped forward, stiffly erect. Opening the door, the boy jumped down and ran to him. Mrs. Thayer descended at that moment. Roan saw her pause. It was the briefest of hesitations, and then she lifted her face and the Major kissed her and they turned to a cottage on the east side of the parade ground, while a striker looked after the baggage.

The Reverend Loftus craned his long neck about and inquired of the striker. "Brother, where is the settlement of Hatsboro?"

"Follow the road past the west barracks yonder."

"I'm obliged to you." And, extending his bony hand to Roan, "Blessed be them folks that sow beside all waters," he strode across the parade, taking the long, militant steps of a reformer, his craggy face set like the prow of a ship breasting the stiff winds of sin.

The crowd soon thinned, and when the stage rolled out for Colbert's Ferry on Red River, the drover the lone passenger, Roan took his baggage and made for the adjutant's office. That harried individual, a first lieutenant, assisted by two toiling clerks, looked up from the knoll of paperwork before him, his face set in long-suffering futility, unrelieved at sight of a new second lieutenant.

"Well, sir," he said, making a motion of tidying up his desk, returning Roan's salute with a flick of his forefinger.

"Second Lieutenant Roan Kimball, 5th Cavalry, reporting for duty from Jefferson Barracks."

"At ease, Lieutenant. Looks like another inspiring day. Ten men from Troop D in the guardhouse for getting soused on rotgut obtained at the quaint little settlement of Hatsboro. Mrs. Agee's spaniel has been breaking down Mrs. Carter's hollyhocks again. Some dumbjohn left the gate open at C Troop's corral last night, which, needless to say, leaves Troop C temporarily unhorsed. Which, needless to say further, does not leave the Old Man in the most jovial of moods." He exhaled vigorously, ruffling the ends of his carrot-colored mustache, puffing out his jowls, and rose to take Roan's orders. He began to read. As he finished, his bored manner faded. He regarded Roan sharply, a sort of sizing up. "You'll find the Bachelor Officers' Quarters on the north side. I'm Barney Lucans." He shook hands. "Better see the Old Man within the hour. Meanwhile, welcome to the dubious climes of Fort Washita."

Skirting the parade ground, Roan took notice of a long line of wagons unloading at the commissary building beyond the south barracks. By now two troops drilled on the quadrangle. The bark of officers reached him crisply on the wind, which seemed ever present on this long-running ridge, and he saw the faces of the men—some Irish and German, young and not so young, all sun-darkened, some burning with wildness, some seasoned to robotlike reactions. From down the west slope sounded the unbroken hammering of farriers' tools. Not one farrier, but many. He was moving into something. He could sense it. A campaign was in the air. He quickened step.

At two o'clock Roan was standing before the post commander, Colonel W. H. Emory, a rake-lean man past middle age, eyes impatient, a harassed-looking man whose thinning crop of gray whiskers clung to the slopes of his long jaws and outthrust chin like stubborn hillside growth. After the usual amenities, he said, "Be seated, Mr. Kimball. I was expecting an older man. But

27

maybe you'll do. There's much to go over. I realize you're wondering about your sudden change of station here. I shall come to that in due order. First, I want to know more about your duty on the Texas frontier. I'll be frank. If it isn't up to what I require and expect, you'll be shuttling right back to Jeff Barracks by return stage."

"God forbid, Colonel."

Emory smiled sympathetically. "I must agree about such duty at a recruit center." From a stack of papers he selected two sheets. "Your service record shows you enlisted at Fort McKavett in Forty-nine at the age of twenty. Saw duty on the Mexican border. Made sergeant at Fort Clark." He seemed to hunt for something. "Here it is. At Fort Belknap, you were placed in charge of the Tonkawa scouts." He snorted his annoyance. "Damn an incomplete report. How long in charge?"

"Two years, sir."

"What happened? Why did it terminate?"

"Well, sir, Colonel McDivitt was trying to break up the traffic in captives carried on by some Kiowas and Comanches and renegade whites. In fact, more whites than it is generally known. We scouted from Belknap to the New Mexico line, and north from Belknap to the Canadian River. We broke up several bands, including some Kiowa-Apaches with captives; busted up a couple of Comanchero outfits in on the game. Rescued some women and children, about half of them stolen in Old Mexico." Roan chewed on his lower lip, concen-

28

trating to summon the pertinent details, at the same time distracted, as if only half of him were attentive, his mind turning to Valerie. Because it was at Belknap that something ended between them, absolute and irrecoverable, and one day when he returned she had gone.

"Commendable," Emory said. "Go on."

"However, we never quite seemed to root out the head of the game. It was like chasing the wind. Then Colonel McDivitt was transferred back East and the scouts disbanded. Belknap was then reduced from four to two troops and I found myself headed for Jefferson Barracks."

"A common story these days," said Emory. "Our western posts are being neglected. The people in Washington are concerned with the growing crisis between North and South—and I'm afraid it's going to worsen." He turned a page and drove a critical eye at Roan. "You're much too modest for your own good, Mr. Kimball. Much too general when I want specific details. If I were depending on your account, you'd be catching that eastbound stage in the morning."

"I don't understand, sir."

"Fortunately, I have been in communication with Colonel McDivitt, now stationed at Baltimore. He says you operate well with Indians. That in the field you become almost like an Indian yourself. That through your efforts with the Tonkawas, twenty-three captive women and children were returned to their families. A considerable achievement. It led to your commission

29

the first year at Belknap. A battlefield promotion, in effect."

And leave back East, where I met her and we got married, Roan mused wryly. When she thought I was a leader of men, before she moved to Belknap and began accusing me of nursing a pack of dirty savages and becoming as a savage myself.

Emory was growing impatient. "For your information, the situation hasn't improved. The Texans are howling for protection, and I don't blame them. Unfortunately, there's much at stake besides those poor innocents being taken captive and held for ransom as high as fifteen hundred dollars a head." He snapped up from his chair and paced to the window, there to pivot around, his voice imparting an ominous quality:

"If we can break up this despicable game in human suffering, there's a chance we can hold Texas for the Union. For as certain as there's sunlight, the country's hell-bent for war." Roan started to speak. A glare from Emory silenced him. "Now, Mr. Kimball, I'm going to reveal something to you the Eastern newspapers haven't got wind of yet. Early last spring I sent a force up Red River to go after the wild bands in their own bailiwick. Our people found them, all right. We got badly mauled. Also lost a hundred head of horses and a fieldpiece complete with caisson and a wagonload of ammunition."

"A fieldpiece?"

"Don't contradict me, young sir. Yes, damnation—a

30

fieldpiece. A twelve-pound Napoleon. They even had the gall to shell our camp one night."

"I've never heard of Indians serving an artillery piece."

"You have now."

"Sounds like Army deserters. We found white men— three, in fact—living with Indians in Tule Canyon."

Emory's taut face wore a curious air. "What disposition did you make of them?"

"Well, sir," said Roan matter-of-factly, "I had them hanged."

"On the grounds of guilt by association?"

"No, sir. Because they were more cruel than the Indians, the captives told us. Because of how they'd mistreated the women. That's putting it politely."

"I see," said Emory, nodding grim approval.

"I still don't understand what you require of me, sir."

"Don't try to anticipate me, Mr. Kimball," Emory rebuked, returning to his chair, steepling his hands, rubbing the tip of a forefinger on the point of his chin. "You said you never got to the head of matters out there. Suggests something, doesn't it?"

"I can think of several possibilities."

"Number one—that you weren't looking in the right places."

"Sir, that's a mighty large world out there."

"Let me pin it down for you, Lieutenant. On the basis of reliable reports from Texas informants and friendly Indians, I have reason to believe the main source of this damnable traffic is not—I repeat, is NOT—on the Texas side of the Red at all."

"You mean it's on this side?"

"Exactly."

"About where?"

"That's where you enter the picture, Mr. Kimball. This time we're going to establish an outpost, a cantonment, on the upper Red to intercept raiding parties headed for Texas. Major Hamilton Thayer will be in command. You will scout from there. Meanwhile, here, you are relieved of all garrison duties. Your time will be amply taken up working with the scouts."

"Tonkawas?"

"Osages this time."

Roan felt the sharp bite of disagreement. "Why Osages?"

"They know the country as well as any Kiowa or Comanche or Tonkawa. Twice a year they leave their villages in eastern Indian Territory and Kansas to go on buffalo hunts. Furthermore, they are traditional enemies of the Kiowas and Comaches."

"Still—" Roan objected. He was developing a strong distaste for the whole reckless adventure.

"You'll understand my choice better when you see the Osages we're enrolling as scouts and arming the same as troopers. They'll arrive any day now."

An old weariness besieged Roan. "So we all go scouting. Don't expect miracles, Colonel."

"I don't expect miracles, but I shall expect results." He had the glittery look of a barracks gambler about to play his trump card at the opportune moment. "Our informants tell us the main figure in this monstrous business in captives is one Sanaco or Scar-Arm. Ever hear of him?"

"Can't say I have."

"You have now. He's our man."

"What is he? Indian or white or both?"

"That's up to you to find out. He shifts around a good deal. Your orders are to get him. Dead or alive." Emory leaned back and Roan recognized the familiar sign of dismissal. "Meanwhile, you will outfit yourself and become acquainted with the Osages, at the same time placing yourself directly under the command of Major Thayer. There is, however, an exception." All at once he seemed apologetic. "When in the field, you will be acting under the verbal orders I've just given you—get Sanaco."

Roan stirred uneasily. "What if my orders conflict with Major Thayer's?"

"Use your own judgment and take the consequences. Frankly, I don't give a damn what it takes so long as you get Sanaco."

"Does Major Thayer know that?"

"He will. Good day, Mr. Kimball."

As Roan came out, a civilian was hurrying up the porch steps to the headquarters entrance. An orderly intercepted the man, who spoke jerkily. "Any word today?"

The trooper shifted uncomfortably.

"I know I was here yesterday. Any word come in

33

today?" He was a sad-faced little man, wearing a patched coat too large for his stooped frame. Shadows darkened his light-colored eyes. He looked all bones and nerves as he continued to pull at his ragged beard.

Emory's clear voice intervened from within. "Orderly, show Mr. Dawkins in."

Expectation lighted the haggard face. Dawkins removed his hat and hurried inside.

"Comes here every day," the trooper explained to Roan, "for news of his little girl."

"Taken captive?"

"Uh-huh. Happened down in Montague County some time ago."

Angling across to his one-room quarters, Roan could feel a familiar frustration. No doubt Major Thayer, who had never fought Indians, would call him in shortly to inform him as to the proper procedure when handling Indian scouts. Later it would be where to scout and when. Emory's almost whimsical preference for Osages was also questionable, when Tonkawas were within two days' ride to the southwest. And as for Sanaco, all Emory had given him was a name.

He removed shirt and boots and stretched out on his bunk, hands locked behind his head. Closing his eyes, he could see Emory's jaw muscles working as he spoke; and Thayer's stiffly erect figure as he met the stage, and Sara Thayer's hesitation, momentary but nevertheless real. A breeze, wandering through the quarters, cooled his face and brow. His senses reeled. Off on the parade ground he heard the soft shuffling of

34

horses—were those unshod hoofs?—and, in moments, the dim undertone of voices. Those sounds faded.

In his next consciousness someone was calling his name and he was breaking out of slumber and sitting upright, staring openmouthed at the tallest and broadest Indian of his experience. A round-faced Indian, diabolically painted, whose head was shaved save for a quivering roached scalp lock that made him loom even taller. A small Latin cross of silver hung from a silver chain around his neck.

Roan, blinking, got up to stand beside the bunk, just as Adjutant Lucans, displaying a devilish grin, stepped from behind the Indian and said, "This is Curly Wolf, headman of the Osage scouts. Curly for short, he says, being a modest fellow. They all just rode in. He wants to meet you."

"Ho," the Osage greeted, eyes smiling. "I have come."

"Ho," Roan said, and held out his hand and felt it being taken, not in the crushing grip of the white man, but in the Indian way he remembered: ceremoniously, his hand pressed, and pumped up and down. He looked up into the sculpture of a massive face, streaked black and yellow, and thick lips and Roman nose and friendly, tobacco-brown eyes. The Indian was naked to the waist, a blanket wrapped around his loins, and when he turned his head in good humor toward Lucans, Roan's gaze went to the Osage's head, to the remnant of his scalp lock, which looked like a buffalo tail, and to which he had fastened a turkey

35

gobbler's beard and the hair of a deer's tail.

"Curly's all painted, ready for war," Lucans explained, tongue-in-cheek. "I told him it'd be a few days yet."

"It'll come soon enough."

"Although Curly's a mission school Indian, he tells me he follows the old ways. Enjoys war. Particularly dotes on fighting the Comanches and Kiowas and Cheyennes."

"Can't say he picks on pushovers," Roan said, and he faced the Osage. "Curly, I'm glad you've come."

Curly stepped closer, his eyes cutting at Roan. He said, "Ho," and placed hands on the points of Roan's shoulders, squeezing, feeling, examining, and worked his hands down Roan's upper arms and forearms and wrists. "Ho-hoooo," he said, approving, stepping clear, and his vigorous nodding set his scalp lock to quivering again.

"Guess you've passed the first test," Lucans observed.

"Hope he doesn't try that on Major Thayer," Roan said.

"It is good," the Osage said, the broad smile splitting his face again. "We will take many horses together."

"Yes. We will take many horses. After you make camp and eat, we will talk about this thing."

"He'll be camped northeast of the post," Lucans explained. "Commissary's taking care of their rations. Lord knows it'll take plenty. Come on, Curly. Let's go see the Big Chief of the Soldier Houses."

36

Curly made the sign for friend, linking his index fingers, and Roan also made the sign. Turning to go, Curly towered a head and a half taller than Lucans, who paused as if detained by an afterthought. "By the way, Major Thayer wants you to work up some drills for the scouts."

"Drills!' Roan echoed. "Hell, they're not enlisting—they're hired scouts—and they don't need cavalry drills."

"My friend, you don't know Major Thayer. He said *drills*."

A moment later there was a rap outside and Lucans craned his neck inside. "Forgot to tell you, Kimball. It's protocol here for an arriving bachelor officer to treat his brother bachelors to a gentleman's evening."

"A gentleman's evening? I believe that calls for the sutler's best brand of swamp tonic."

"Ah, I see that you've experienced similar initiations," Lucans said, wagging his head sagely.

"We'll have it here after taps."

Lucans grinned fiendishly. "Lieutenant, you speak the language of our post," and, bowing with ceremony, he departed.

They came trooping in after taps, expectancy lighting their tanned young faces. A handful of the usual West Pointers whom Roan had met at mess. Only one officer was older than Roan, First Lieutenant Charles Jernigan, unsmiling, his hair ash-colored, parade-ground erect, high-strung, apart from the friendly banter. But under his indifferent surface, Roan sensed a bitter discontent. At the moment he was exchanging a desultory conversation with Adjutant Lucans. Roan recognized the old signs: a fortyish first lieutenant, sour as hell because he wasn't a captain or more. Roan hardly blamed him.

Young Cass Povich came over, all sly grin. "Hear you're quite an Indian fighter, Kimball."

"I hadn't heard," said Roan, grinning back. "Let me pour you another drink, Lieutenant."

"Don't mind if you do."

Povich downed his whiskey in one gargantuan swallow, reddened, let go a long breath and said a bit thickly, "Tomorrow, I become Post Engineer. A distinct honor, sir. My first duty, Adjutant Lucans has informed me, is the proper and immediate disposal of untold tons of horse manure. Also, I am to superintend the daily removal of all post garbage. Another distinct honor."

"You have my congratulations," Roan said, straight of face. "I received the same high honors at Fort Belknap."

Povich slapped him across the back. "Brothers all— bound by the mystic bond of the horse corrals." He swiped at the ends of his cultivated blond mustache and leaned in, his manner confidential. "Yet events of importance do occur around here, Kimball. You should see the white captives the Indians bring in, when the ransom money changes hands."

Although his voice was pitched low, Roan saw heads turning. The voices stilled. Jernigan said, "Aren't you

38

exaggerating, Povich? We've had only two exchanges of captives within the past six months. Delawares brought them in. A third is in the mill."

"Delawares?" Roan said. "Not Comanches, not Kiowas?"

"Delawares—the great Entrepreneurs of the Plains," Povich said dryly.

Jernigan threw him an overbearing look. "What Mr. Povich means is that Delawares often serve as go-betweens, though it's gross exaggeration to infer we have a thriving exchange of captives." An expression of self-righteousness colored his face. "I wish to God there were more, so more captives could be freed. In the two instances, we contacted the families in Texas. In each case, a member of the unfortunate family came here. I myself, as legal adviser to Colonel Emory, helped them work out the ransom arrangements."

Povich was helping himself to another whiskey. "Arrangements up to fifteen hundred dollars. Nice little profit for somebody."

"Whatever the price," Jernigan snapped, "wouldn't you say that's preferable to letting children grow up in savagery?"

"I dunno." Povich waved his glass. "You never hear the young Indians complaining."

Jernigan threw up his hands. "Your remarks verge on adolescence, unbefitting an officer and gentleman."

Povich's sweat-filmed face went crimson. "Care to back that up sometime with sabers?"

"Stop it—" barked Lucans, striding between them.

"There'll be no more of that, gentlemen. Mr. Povich, I shall discreetly fail to recall that you said that. All of you do the same." He trailed his gaze over them. Jernigan appeared more withdrawn than before. Povich, with a sheepish gesture, pulled at his mustache. "It's time to go," said Lucans.

There was a stretch of silence, and then Jernigan, very erect, walked out. The rest shook hands with Roan and left. All but Povich, who hung back, murmuring, "The Delawares always have a white renegade or two along. Tell me, why do they come as far as Washita? Why not Forts Belknap or Richardson or Griffin? More money changes hands here—that's why . . . Sorry I spoiled your party, Kimball."

"You didn't. Good night and good luck."

CHAPTER 3

Soon after dinner an orderly found Roan. "Compliments of Major Thayer. Says for you to mount up with him at headquarters to inspect the Osage camp."

Riding that way minutes later, Roan thought of the Tonkawa scouts' village on the Salt Fork of the Brazos at inspection time. Of prim officers noting the scouts' seeming shiftlessness, their lack of order, the smoky, mesquite-wood campfires, the smell of meat cooking, the flies, the numerous dogs, the children running free. The Major was in for some surprises today if he expected a camp along military lines.

40

"It's time we reached an understanding with the Osages," Thayer said crisply, coming to the point. "They must know what is expected of them as a military unit under my command."

"Indian scouts follow pretty much the same pattern, Major. They look disorganized, yet they see things a white man often overlooks, and they'll cover double the ground a good trooper will. On the whole, I've found them dependable."

Major Thayer had a clipped fashion of speaking, a formality that complemented his stiff-backed erectness; and heavy, sandy brows like layers of bedrock overhanging the gray chambers of his eyes, and a prominent nose, high-ridged and broad, which filled out Roan's impression of a stolid mien—unswerving, unimaginative, cold. He brushed at his severely trimmed mustache. "I have yet to be convinced of that, Mr. Kimball. As for organization, I propose to do something about that before we leave for upriver."

Roan left the matter there. Why argue with a man whose mind followed the narrow limitations of a drill book? Jernigan joined them. The Lieutenant nodded coolly to Roan and attached himself to Thayer's side as they rode off, chatting amiably with the Major about the forthcoming campaign, the effect of weather on grain-fed mounts, the delay over the lack of wagons. Roan began to sense a tiredness as he recognized the familiar approach: a junior officer, an older one at that, posturing for the commander's benefit; even worse, Jernigan was going on the expedition.

41

The Osage camp, several miles northeast of the post, occupied an oak-studded knoll. The Indians, some twenty of them, had constructed brush arbors and there were also some canvas tipis, which represented the hasty efforts of the commissary officer. But canvas tipis were as ovens in June and it was under the cool arbors where the Osages reclined and cooked. They had, Roan saw, dug a pit and over it hung strips of beef on a framework of bows. The aroma of sizzling beef reached him, making his mouth juices run. Beyond, a few youths loose-herded the Osage horses.

The arriving officers were ignored, apparently unnoticed. Thayer threw a censuring look about. "Their horses aren't picketed and they don't even see us. Scouts should be alert at all times."

"They see us, all right," Roan said. "That's Curly, their headman, getting up now."

Thayer halted, sniffing, just as Roan breathed the new smell. A boiled smell. A stink, yet tantalizing as Roan remembered.

"What in God's name is that foul stench?" Thayer demanded.

Roan masked a smile. "They're boiling tripe. Tastes far better than it smells. I've been told the French eat it too."

Curly, a stately figure advancing to greet them, resembled a magnificent, half-naked giant. The tiny silver cross on the silver chain around his neck glistened against his copper-hued skin. He smiled broadly (he was always smiling, Roan thought), minus his

42

gobbler-beard-deer-tail roach, which left only the shaved crest of his scalp lock on top and the remnant of his hair hanging like a buffalo's tail.

"Major Thayer . . . Lieutenant Jernigan," said Roan. "This is Curly Wolf. He's a great warrior. A great taker of horses."

"Ho," said Curly, nodding at the obvious flattery, slanting his great head at them, enjoying every word.

"This man," Roan said, inclining his head at Thayer, "is the chief of the pony soldiers who will go up Red River to build a soldier house. You and your friends will scout for him."

When the officers dismounted, Curly took Thayer's hand and pumped it again and again, and repeated the ceremony with Jernigan, while they stood ill at ease; sweeping his hand toward the arbors, his dark brown eyes warmly generous, he invited them to share his camp.

Stronger, Roan breathed the unmistakable smell; now he saw the cooking pots. At Curly's invitation, the officers sat on a seal-brown buffalo robe, Roan at one side, Major Thayer between him and Jernigan.

And, softly, the Osage said, *"Tomsheh,"* his tone relishing, and pointed at the pots. So that's what the Osages call it, Roan said to himself, feeling an old hunger.

Thayer jerked an eyebrow at Roan. "He's inviting us to eat with them," Roan explained. "We'll insult them if we don't. Tomsheh is a great delicacy."

"I can think of a more suitable term."

43

Taking a sharpened twig, Curly speared a light-colored, spongelike piece and, eyes anticipating, handed meat and twig to Thayer, who, hesitating, accepted gingerly. In turn, Curly passed servings to Jernigan and Roan. All the remembered succulence returned to Roan as he bit into the rubbery mass and forgot the smell and settled down to gorging himself.

Thayer was nibbling uncertainly, his nostrils pinched. Jernigan dropped his piece on the robe and stabbed it again. The Osages, who had not helped themselves until their guests were served, pretended not to notice; to stare was bad Indian manners. After a few tentative bites, Thayer put down his portion, rose and went out to inspect the Indian horses. Jernigan, in relief, and ever the imitator, seized on the moment to follow the Major.

Finished, Roan stepped over to a pot and stabbed another piece, catching Curly's approval as he did, and returned to the robe. When that portion was consumed, he said to his host:

"These white men are new to your ways. They will learn in time."

Curly shook his head in denial. "The Heavy Brows will never accept our ways. We must accept theirs." He turned to watch the officers. "Some scouts rode west early this morning. Two riders are coming to Soldier House on Hill. One white man. One Indian."

"A Kiowa?"

"No Crazy-Knife. This one's trader-Delaware. Ho. I

was going to tell your chief over there this new thing."

"I'll tell him."

"Say nothing. He will rush out there, this new chief. Scare our game away. Let this white man and trader-Delaware come in. They will."

"When?"

"Tomorrow. Be like the coyote. Wait." Curly's thick hands were slick with grease. He wiped them up and down his deep chest. "I have had talk with Big Soldier House Chief. He says your tongue is straight. My tongue is straight too. We are friends." Roan rocked back and forth, nodding, knowing he must not interrupt. The Osage went on after a moment. "Soldier House Chief told me this captive thing is bad." Curly began playing with the cross. "Jesus people at mission school when I was young boy told me it was bad. I believed them. I believe Soldier House Chief. He says he wants to rub out this bad thing, this evil."

"It is bad," Roan said. "I need you and your warrior friends to help me find the man who causes much of this bad thing, this making slaves of women and children. I am told his name is Sanaco and also that he is called Scar-Arm. Ever hear of him?"

The dark eyes changed, amused. "Would buffalo herd bull hear wolf snapping at his heels?"

"Ever see Sanaco?"

Curly smiled, not only with his lips but also his eyes. "No, my friend. But one of our tribal elders saw Sanaco when Sanaco was go-between when Osages held a Kiowa prisoner. It is said Sanaco's left arm is

45

bad-scarred. The scars go round and round his arm, from a rope twisted there when a wild horse dragged him."

"Is Sanaco Kiowa or Comanche?"

"Ho. I do not know this thing. My elder saw him in the dark of a lodge."

"When did he see Sanaco's scarred arm?"

"My elder saw nothing. It is the Kiowas who say Sanaco's arm is bad-scarred."

"Did Sanaco talk Osage that time?"

"He spoke Kiowa. Some say he is half Kiowa, half Mexican. Some say he is half Comanche, half white. Who knows? I would take his hair, if I could, because I am Osage. Because Sanaco, whatever he is, runs with the Cut-Knives. Always my people have fought the Cut-Knives and Snakes, the Comanches." He became thoughtful. "We will look for Sanaco. That is good. Maybe we find him. Maybe big fight. Ho."

The two officers were coming back. Thayer's crisp voice, couched in complaint, reached Roan. "Fine horses. Better than we're mounted." Roan winced as Thayer, coming under the arbor, addressed Curly, his manner suggesting the Osage had little authority. "I want you to start training your warriors to fight like ours."

The Osage's smile thinned. "We are Osages. We fight like Osages. Not like pony soldiers, who ride in lines. Like buffalo going to water."

Thayer, brushing at his mustache, chose a more cour-teous approach. "We will talk about that," and he made

46

a covering effort of tolerance. "Thank you for the feast."

"We Osages feed everybody who comes to our camp," Curly said, his smile further strained. "Even our enemies, if they come in peace."

No word was said as the officers mounted and trotted off. Finally, Roan said, "It's easy to underestimate Indian scouts, Major."

"They are slovenly heathens. They loll about camp like hogs."

"Curly went to mission school. He's a Christian. That's one reason why he wants to help stop this traffic in captives. And I daresay the Osages know more about what's going on beyond the post than we do at this moment."

A lofty look seemed to heighten Thayer's posture in the saddle. "You're on the verge of impertinence, Mr. Kimball. When I need your opinion, I'll ask for it." A keenness moved in the cold depths of the gray eyes. "Do I detect a hidden meaning behind what you just said?"

Damn the man, he missed nothing. Were he Colonel McDivitt and the circumstances different, Roan would tell him what Curly's scouts had learned. "You do not," Roan heard himself replying.

"Then let there be none, if you are to remain in my command."

"Colonel Emory told me that when I'm in the field I act under his verbal orders."

"Which are?" There was the lofty look again, enough

to make a man long to smash it.

"To get Sanaco at almost any cost."

"We'll see about that, just as we shall see about sprucing up your pack of gut-eating Osages. Now, Mr. Kimball, before I dismiss you for the remainder of the day, you can think about organizing the scouts into some remote semblance of order."

Riding next morning to the Osage camp, Roan found only the few herd youths. Where, he signed, are the warriors? A boy gestured west.

Roan cut more rapid signs: When will they return?

The fluent brown hands, slim and graceful, formed the sign for sun going down. Roan, understanding, turned back for the post, riding along in a preoccupied state.

The racket of a horse rolled toward him, shattering his musing. A woman rider. She wore a blue riding habit. A plume slanted from her ridiculously small, stylish hat. And then, seeing the liquid of Sara Thayer's eyes, and caught up in surprise, he became aware of a powerful but controlled pleasure.

She recognized him at the same moment, and he saw again the warm cheerfulness of her. Looking past her, he asked, "Where's your escort, Mrs. Thayer?"

"I have none. I'm supposed to be riding near the post."

"It isn't wise, even in peaceful Chickasaw country, for a woman to ride alone."

"Unwise, though you say the country is peaceful? You are being overly gallant, Mr. Kimball." After those first moments of recognition, he saw that she had thrown a cloak of stiff propriety about herself.

"I'm thinking of the riffraff whites who plague Indian country. Hatsboro's full of them."

"You sound like my husband."

"I agree with him on that point, Mrs. Thayer."

She shrugged her annoyance.

By now the rising sun was bearing down and the wind had a breathless heat, and he sensed an impasse in their conversation. "There's a spring nearby," he said, unable to think of more to say. "Would you like a drink before I escort you back?"

She shrugged again.

Roan guided them to a grove of oaks. Dismounting and reaching up to hand her down from the sidesaddle, he saw her brief uncertainty. She came down lightly, no more than brushing him, after which each stood well back, like careful-eyed adversaries, it occurred to him.

"You are very correct, Mr. Kimball."

"I respect you." Now, he sensed, was the time to show her to the spring. Now. Instead, he said, "I have met your husband."

"And . . . you have formed an opinion?"

"None as yet."

She gave him a dubious scrutiny. "Are you trying to spare my feelings?"

"I've served under all sorts of officers."

"I see, you evade, which is just as well," and her agitation sudden, "because I've come here—because of

49

what I just said—I hope you don't think me a bad wife. I try not to be."

"Bad? I think you're very human. A very fine woman."

Her stiffness vanished, leaving her face quite warm and appealing. "It's good to talk to someone. Someone who listens. Someone you can trust."

"A man needs that as well, Mrs. Thayer."

She canted her head just slightly at him, a provocative motion. "Must you keep being so formal? You may call me Sara, if you wish."

"Thank you. My name's Roan, if you remember?"

"I remember." She offered an impulsive gloved hand. "So it's settled."

"Fair enough," he nodded, conscious that he was smiling, and that he still held her hand.

It was happening. He could feel it funneling up through him as he got the lavender scent of her, the clean-woman scent of her, dashing away the final vestige of parlor-bred formality between them. Her face was close and he leaned down and touched his lips to hers, lightly, more of a caress than a kiss, and straightened up and released her. Although he hadn't felt her lips respond, they were warm and tender and she had not turned away from him.

"Did that just happen too, Roan?"

"I think not. I intended it."

"You're being honest again." A sigh escaped her. Her liveliness went out. "I must go."

"Yes, you must."

50

She was mounted before she spoke again. "Don't let me burden you, Roan."

"You're not."

"I don't want to make you unhappy."

"You're not."

She reined to leave, and he followed. "No," she said emphatically. "It wouldn't do for you to be seen escorting me. I would receive the direst accusations."

She rein-quirted her horse, which jumped, startled, and bounded away galloping.

Roan followed her with his eyes until a crease in the browning prairie enveloped horse and rider. He continued to watch her until she appeared on the far slope, the horse traveling at a dead run, until he saw her no more.

All hurry left him. He felt strangely tranquil and content, fulfilled, powerfully alive, and he was thinking how odd that he felt no guilt, none whatever. Was it because she had been denied happiness for so long?

Sometime later, he was passing headquarters when Adjutant Lucans rushed out and hailed him:

"Where the hell have you been? The Old Man wants you front and center. Something's up. We've got company."

"What do you mean."

"No time to explain. Get in there."

Roan noted the horses tied at the rail. Two wild-looking bay mustangs, small and wiry, their dark manes and tails uncommonly long.

Entering, he picked up Colonel Emory's distinct

51

voice. ". . . Let's proceed, gentlemen. Major Thayer . . . Lieutenant Jernigan . . . I believe you're acquainted with Mr. Samuel Dawkins."

Roan found a bench. Major Thayer sat on Emory's right, his manner coldly official. Lieutenant Jernigan was a stiff shape on Thayer's right, his air imitative of the Major's. Dawkins, the Texas civilian, occupied a chair to Emory's left. He seemed alone even here, and Roan felt a pang of sympathy for this distressed man. Dawkins kept twisting at his hat brim. With his extreme gauntness, he gave the effect of a gnarled mesquite, shaped by wind and sun and cold. His thinly bearded face was lined about the mouth. His light blue eyes, shadowed with fatigue, darkened further as he fixed his attention on the Indian and white man seated before the Colonel.

The Indian's dress put Roan in mind of a poor white, brownish linsey-woolsey pants and faded gray shirt, his hair hacked short. He stared at the floor, apparently without interest, but there was a keenness about him, a total awareness of what was going on.

The white man, in his late thirties or older, had a mass of wavy reddish hair hanging to his shoulders. A man wholly in charge of himself, assured and strong-willed, his arms folded, his massive head thrown back. His nose stood out, effecting a solidness to his bold face, and his bluish eyes were alert and piercing. A thickset man wearing fringed buckskins, who had yet a softness as betrayed in the puffiness of his bush-bearded face, and the full, pinkish lips and the plump hands.

Now the white man stood and cleared his throat. "Well, Colonel—we found the little Dawkins girl. All we need is the money to buy her from the Kiowas. Just two days' ride from here."

Dawkins lurched forward to rise, but sat back as Emory asked, "Mr. Shell, how do you know she is the little Dawkins child?"

"Says she is. Says her name's Emily. Says she was captured nigh two years ago. She's bright as a new dollar."

"Does she know where she was taken?"

"All she knows is it was near Red River."

"Give us her description."

"Blue eyes. Yellow hair."

"How old is she?"

"About nine or ten, I'd say."

"Mr. Shell, many little girls have blue eyes and yellow hair. And an intelligent child might say anything to get out of an Indian camp."

Shell's face underwent a subtle change. His next words had a pouncing quality. "She's got a scar on her left cheekbone."

Dawkins jumped up, shouting, "That's my Emily! She got the scar when she fell on an ax when she was four." He was pleading to Shell, "Is it kinda crescent-shaped, high up on her cheekbone?" dabbing at his own cheekbone as he spoke so hopefully.

"That it is," Shell assured him, and he appeared to draw further on his memory, squinting his eyelids, squinching his mouth. "It's dim by now. Man'd hardly notice it first glance, but it's there, just like you say."

53

"God bless you, Mr. Shell. God bless you."

Slumping, Dawkins buried his face in his hands, audibly weeping and shoulders shaking. Emory, for a long moment, favored him his sympathy, and then, as if he must go on, he asked:

"Do you have other proof, Mr. Shell?"

"Figured you'd ask that. Don't blame you. Man's got to be certain." With a positiveness that spelled triumph, Shell drew something from his shirt pocket, and as he laid it on the Colonel's desk, Roan heard a faint metallic rattle.

Dawkins sprang catlike to the desk and snatched up the object, his eyes wildly devouring as he turned it over in his trembling fingers. "It's the locket—my wife's—Margaret's. Her name is carved on the back right here. Emily played with it a lot. Had it on the day they took her." He fell to weeping again, which continued unbroken for some moments. A deep pull of breath and he took a grip on himself and said, around, "Excuse me, gentlemen. It's just been a long time, is all, and now Mr. Shell and his Delaware friend have found her for me."

"Call me Kirk," said Shell, displaying his advantage for the officers to see. "I don't like fancy handles."

"How much do the Kiowas want?" Emory broke in.

Shell hooked a thumb in his belt and looked the Colonel in the eye. "Fifteen hundred dollars—every cent in Mex dollars."

"The last time it was twelve hundred," Emory said, suspiciously. "Why the big jump?"

54

"The Kiowas are stirred up. They lost a heap of warriors last season."

Pleadingly, and for Shell alone, Dawkins said, "Three months ago when I first came here, I thought I could raise some money. I went back to Texas and offered my stock for sale. It didn't bring much. I put up my farm for sale—nobody wanted it. Land's cheap. Well—" he said, a desperation hanging in his voice.

For the first time, Shell lost some of his cocksureness. He turned to Emory, who said, "Fifteen hundred dollars is a great deal of money on the frontier. So's a thousand or five hundred."

"I don't set the ransom prices. The Indians do. You know that."

"Where is the child at this moment?"

"Right now," said Shell, cocking his head, "little Emily Dawkins is in a Kiowa camp about two days' ride from here."

"I asked *where*. Not *about where*."

"That I won't tell you," Shell flung back, unafraid. "Reason is you might go bustin' in there an' get little Emily killed. Them Kiowas'd cut her throat the very second they caught sight of you horse soldiers pilin' into their camp." His bargainer's voice took an unbudging stand. "It'll take fifteen hundred to break her out of there."

"By chance," Emory asked quietly, "would it be Sanaco's camp?"

"Sanaco? Who's that?" Shell sounded just mildly puzzled.

55

"Perhaps it's only a name."

"Look here, Colonel. I been all over hell an' back on the lookout for this little girl—now you throw dust in my face. Sanaco? Who the hell's Sanaco? Wasn't everything up to snuff time before, when I brought in the little Parham boy?"

"Judge Parham is a man of considerable means. Mr. Dawkins is a poor farmer."

"If you doubt my word, Colonel, I remind you I've been a government scout. Was for years. Saw my last service at Fort Belknap back in Fifty-seven."

"All I'm saying is that fifteen hundred is out of reason in this case. Mr. Dawkins can't raise it. Few people on the frontier could. It's impossible. By the way, what do *you* get out of this, Mr. Shell?"

Shell smiled, an ingratiating smile, and turned his head left to right for all to see that he wasn't flustered. "It's whatever I can bargain outa them red devils later. What I get, I earn. A man takes his chances. I don't hold onto my topknot by bein' meek."

"I'd give you ten times what the Kiowas do if I had it," Dawkins said fervently.

"Thank you kindly, Mr. Dawkins," Shell replied, bowing his head at him. "You're a fair man."

Colonel Emory slapped the edge of his desk. "We've reached a dead end, gentlemen. Any suggestions, Major Thayer?"

"Yes—that Shell persuade the Kiowas to reduce the ransom."

"They won't budge," the white man vowed. "It's fif-

56

teen hundred or they keep the kid."

"Lieutenant Jernigan?" Emory asked.

"Ask them to cut it to twelve hundred," the Lieutenant suggested, quick to ape the Major.

"Twelve's as big a mountain as fifteen," Dawkins said, downcast.

Roan was standing, struggling with a baffled wrongness, when Emory noticed him. "What is it, Mr. Kimball?"

"I suggest we cool Mr. Shell's heels in the guardhouse until he's ready to parley again with the Kiowas."

Shell heaved about, angry astonishment jutting into his face. "What's your say in this, soldier?"

"That won't be necessary, I'm sure," said Emory, his voice meaningful. "Mr. Shell's a reasonable man." And, facing Shell: "Since you sympathize with Mr. Dawkins' plight, you will parley again with the Kiowas, won't you, as a humane gesture?"

Shell matched him, stare for stare. "Let's get down on the taw line, Colonel. What's your offer?"

"Mr. Dawkins is prepared to offer one thousand dollars in gold and silver."

Dawkins strained forward, speechless, and glanced sharply at the post commander.

"One thousand," Shell repeated, belittling, scornful, his mouth dropping. "They won't swap for that little dab." The Delaware had cocked his head, Roan saw, absorbing every word.

"That *little dab* of which you speak," Emory said,

"happens to represent a fortune to a good many men. I want you to parley on that figure." And with a persuasive relaxation of tone: "You can for the life of a helpless child."

Emory had him boxed and Shell, knowing it, forced an expansive smile. "They won't budge a hair, but I'll try. You'll see I'm right. I know Kiowas."

"Thank you, Mr. Shell. We are indeed grateful. We'll expect you back in a few days."

As if to balance Emory's decorum, Shell reached for his hat on the floor, bowed, murmured, "Gentlemen," and with a jerking of his head for the Indian, filed outside, the Delaware following.

Dawkins' puzzled voice came hushed. "Colonel, I told you five hundred is every cent I can raise."

"I know you did," said Emory, placing a hand on Dawkins' shoulder. "We'll manage something. Throw in some horses. Take up a collection. Let's see what Shell brings back."

"Why wait?" Thayer snapped. "I suggest we trail Shell to the Kiowa camp and attack."

"Attack?" Emory jerked around. "And risk having the Indians kill the child? Shell's right about that."

An instant flush stained Thayer's neck and face. He became more erect and said no more, swallowing his affront. Emory, seeing, said in understanding, "Think nothing of it, Major. That's what we'd all like to do."

Roan was standing in the doorway, watching Shell and the Delaware riding westward across the parade, bound for the downslope road that wound through the woods to Hatsboro, when Emory addressed him curiously:

"What made you speak up, Mr. Kimball?"

"One thing. Shell wasn't at Belknap in Fifty-seven. I know—I was."

CHAPTER 4

The group dispersed. Roan found Dawkins on the porch, alone, gazing sightlessly across the rectangle, a faraway expression saddening his eyes.

"You've had a long wait," Roan said. "Now you're getting close."

"Maybe. My Emily was six years, four months and eleven days old when they took her. Her birthday is April 7. A springtime child. I keep wondering how she looks. How much she's grown. If she'd even know me."

"She will. Mind telling me how it happened?"

Dawkins shortened his looking, studying a place on the floor, working the tip of his left boot there. "I was gone with my two boys over to a neighbor's. Not far. Indians came. Killed Margaret—my wife—took Emily. That's it in a nutshell."

"All Indians?"

Dawkins slung about, shaken out of his brooding. "My God, man, who else?"

"Some white men figure in this game as well, Mr. Dawkins. It's a lucrative business at times. I've seen how it works. Else why do men like Shell show up?"

"Mr. Shell's my friend. He's trying to help." The Texan's eyes flashed. "I won't have you talking him down."

"I'm not questioning what you say. I thought maybe a neighbor had seen whites among the raiders."

"Nobody saw 'em."

"After that, what?"

"I followed their tracks. Lost the sign at Red River."

"An old story," Roan nodded.

As if another man's understanding drew him out, Dawkins fell into a reminiscent mood. He said he was from Middle Tennessee; had brought his family down the Texas Road through Indian Territory into Texas. At the home of a sister near Bonham his sons awaited him, and he guessed they were tired of his absences long ago. He talked of lean crops, he talked of horses, and he talked of the stand Texas was likely to take if war came with the North.

Roan listened until Dawkins took his leave, a solitary figure trudging head down toward his wagon, parked south of the commissary building.

Roan rode to his quarters, unable to free his mind of the man's plight. Meantime, detached from garrison duties and the Osages out on scout, he was on his own. His eyes chanced on his saddlebags, packed with rations for scouting. An impulse grew. Taking a blanket off his bunk and picking up the saddlebags, he left quarters. In moments he was saddling for Hatsboro, down the long slope past the westside stone barracks, following the narrow road squeezing into the thick woods, there to lose itself to the naked eye until Roan entered the oak timber.

To his right he could hear firing on the target range. A strident voice would shout a command, followed by a volley of carbine fire. The road, snaking on through the dense woods, took him to a spring dug out in a draw. Dismounting, he watered his mount and climbed to the saddle.

Walking his horse up the other side of the draw, he flinched from the burr of a bullet and heard the report of the weapon. Instinct drove him spurring off the road into the oaks, where he flung about searching, expecting some fool recruit to come blundering down the draw. Was that a carbine? He wasn't certain. What he wanted to think, he realized, was that it was a stray shot from the firing range, yet the severe voice of experience told him otherwise. As he watched he heard, barely audible, the padded movements of a horse, dimly, slowly, now faster, moving away on the soft leaf mold of the woods.

He charged up the V of the draw, raising a clatter of gravel and loose earth, up a crumbling red bank and into the timber, where rank upon rank of oaks forced him to rein down. He picked his way, hearing no horse racket to follow, and when he broke out of the woods and saw the target range and the huddle of troopers a hundred yards away, no horseman was in sight.

Lieutenant Cass Povich, young, bluff, zealous, impatient, bored, was striding up and down behind a kneeling platoon, his voice like a grindstone. "You dumbjohns—you squeeze the trigger—you don't jerk it. And the targets are there," pointing west, "not there or there," making sweeping gestures north and south. Seeing Roan, he barked an "at ease" and came forward, welcoming the respite.

"Lord help us if we ever get in an Indian fight," he lamented, striking a doleful face. "These recruits couldn't hit a bull at three paces with a handful of shelled corn. What brings you out, Kimball? Aren't all officers in the Major's expedition excused from garrison duties? Or are you checking up on me? I did so well as Post Engineer, they're taking me along."

"Did a rider just come this way?"

"Not by us, though one could have skirted through the woods unseen. Something up?"

"Maybe."

"You look more than maybe. You're mad as hell. What is it?"

"Somebody took a shot at me on the Hatsboro road."

Povich covered his face with both hands and groaned. "Maybe it came from here. I tell you no living thing is safe within four hundred yards."

Roan was gazing back toward the timber. "Couldn't have. It came from up the draw—that's north. I heard a horse going off."

"Which way?"

"North, I thought. Then east."

"By God," Povich muttered, outraged.

"Just forget it for the present, will you? No word to

62

anyone. Good day now and good shooting."

Povich was right. He was angry, and it stayed with him as he scouted back to the road and turned for Hatsboro. After several hundred yards, the woods fell away to a stump-studded clearing that spread ugly ruin on both flanks of the road, made uglier by the clutter of log shacks and piles of refuse, chiefly bottles and kegs and barrels. The unmistakable signs of what troopers called a "hog ranch," always just beyond the post boundary and therefore untouchable. Every Army post he'd known had one. Offering dreadful whiskey, various gambling games in which a trooper seldom won, unless to lure him on to a more certain parting of his pay of thirteen to sixteen dollars per month, depending on years of service, and the company of jaded women. The pretension of a sign—SALOON & GEN. MDSE.— drew his attention to a log building longer than the others. He scanned the horses tied there, recognized none, and it passed through his mind that he had expected to find the mustangs of Shell and the Delaware.

As he entered, the discordant notes of a harmonica drifted to him from around the far corner of the building. Behind the bar a white man, portly and keen of eye, glanced up and stiffened apprehensively. "Come right in, Lieutenant. Everything's nice and quiet."

"At this hour, sure."

"None of your boys around here."

"Don't worry. They'll report soon after taps."

Two young mixed-bloods sat drinking at a table. In a back room he could hear cards being shuffled and the chatter of voices.

"Have a drink on the house, Lieutenant."

Roan shook his head no, his eyes drawn to a sharp-featured woman leaving the back room. Behind her tired eyes stood an embedded boredom. She leaned her slack body against the end of the bar, and Roan saw her, with effort, try to call back some dormant spark of gaiety. "Better have a drink, soldier."

Roan ignored her to ask the barkeep, "Anybody ride through here the last few minutes from the east?"

"I can't see everything that goes up and down that road."

"You didn't answer the question. Did you see anybody?"

"Not a soul."

Roan considered him with dry humor, thinking why would he reply otherwise?

"Better have that drink, soldier," the woman insisted.

Irritated, the man turned on her. "Go back and watch the game, Maud. See if they need anything."

"If you ask me, this whole shebang needs something. Like a graveyard after Fort Smith. Another poker hand like that last one an' Barney'll be down to his socks."

Enough, Roan thought, and moved past the woman to the back room and looked inside upon three white men, all strangers, around a table, one listlessly dealing cards. He turned away and was outside when the tuneless notes of the harmonica reached him once more, causing him to heel about on a vague recognition. Rounding the corner, he nearly stumbled on a figure that seemed all arms and shank, folded like the bars of a cot against the log wall. Despite the hat slanting over the brow and the hands cupping the harmonica, Roan knew him.

"Hello, Reverend."

The Reverend Noah Loftus rose cranelike and shook hands. "It's the Colonel."

"Lieutenant. How's your work going here?"

"Poorly. Poorly. Nobody to preach to much during the day, an' them at night won't listen, they're so full of wildcat whiskey. What can I do for you?"

"Looking for a man that rode by here or stopped in the last few minutes, coming from the east."

"Saw one fellow half hour or so ago. A soldier."

"Did you notice his rank?"

Loftus looked sheepish. "You know me, I can't tell a general from a private. I didn't pay him much mind, though I'd know him again if I saw him. Anyhow, he rode to that cabin over there. Stayed a bit an' rode off east."

"Take the road?"

"Reckon I was dozin' a little about then."

"Which cabin?"

"One right over there by the edge of the woods where them two's comin' out right now."

Roan followed Loftus' gaze, recognizing Shell and his Delaware counterpart as they mounted and cut rapidly for the road. With a glance, Shell dismissed

65

Loftus and Roan. A second, longer appraisal, and he rode straight at them, his eyes bulging at sight of Roan, calling, "You don't give up, do you, soldier?"

"Not till you deliver the little Dawkins girl."

"Butt in, Army style, you'll spoil the game. I'm the only white man the Kiowas trust."

"Same as Colonel McDivitt trusted you at Fort Belknap?"

"What's in your craw, soldier?"

"You didn't scout for McDivitt in Fifty-seven. I was at Belknap in charge of the Tonkawa scouts. I never saw you or heard your name."

The pinkish face flamed. "Still don't savvy, do you, soldier? I'm the only white man that knows where that poor little girl is." A self-effacement seeped into his tone. "I'm the one man that can free her."

"I just hope you do that."

"I will—if the goddamned Army'll stay out of it." Shell quirted his horse away, the Delaware following.

Watching them disappear where the westward road left the clearing and bent into the timber, Roan brooded, "How long you aim to fight this hellhole, Reverend?"

"Long as I got breath. The Lord's work never comes on a silver platter."

"You won't save many souls here. If you starve out, come to the post. If I'm not there, look up Adjutant Lucans."

"Thank you, brother." Loftus was watching the westward road also. "You aim to follow them two?"

66

"If you can joust the devil here, I can grapple with him in the wilderness."

When Roan rounded the bend in the road, he met only the emptiness of the serpentine traces coiling like an outflung rope down to the river, the Washita. He rode into the rusty-brown water, summertime-low, and when he crossed he saw the wet hoofprints darkening the reddish bank. Reaching the first rise above the river, he spotted the dust of two riders.

He fell back, content to keep them in sight, no closer.

As the afternoon burned on and the country leveled off and the road diminished to a faint trail, he realized that the two were veering northwest, no longer hurrying, and presently there wasn't even a trail.

The sun hung low when he lost sight of them, gone like dust tails, as if the vastness had swallowed them at a single gulp and now mocked him to find them. Haze closed upon rolling hills that clumps of thick timber made dark and shaggy.

He was beginning to feel unwise, a victim of his own rashness, when a horse nickered. Into a clot of oaks he hastened. Hearing no more, he tied up and worked forward to the crown of a timbered hill and saw, below, tents and horses and moving figures.

An increasing puzzlement nettled him while he watched a man lead three horses to a creek and back. Where were the Indians, the fearsome Kiowas Shell had kept harping about, flourishing their presence before Colonel Emory like a threat of doom? More horses were led to water, more figures moved about the camp.

A brush of sound rubbed faintly at Roan's senses and died on the wind as he concentrated his interest on the camp's activity, which struck him as unusual this latening hour when cooking fires should be licking high.

Again the brushing, as subtle as a whisper, ran prickling up his spine and neck, and he felt uneasy, the nakedness of not being alone, a sound obscure no more, and behind him, and he hurled himself about flat with his carbine cocked at the ready.

Less than a picket rope's length away, the silver cross dangling incongruously below the bronze trunk of his neck, crouched the immense shape of Curly Wolf, smiling hugely. "Ho," he said. "You have coyote ears. Next time I will touch you before you can turn."

Roan swung the carbine aside, set the hammer on safety. "Next time you'd better speak up. Come over here. Tell me about this camp."

The Osage, pleased with himself, pressed down alongside Roan. "They moved camp here this morning."

"Where are your scouts?"

"All around. We saw the Heavy Brow and the trader-Delaware ride in."

"What else have you seen?"

"A little white girl."

"How many Heavy Brows?"

"No more Heavy Brows."

68

"They look like Heavy Brows from here."

Disdain roughed the Osage's voice. "They're off-breeds dressed like mixed-bloods."

"Off-breeds?"

"Not Osages."

"If they're not Osages, they're off-breeds? Is that it?" And the Osage nodded, unable to see the humor of Roan's question.

Still, there was much down there that puzzled Roan, and he asked, "Where are the Crazy-Knives? The Heavy Brow who just rode in calls himself Shell. He told the Soldier House Chief there was a big Crazy-Knife camp where the little girl is held."

"He lied. No Crazy-Knives here." Curly drew a circle in the air. "We been all around. No Crazy-Knives."

"The Heavy Brow Shell is trying to sell the little white girl. When the Soldier House Chief said Shell's price was too high, Shell said he would talk again with the Crazy-Knives, who own the little girl."

"He lied. No Crazy-Knives."

Roan could see tents coming down and packs being tied on mules and horses. "Something's wrong, Curly. Why are they breaking camp?"

"He is afraid, this Heavy Brow you call Shell. He looked afraid when he rode in, the way he quirted and spurred his poor horse. My friend, this Heavy Brow and these off-breeds are going long way from here. I don't like this thing."

Roan said nothing for a moment. "If we let them go,

69

the child will never see her people again."

"That is bad."

"We have to stop them, Curly."

"That is good." The Osage made a wolflike movement to go at once.

"Wait, Curly. There can't be a big charge and much shooting. The little girl will get hurt."

"How you fight if no yell, no shoot?"

"Tell your scouts to approach the camp from the west and north. Tell them not to charge. Just draw fire and stay out of range. Tell them to keep yelling. Make the off-breeds think they're getting ready to charge. While that's going on, you and I ride in from here and take the little girl. That's all. This is not a scalp raid."

"What if off-breeds try to stop us?"

"Don't let them."

A great surge of satisfaction rolled across the massive features, and Curly faded back into the woods. When he returned shortly, he was leading his mount and Roan's and carrying a round blue shield on which fetish designs were painted. He became stationary, his attitude listening.

"They're still packing," Roan said.

After a minute or so, a whippoorwill's call rose, far off, plaintive, clear. Curly quartered about, an added keenness to his animal patience. Another call came, and after another pause another call and another.

"Look," Curly said. "Get on your horse, my friend."

Mounted, Roan saw the first scouts showing themselves as decoys, heard the first wild-shrill gobblings

70

on the prairie. A shout shook the camp into action. The packers went to grabbing at rifle scabbards.

Roan spurred into a run. Curly drew the blue shield against his body. Rapidly, the figures and the horses and mules in the woods became life-size, the "off-breeds" kneeling and firing, others grabbing at loose reins and halter ropes. As yet Roan saw no small girl among them.

"Over there," Curly yelled, and Roan, cutting that way, marked the little shape behind a stack of packs.

In a breath they were rushing through the outer timber, into blooms of powder smoke and the milling confusion of loose stock and darting men. A bronze-faced man, features contorted, seemed to sprout from the ground on Curly's side. Curly whooped and struck with his war club. The man fell spinning under the Osage's horse, his trampled rifle clattering.

Before Roan, suddenly close, materialized the packs and the small figure cowering there. He dropped to the ground and scooped her up, feeling her doll-like light-ness, her thinness, seeing the terror living in her face. A man ran shouting to halt him, rifle swinging. Curly jumped his horse across and rode the man down.

By then Roan had swung his slight burden to the saddle; with Curly gobbling great cries, he tore out of the timber.

He reached the foot of the lookout hill before he realized that Curly wasn't following and that something unexpected was happening back there. For the camp Indians were scattering like quail, fleeing from giants

71

on horseback gobbling like mad. Meaning struck: The Osages had charged after all, and he wondered why.

Hearing a dim cry, he remembered the child he held, and he dismounted and sat her down gently, saying soothing words over and over, then sensing that she didn't understand, else she was too frightened to comprehend. He tried smiling at her, but neither did she smile back. One thing he could see was her fear of him as she shrank back.

"Emily," he said softly, carefully. "Your name is Emily. Remember? Emily Dawkins. Your father is waiting for you at the fort. We're taking you there."

She revealed not the faintest understanding, not the slightest lessening of her fear, and he said no more for the moment.

In her ragged dress, crudely fashioned from cheap trading cloth, she looked so forlorn, so slight, so wretched, the dirty mat of her pale yellow hair hacked off, her slim face betraying a pinched cast, her light blue eyes baring a submissiveness that tore at him and raised his anger. She was shivering. He peeled off his jacket and folded it around her, patting her as he did so, vaguely alarmed. Again she shrank away from him.

A single horse clattered up hard. It was Curly, grinning like a giant pumpkin.

"Why'd the scouts charge?" Roan demanded.

Curly looked hurt. "This bad thing happened. Offbreeds wounded one of our scouts. Everybody heap mad."

"Who was wounded?" Roan was skeptical.

"Traveling Elk."

"Wounded bad?"

"Not bad, not little."

"Curly, the scouts disobeyed orders. That's bad." Yet he wouldn't report such to Major Thayer; if he did, he'd receive a mass of foolish restrictions he couldn't put into effect, which he wouldn't if he could. Nevertheless, he would have to make a full report and numbers always impressed green commanding officers. "How many off-breeds did the scouts kill?"

"Brave they fought for off-breeds. We took the hair of four."

"Where's the Heavy Brow?"

"Got away," Curly said, abashed. "With the trader-Delaware."

"We'll go back a way and make camp for tonight."

At Roan's order next morning, Curly sent a scout ahead to the post with the news of the captive's rescue. Because of the child's puzzling fear of him, Roan had her put aboard a gentle mare taken at the camp. Throughout the day she said nothing.

As the scouts trailed across the parade, Roan saw Dawkins among a group of officers outside headquarters, his chin outthrust, leaning forward, eyes hawking, hands pressed against his thighs. Roan reported to Colonel Emory:

"Here she is, Colonel. Shell was pulling out, and there were no Kiowas. Just a camp full of mixed-bloods dressed like whites. We took her. Shell and the Delaware vamoosed."

73

Emory stood back and Dawkins, his eyes strangely bright, seemed to float on airy feet as he literally skipped past Emory to the child. Transfixed, he said, "Emily," and choked. "Emily—I'm your father." He held up his arms.

She pulled back, clinging to the saddle, and Roan saw the same fear renewed. With careful tenderness, Dawkins loosened her hands and took her in his arms, while raindrop tears coursed down his cheeks. When her feet touched the ground, she pushed back again. The two of them froze like that, apart.

Emory said, "Gentlemen, let's go over here," and when they were out of earshot:

"Mr. Kimball, I want an immediate detailed report covering these unusual circumstances. What else happened?"

Roan told him, omitting only the Osages' charge, meanwhile seeing Major Thayer's censure forming with Emory's.

"I see no logical reason for Shell to break camp," Emory responded, scowling.

"Maybe he got cold feet."

"Why? He had nothing to fear from us. He could have brought the little girl in if the Kiowas had agreed to the reduced ransom, or he could have returned without her if the Kiowas hadn't agreed."

"But there were no Kiowas. He lied."

"Why did he? It wasn't necessary."

Roan scanned the intent faces. Should he tell the rest? About the man in uniform riding to Hatsboro and

74

the conference with Shell and the Delaware? He decided not and shrugged. "I think he made up the Kiowas so they could be blamed if he turned down the one thousand. Something caused him to change his mind."

"Has it occurred to you," Major Thayer took up the questioning, "that Shell was breaking camp to bring the child here?"

"Not that late in the day, Major. He was hurrying to go the other direction."

"Do you realize you've caused the serious loss of the one reliable go-between we had with the Kiowas?"

"I know we have the little girl. We wouldn't if we'd stood by and let Shell pack her back to Indian country."

"Here's Dawkins," someone said, and Roan turned to see the Texan leading the child across. But something was wrong with Dawkins' face, and the child was crying and confused. He kept trying to comfort her with clumsy pats.

"If you want an escort to Colbert's Ferry, you may have it," Emory assured him.

A mask of sadness and disappointment enveloped Dawkins' tired features.

"Is something wrong?" Emory asked.

Dawkins shut his eyes as if against pain.

"What in heaven's name is it, man?"

"Colonel, this poor little waif isn't my Emily."

"Did she say so?" Emory was aghast. "Did she tell you another name?"

"Tell me?" Dawkins moaned. "She's been a captive so long she's forgotten any English she ever knew."

"We can fix that. The Osages can talk to her in Kiowa." Dawkins lifted a weakly imploring hand. "I know without that."

"How? Speak up."

"It's the scar, high up on her left cheekbone."

"That fits the description."

Dawkins turned to gaze at the weeping child, patting her again as he did. "Except hers was put there not long ago."

"Put there?" Emory was shocked.

A furious light ignited Dawkins' eyes. "Cut there—it looks. It's too recent—too red—to be an old scar. Maybe that explains why she's afraid of white men. Why she'll scarce let me touch her. Why Shell, maybe, lost his nerve. Yet how could I say she wasn't mine, when I hadn't seen her goin' on four years."

"Dawkins, this is difficult to believe."

"She could be my Emily—blue eyes, yellow hair. She looks like I think Emily would look. But she's not. I know—I feel it. I know as a father."

"Only you can decide," said Emory, not hurrying him.

"I've decided, Colonel." Dawkins seemed to cast a burden off his stooped shoulders as he stood more erect. "I want that escort today. I'm taking this poor child with me, so she'll have a home same as my Emily had." He paused, as if considering, and Roan saw the tired eyes settle on him and heard the tired voice saying, "Before we go, I want to see Lieutenant Kimball alone."

When the others had moved away, Dawkins fumbled in his shirt pocket, and when he brought his hand forth, it was clenched into a fist. He pressed an object into Roan's palm—the locket, Roan saw—and the tired voice, vibrant with hope, said, "If you find my Emily, show it to her. Maybe it'll help her remember who she was once and the joy she had as a small child."

CHAPTER 5

In the days that followed, riding out and back from the Osage camp, Roan learned that it was one matter to avoid Sara Thayer, another not to think of her. But it had to stop. He knew that; common sense so dictated. Now and then he would catch sight of her. She was always alone, no doubt against orders, at gallop or canter or trot, more often than not riding at random across the open world of the dun prairie, which made her seem more remote and unreal than ever. Each time he saw her he did not change course toward her, and likewise he sensed that she did the same. And so it was over, he thought. At the post he shunned officers' charades and card parties, the numerous going-away functions being given in connection with the expedition's approaching departure.

One afternoon, returning to the post, he passed the spring and, instead of following his usual route, he obeyed a whim and turned south, a circling way that would bring him to the fort within the hour.

Here the prairie rolled and clumps of thick timber shortened his view ahead. Thus, he chanced upon the woman rider suddenly, just as she was riding past a stand of timber parallel to him. He stopped. At the same time she noticed him and stopped. Roan saw her hesitate as he was hesitating, and start to go on as he was and stop again. Suddenly their actions struck him as absurd. He reined toward her and saw that she was holding up.

"Mr. Kimball," she said, smiling, "I do believe you've been avoiding me."

"I have," he said a little painfully. "But not from disrespect, I assure you. Not because I wanted to."

Pique sharpened her tone. "You are continually speaking of respect."

"Every woman wants respect. Every woman wants to be looked up to—doesn't she?"

"But not ignored."

"I'm sorry."

"Don't apologize." She was holding her head quite high. "In another moment you'll be bowing and scraping like one of our puppetlike junior officers."

"You misplace me. I'm not a West Pointer. I came up through the ranks. One reason why the Major frowns on me."

He saw the suggestion of a smile, an openness that relaxed her even features. "That's closer to the truth than you might think. Many West Pointers are like that, but not all. Colonel Emory, for one. Speaking of the truth, I miss our talks. There's no one I can talk to."

"No one?"

"Nothing has changed. Nothing will change, because my son worships his soldierly father and I dearly love my son."

"Another reason why we shouldn't see each other," he said.

"Not even to talk?"

"You see, I find it hard not to think of you as a lovely woman."

"Is that so wrong?" She was teasing him again.

"It could make you unhappy, more than you are now, and I don't want that."

"You flatter a woman without intending to."

"I speak the truth, Sara."

"I believe you. Well, I'm also shameless," she said, gazing around. "After riding two hours, I should like a drink of water. I said that knowing you would hesitate as you are hesitating now."

His laughter erupted. "You don't give a man time to answer. Well, a drink it'll be."

They rode toward the spring, saying no more, and she dashed ahead and dismounted and was taking a tin cup from her saddlebag before he could step down. "I hope," she said, "you are aware that a scheming woman would have waited for you to assist her down?"

"I noticed."

He filled the cup for her at the spring and brought it

to her and she drank and said, "I come here often. This is my place of dreaming. My tryst with my other self. I've often seen you riding by."

He stared at her, surprised.

"Now you know I've been avoiding you also."

They laughed in concert; at last the restraint between them was broken.

She sprinkled the last of the cup's contents on the grass, returned it to the saddlebag, and turned back to him and gazed at the glistening spring, the trees, and the open sky. "Here I feel free. Peace of mind. It's the most precious state of being, the most needed. I love this little jeweled spring and its shield of sturdy oaks. It's so lovely here. And to think I shouldn't know it had you not shown it to me. Thank you, Roan."

"I'm glad it's brought you pleasure."

She made a whirling movement of delight, spinning about and facing him. "Lord Byron wrote: 'I live not in myself, but I become portion of that around me.' How true!"

"I'm not familiar with Lord Byron, but the other day an Osage told me: 'Where the wind is free, I am free. Living like a Heavy Brow, I grow weak and pale and start to die.'"

"A primitive Byron. How perceptive. What Osage?"

"Curly Wolf, the young headman. A strange mixture of Christian and savage. He told me he's been in a dozen fights and taken some twenty scalps. Mostly Pawnees and Kiowas, and white men intruding on the Osages' reservation. He loves children. The little girl

80

we rescued wasn't afraid of him at all. But she was afraid of me. She's afraid of all white men, though no doubt Sam Dawkins will win her over before long."

She was pensive. "Oftentimes I think, too, of these lines of Byron's: 'The thorns which I have reap'd are of the tree I planted; they have torn me, and I bleed. I should have known what fruit would spring from such a seed.' That is my life, Roan. I blame no one—no one. I want no sympathy from you or anyone."

He met her eyes, seeing her betraying loneliness that always caught him by the throat. Not realizing that he was moving, he felt himself taking her gloved hand, felt the touch of her spreading all through him.

"Sara," he said, very low, "listen to me." Seeing the lovely eyes growing wider and wider, and the intensity there, the waiting, as if she knew what he was going to tell her, yet fearful he would, he spoke almost roughly, "Will you return East—maybe St. Louis—go through the hell and stigma of a divorce—marry me?" It had flashed out, an immense force breaking loose, unmanageable, beyond his grasp, raw and true. "I'll resign my commission if necessary. We'll go somewhere and start a new life."

Confused, she withdrew her hand, and he saw that she was shaken, stirred by dread and fear. "I have my son to think of."

"You also have your own life to think of. I will make Jamie a good father. I will make you a good husband. I love you. I will make you happy. I'm no halfway man."

Her eyes gave her away, even as she said, "Jamie worships Hamilton. I can't, Roan. I can't. I've thought of running away, but I can't do that either because of Jamie."

Watching her, Roan was conscious of a dead silence that capped everything.

"Roan, what did you expect me to say?"

"What any good mother and loyal wife would say, I guess. Just what you said."

She took his arm, an imploring gesture. "I led you to think otherwise, didn't I? That possibly we could be together? That would be so wonderful. I'll always remember you asked me."

He'd never seen such womanly sadness, such earnest sincerity. Certainly never in Valerie. Touched, he traced the outline of her cheek with the tip of his forefinger. "We'll have our talks," he said. "I understand."

"I wanted you to say that. Oh, Roan, you are good to me. You are good *for* me."

"I'm not at all sure about that."

He didn't expect her suddenness, her impulsiveness, the silkiness of her completely against him, the lifting of her face, her eyes half closing, veiled under the long lashes, her head turning now and lifting higher, her full mouth giving and seeking. He bent his head and reached around her, feeling the softness of her lips, parting after a moment and all her sweetness therein for him, aware of the scent of lavender about him. His head swam.

He raised his head after an interval. Neither stepped

back. He continued to hold her.

"Your arms feel so good," she said. "So warm and strong and yet gentle. Here—now—anything seems possible, even though I know nothing can be, really."

"Don't think about anything now," he said, and held her until at last she said, "My hat—I think my hat has fallen off."

As he picked it up and handed it to her, conscious of his stifled, uneven, shallow breathing, a faint rumble drummed at his drugged senses. "Hear that?" he asked.

"What is it? Yes."

"Wagons," he said, knowing, and annoyed, realizing that the moment was over. He went past the horses to the edge of the oaks. From there he saw a line of bobbing canvas tops, swaying like hooded caterpillars squirming along the Fort Smith road, bound for the post. He walked back to her. "It's the extra wagons we've been waiting for. You know what it means? We'll be headed upriver in a few days."

"Yes," she said, a little mysteriously, he thought.

He regarded her sharply. "What do you mean?"

"I thought you knew. We're going. Jamie and I."

"You're not."

"Other officers' wives and children are going as well."

"It's poor judgment. I'm surprised that Colonel Emory would approve it."

"Aren't you glad?"

"Not there—it's no place for families. You could stay here, you know."

"But I'm not."

"Just why are you going?"

"Roan," she said softly, earnestly, "don't you know? I told you I'm shameless. I am. It's to be near you. If that's all there is to be for us, which is so little, then I won't take less."

The stifling sensation came upon him again. He said, "Sara—" and could say nothing more.

"Roan, I've just found out something about myself. This very instant I have." She was looking straight at him, no longer afraid. "I've known for some time that I love you. I think I began to that evening when we raced across the meadow together. And now— although I know it sounds impossible and I know it's wrong, in a way, though I love you—I'll do anything but what you asked of me. I can't ruin Jamie's life as I have my own. That's the only thing I won't do for you, Roan."

All he seemed to see was the glowing luminosity of her enormous green eyes, different even from moments ago. He could feel his face knotting as he stepped deliberately to her, as her features lost clarity and he felt the blinding crush of their bodies.

He was moving through the strangest haze, a dream state without darkness, without end. He realized slowly that he was near the gleaming spring. There he felt her go limp, and suddenly she was slipping from his arms. He bent and caught her and held her, and still all he saw was the ivory paleness of her small, perfect face tilting back, her mouth turned for his, her eyes glazed. And time had no meaning.

"I don't know how I'll feel tomorrow," she said, and opened her arms for him.

CHAPTER 6

After breakfast until tattoo, the farriers' hammers raised a continual din in the shoeing sheds below the west barracks. Supply sergeants rushed here and there, burdened with lists. Troopers oiled saddles and weapons, mended and polished gear and trappings. Details drew ammunition from the stone magazine; others loaded sacks of grain and boxed rations at the commissary building. At the officers' cottages wagons were drawn up to take on household articles of the departing families.

Roan could show only his silent disapproval of the last preparations, realizing that these Army people, for the most part accustomed to the comfortable Eastern posts, had little understanding of the trials that awaited them. Fort Washita, established to protect the Chickasaws and Choctaws from marauding Plains Indians, provided inadequate training for the far sterner demands ahead, in as much as the post had never experienced a single Kiowa or Comanche scare.

At the moment Sara Thayer was directing the loading of an exquisite little dressing table of dark red wood that gleamed like wax in the sun, while the boy, Jamie, ran about as restless as a terrier.

Two days had passed since the chance meeting near the spring. Seeing her again, Roan asked himself why he felt no merciless lashings of guilt. Was it because his strongest wish was to see her happy? And indeed she looked happy now, truly happy, as her warm, considering voice cautioned the troopers, as she complimented them on their carefulness.

He honestly believed he could recall every word she had spoken at the spring, and every gesture she had made, and every expression, and he wondered why he could, why each detail lay so remembered in his mind. And he remembered her utter calm afterward, her sweet-voiced finality:

"Roan, this is something for me to keep, to cherish. I have that. No one can take it away."

He was thinking of many things. "It has to stop."

"Yes, it must," she agreed, her feeling breaking through. "If not, it will consume us both. I love you too much to destroy you."

"Just don't be sorry."

"I'm not. I won't be. I had a dream and it was good— it was true, it was real. It's gone now. But I shall hold it dear. Remembering the good helps one endure the present."

He ached to hold her again, and he sensed the same in her. Time struck hard at him. He glanced at the lowering sun. There was nothing left to say as each stood there, at loss, deliberately apart. Without speaking, he lifted her to the sidesaddle. A moment and she was gone from him.

He blocked the scene from his mind and was riding past, when she waved and called, "Oh, Mr. Kimball."

He stopped.

Something reached out between them, even here; he sensed it, he saw it living in her eyes. She said, "Jamie's dog, Trixie, has disappeared. She's black and white."

"I'll look," he said. Look he did, riding completely around the post, and down to the stables and back. Returning, he reported his lack of success.

"Thank you, Mr. Kimball."

That was all.

Roan divided his time, henceforth, between the post and the Osage camp, endeavoring to carry out Major Thayer's orders from "drills" on one hand and, in exasperation, meeting the Osages' evasive responses on the other. Curly explained, "Why ride in straight line like Heavy Brow pony soldiers and lose many of our best warriors if a fight comes? Why ride this foolish way when there are no Crazy-Knives to fight? Or no Snake people—the Comanches? Tell Stone Face [their name for Thayer] we will fight when the Crazy-Knives show up, and we will fight our own way. Tomorrow we eat tomsheh. You come alone."

Roan did prevail on his charges to accept a form of discipline, to ride in two bunches, Curly leading the first, the stately Traveling Elk, recovered from his slight wound when cavorting before Shell's camp, the second. "Even this is foolish," Curly said. "We know how brave we are."

Roan despaired of further instruction. Army orderliness simply wasn't their style. Each warrior was an individual, to ride as he chose, to fight when his power or medicine indicated the signs were propitious.

On the morning of the tomsheh feast, Lieutenant Jernigan arrived while Roan and the Osages were eating under the shaded brush arbors. Although Curly sat facing the trail, he gave no recognition of welcome as Jernigan dismounted. Jernigan had a prancing walk as he entered the camp, sniffing distastefully.

"Mr. Kimball," he said, "Major Thayer asks if you have drilled the Osages for proper inspection at the final review tomorrow?"

"We're ready," Roan said, wiping his hands on a tuft of grass and getting to his feet.

"I request a more specific answer, Mr. Kimball."

"What specific does the Lieutenant have in mind?"

As Jernigan appraised the camp and the reclining Indians gorging themselves, aversion shaped along the line of his embittered mouth and in his eyes. He clasped his hands behind him and assumed a stiff-backed stance, his basset legs too short for his long torso. "Major Thayer expects them to ride past as a troop in line—a straight line, I may add. Think you can manage it?"

"As scouts, yes. As a troop of cavalry, no."

"Just what does that ambiguity mean?"

"In an irregular line, Lieutenant. In a bunch. Like a pack of wolves hamstringing a buffalo. The way

Osages charge. Hell-bent for hair."

"Major Thayer will be highly displeased."

"You can't drill Indians like wooden soldiers. It's against their nature, if no one has told you."

"I'm beginning to see why," said Jernigan, sweeping the camp and its occupants another scathing look, "when I find all of you in camp, feasting, at eleven o'clock in the morning."

"They did all right when they rescued the little Texas girl."

A portion of Jernigan's aplomb deserted him. "I still maintain that Shell was preparing to return to the post. That your attack was premature. He fled to save his life. I have presented my views to Colonel Emory, who himself says Shell was our best go-between with the wild tribes."

"Shell's claim. As a matter of fact, he's just a fat vulture preying on helpless women and children. What's more, he cut that scar on that child to make her fit the Dawkins girl's description."

"An echo of the words of an old man addled by grief."

"You're blind not to see through Shell."

"By God, sir, you had best watch your tongue."

"Don't tell me what I know. I had three of Shell's kind hanged sky high in Texas."

Jernigan drew himself up, pale with anger. "I suggest you mend your insubordinate manner under Major Thayer."

"Hold on now, Lieutenant. You forget that in the field

I'm on my own. Complete freedom of action. Colonel Emory's orders."

"You can also hang by those orders, if you go wrong."

Roan turned his back and stepped to an iron pot and speared a piece of dripping tomsheh, and said carelessly, "See you at the review, Lieutenant."

Jernigan pivoted on his heel, striding swiftly, back arched, to his horse.

"I don't like that man," Curly remarked when Roan returned to his seat. "He has weasel eyes. He is your enemy, my friend. Better kill him when you can."

Roan shook his head and turned to his dinner. Tomsheh had never tasted better.

In preparation for the review, the Osages painted their faces and attached the roaches of turkey-gobbler beard and deer-tail hair to their scalp locks and donned their best buckskin leggings and moccasins. Curly Wolf spent an hour at his grooming, streaking his broad face black and yellow, diabolical lines that converged at the corners of his mouth. With his roach quivering and the tail feather of a golden eagle tied to his fragment of natural hair, Curly looked a head taller to Roan, a fearsome aspect replacing his usual genial mien.

The Osages' arms were an assortment of muzzle-loading rifles and carbines, among them several ancient Hawkens, with powder horns and bullet bags. To Roan's reminder of the promised Springfield carbines, Colonel Emory had explained with regret, "We have no carbines to spare. Every extra weapon between here and the Mississippi is being called in by the War Department."

That afternoon Roan could hear the band playing *Hail, Columbia* as he and Curly and Traveling Elk led the scouts toward the parade ground. Thayer's memorandum for the day, delivered that morning by a noncom, said each troop was to proceed past the reviewing staff at an "orderly gallop in the best prescribed manner." The scouts, passing last, would "proceed in the same orderly fashion."

It was going to be quite a show, Roan saw, with the proud families gathered on the north and south sides of the parade ground, and the troops, by fours, each bearing its swallow-tail guidon, trailing in now to the assembly point. He took the scouts past the last troop dismounting on the north and signed for the Osages to dismount.

Observing the center of the parade, he saw Colonel Emory and staff drawn up, Major Thayer and Lieutenant Jernigan there as grim as stonework. A command came rolling down, "Prepare for inspection." Shortly, a barked "Right—dress! Front!" and commanders passed down the lines of dismounted troopers, each man standing to the left of his horse, face set to the front, body erect, chest on a line with the horse's mouth, reins held with the right hand six inches from the horse's muzzle.

Roan felt a tug of respect. Thayer had drilled these men well. Meanwhile, the Osages stood around like indolent copper gods, enjoying the ceremony of the Heavy Brow soldiers, while their Plains-bred horses nuzzled the flinty earth for nonexistent blades of grass.

Adjutant Lucans received the report of each company captain. The chief trumpeter raised his bugle to his lips and blew "Mount" and the men swung to saddles. Roan waved the Osages to horse, thinking that, for big men, they had the grace of cats.

He heard the band sound off and Emory's hoarse, "Pass in review," and the bandsmen swinging into a trot march. Now: "Foors right—march! Fooo—ward, march!" And the lead company moved out.

"Left front into line. Trot—march! Gallop—march!" There was the rattle of bit chains and the squeal of oiled saddle leather as the first troop obeyed with flawless precision, after it troop by troop, dressing to the right as it rode past the reviewing officers.

As the last troop galloped by, Roan led off at a trot, the cadence of unshod hoofs picking up behind him. He spurred into a gallop and so did the Osages. Something about their hard coming warned him, belatedly, that the hoof racket sounded too fast. He heard a chilling screech, and his mount tore ahead running. The onrush of horseflesh behind him forced him on, unchecked, riding the crest of a violent wave, and a backward glance revealed the Osages riding all over their mounts, switching ends, hanging from the flanks, howling like demons.

He was beyond the reviewing staff before he could bring his horse under tight control; quickly, he reined down to gallop, then trot, and led the Osages about in an abrupt, dust-raising turn, aware that now they behaved as orderly as any troop. To his relief the families had scattered to the porch of the south barracks.

He dreaded to look across the parade. He did and was shocked to see horses rearing and plunging, troop formations broken and riders unseated, others afoot, tugging on the reins of walleyed mounts.

Roan froze, hunched in the saddle. The only course left him was to wait here, wait and catch his merited hell.

Curly towered up beside him, beaming pride. "We show Stone Face how Osages ride. Hooo."

"You showed him, all right," Roan said miserably, yet he couldn't locate the righteous anger he wished to vent on his primitive charges.

Over there, at last, the reviewing staff had its horses under rein. A rider detached himself and raced across. Lieutenant Jernigan pounded up, eyes glittering wrath, or was that relishing malice?

"You've done it now," he shouted at Roan. "Get yourself over to the Old Man."

On the way over, Roan foraged through his mind for plausible excuses and found not one. By any judgment, he had failed to lead the scouts past in orderly manner and had shattered what was planned as a final, impressive review. Roan saluted and waited, inwardly braced for the storm, though there was no hint of that in Colonel Emory's composure. Major Thayer was scowling until his thick brows almost touched. He kept swiping at his mustache. His eyes were as pale as ice.

"Mister," Emory began, "that was a most extraordinary exhibition of riding and noisemaking."

"I'm afraid it got out of hand, sir," Roan answered, at the same time desiring to protect the Osages. "The scouts were trying to demonstrate how well they can ride."

"You ruined the review," Thayer shot out. "You demonstrated a decided lack of judgment, Mr. Kimball." He turned to Emory. "With your permission, Colonel, I should like to request that Lieutenant Kimball be replaced as officer in charge of the Osage scouts."

"I think not, Major."

"But, sir, the scouts are ill-disciplined. You saw how they broke up the review."

"I'm thinking of something more important than a review." Thayer became very still and stiff; for a moment Roan thought he was going to object further, until Emory went on reflectively, "A simulated maneuver such as the Osages executed—whooping and charging—is exactly what your men may be faced with in the field on Red River. However, I trust by that time they will have learned how to control their mounts."

"Colonel, sir, I respectfully disagree."

Emory's voice had a stringent curtness. "Instead of removing Lieutenant Kimball, I think we should look on today's disruption as a needed field exercise. In fact, I find the demonstration useful to us all, a rather grim reminder of our unpreparedness for fighting Indians. Good day, gentlemen."

CHAPTER 7

Promptly at seven o'clock next morning, preceded by Second Lieutenant Roan Kimball and the Osage scouts, Major Hamilton B. Thayer's command pulled out of Fort Washita for the upper tributaries of the Red River.

Passing through Hatsboro, Roan saw its motley inhabitants turned out to watch. One man, flicking a switch, sat a bony mule of advanced years. With a clap of heels, and his ungainly long legs skimming the ground, the Reverend Noah Loftus joggled out to the head of the scout column.

"Just come out to wish you luck," he said. His hoarse voice was gravelly, down to a croak.

Roan regarded him keenly.

"Don't you aim to build a fort on Cache Creek?"

Roan sighed, realizing he should have known the command's objective would leak out. Hatsboro heard everything. "So word's got around, has it?"

"If a bedbug switched barracks, they'd know it next morning in Hatsboro. I peer at it this way, Brother Kimball. My work is finished here. I've preached till I'm plumb wore out. Not one immortal soul has Noah Loftus saved. I've tucked in my tail feathers. I'm licked by whiskey an' cards an' painted women. Now that tells me something. It's about time to move camp. Pagan Indians will be comin' to your new fort. Before long Noah Loftus will sashay out there to fetch the good news to the heathens. What do you say to that, brother?"

Roan, reluctant to encourage him, said, "It's a long way. It's wild country. We're going far up the Red."

"The Apostle Paul went to Antioch, didn't he?"

The man's absolute sincerity got to Roan. A weaker person would be asking to tag along with the column. Roan stuck out his hand. "Good luck, Reverend. Hope you have better luck than Paul and Barnabas had. Follow our trail. Don't sleep by your fire at night."

Once across the Washita, Major Thayer moved the column leisurely by the book, halting ten minutes of each hour, nooning for an hour, causing Curly to grumble at the end of the day, "Stone Face moves like stone."

Far out on the second day the scouts came upon a cabin and cornfield and garden patch. Brown-skinned children scattered before the approaching horsemen, and dogs snapped at the heels of the horses. An Indian filled the doorway, on his wide, full face the wariness of one used to the unexpected. He gripped a rifle. He shouted at the dogs, which slunk close to the house.

"Chickasaw," Curly said under his breath to Roan.

"What you want?" the Indian in the doorway asked.

"Water," Roan said.

"Spring's yonder."

96

As he started off, Roan held up to avoid riding through a detail of large spotted pups trailing a weary female. Judging by her snapping behavior, she was trying to wean her hungry litter. He pointed to a sturdy male pup. "How much?"

"Too many dogs now. Take him."

Dismounting, Roan gathered up the pup, looked him over, and gave the Indian a dollar. Leaving the Osages at the spring, he backtracked for the column; seeing the headquarters advance, the noncommissioned officers and orderlies and the standard-bearer, and behind them Major Thayer and Lieutenant Jernigan, now his adjutant, Roan swung wide to quarter in on the command, riding down it until he found the ambulance in which Sara Thayer and Jamie rode.

The boy's eyes, fixing on the pup, became enormous. "He'll make you a good squirrel dog," Roan said, handing the squirming pup across, and departed on the gallop.

Before supper, Roan took a walk along the bivouac. Passing the Thayer ambulance, he saw the Major's striker busy at chores and Sara stirring something in a kettle. Jamie and the spotted pup wrestled under the wagon. An emptiness caught Roan and also his disapproval. A hundred campfires were announcing the command's presence here tonight; by tomorrow every Plains Indian within fifty miles would know. Sara and Jamie and the other families had no place here. If Thayer were going to establish a permanent fort on the Red, that normally assured adequate protection and living quarters for the families; as it was, his orders called for a cantonment, a collection of temporary quarters at best, a crude stockade and blockhouses.

He went on a way, listening to the pleasant hum of voices at ease. Strolling back, he was drawn closer to the wagons by the high, carefree excitement of children at play. One was Jamie. Judging by the racket there, it appeared that all the children around the wagon wanted to hold the pup. And, seeing them and hearing them, Roan could not but think of the little Dawkins girl. Was she still alive? If so, in what remote camp? Blue eyes, yellow hair. Thin-bodied after these years of fetching water and gathering wood. Why had Shell substituted the other child? Did that mean that Emily Dawkins was dead?

That likelihood weighed on him as he angled back to the Osage camp.

Summer twilight idled long after the hungry Osages, camped apart from the command, had eaten and taken their rest. Roan propped his head on his saddle and closed his eyes, attentive to the murmurous ebb and flow of the scouts' unhurried talk. He was beginning to pick up some Osage words, for he gathered that nothing of note had happened during the day. No strange Indians sighted by those scouts working farthest out. No buffalo. The Osages were hungry for meat.

"Where your people?" Curly asked him.

Roan sat up, surprised that the Osage had asked. Roan made the sign for gone, passed on, and pointed toward Texas. Curly nodded, said, *"Tejano,"* and Roan nodded.

"Indians killed my father," Roan said, and awaited Curly's reaction.

Curly's eyes moved in inquiry. No more. His Indian manners forbade him to interrupt when another person was talking.

"Comanches, I think," Roan explained. "Maybe Crazy-Knives. Both tribes had war parties raiding around there."

The smoky-brown eyes got glittery, then solemn. "Ho. You must kill one Comanche, one Kiowa."

"I don't know who did it."

"Any Comanche would do. Any Crazy-Knife. You must do this thing for your father."

"To kill just any Comanche or Crazy-Knife?" Roan shook his head in disbelief, in refusal.

"You have wife?"

"Once. Not anymore."

"Dead?" Sympathy engulfed Curly.

"She went back to her people. Back where the sun rises."

"My friend," said Curly, suddenly slapping his hands together, "your people are dead—you have no woman—so we Osages adopt you now. We like you. You understand us. From now on your name is One-of-Us. Ho. It is good."

"One-of-Us," Roan repeated, nodding, nodding, contracting his mouth. "That is good. I am honored. We will be friends the rest of our lives and always the

99

smoke of our fires will rise straight to the sky." His voice thickened. Curly, impulsive, generous, primitive Curly, had caught him off guard.

Near dawn. A dim rose-colored hue flushing the east. Wooded hilltops shaggy blurs against the changing light. A breeze out of the southwest rustling the prairie grass, conveying sweet scents. Around Roan, sitting up in his blankets, the faces of the Osages suggested dark, copper masks, broad, strong, impassive, serene. As one, the Indians left their robes and blankets and slipped toward the East, moccasins brushing the wet grass. Some wore small bells that tinkled. He waited, finding himself with head bowed, and as the first blade of true light split the sky, he heard beseeching voices chanting the Rising Song to Wah'Kon-Tah, the Mystery One. *Ahhhhhhh . . . Hooooooo . . . Ahhhhhhh . . . Hooooooo*. The chant, long and unbroken, rose quavering and high-pitched, as earnest in petition as that of small children. The chant wailed on, and he thought: Guard them against their enemies. Make them brave. Bring them meat. That's what they're praying for.

The prayer-song ended as abruptly as it had begun, and for a briefness it seemed to Roan that the breeze carried it on. As the Osages turned back, Roan realized that he had never failed to feel reverence when he heard their prayer-songs, morning and evening; and the insight bore upon him again that these men, primitive by other standards and beliefs, had a faith that made them unafraid of death, especially death in war. He was aware of an enormous respect for them, for

100

they were also generous and they loved children. On the way back after the raid on Shell's camp, Curly had treated the homeless, frightened white child with the gentleness of a woman.

Long before the command stirred forward, the Osages went drumming forth, fanning out, watching right and left and ahead. It was around seven o'clock before Roan heard the trumpet sound "Mount." At last the command was in motion.

An Osage named Runs-Against-the-Sun was riding in front, a young man, hungry for war honors, alert and prone to excitability. He would dash to the next fold of prairie, outlined there, hoping the enemy saw him, inviting them to fight him if they dared meet one so brave and strong. More often than necessary he dashed back to tell Curly what he saw.

"Ho," Curly confided to Roan, "if red-tailed hawk flies over, he will tell us. If coyote shows himself, he will tell us. If antelope runs, he will tell us. But this thing is good. He will make good warrior in time."

The afternoon was half spent when Runs-Against-the-Sun, following the deep scour of an old buffalo trail meandering southwest, flung his horse about violently and cut one rapid circle after another.

Curly stopped to observe. A little time passed. He said, "No enemy is close or he would rush back here. Let us wait. Although this young man has found something, he must learn not to signal danger unless danger is close."

Never ceasing his circling until Curly and Roan

approached, Runs-Against-the-Sun raced to the trail and pointed. Roan saw a slender stick stuck upright into the softer earth beside the trail, pierced to it a leaf-shaped piece of flesh, flat and light-colored. With Curly, he dismounted to examine it. Runs-Against-the-Sun, down with them, stood back to await his leader's approval.

Roan, feeling gray nausea kick his stomach, recognized it just as Curly said, "This thing is white man's ear—taken this morning. It's Crazy-Knife mark."

"Their message is plain," Roan said, making a throat-cutting motion.

"Ho. Ho. Heavy Brows go back. Stone Face better watch horses tonight."

The advance clattered up and halted, the noncoms staring curiously at the grim object beside the trail, followed shortly by Major Thayer and Lieutenant Jernigan.

"What's the delay?" Thayer, ever curt, directed the question at Roan, who cocked his head at the stick.

"Just a brief one, Major. Nothing unusual. Curly says it's an old Kiowa custom to take an ear. They're warning us to go back."

"You mean they're trying to bluff us?"

"I wouldn't say they're bluffing, Major."

"We'll proceed as planned, of course. Meanwhile, I hardly think one piece of flesh"—he searched for the precise sarcasm—"symbolic of savage intent, warrants holding up the entire command."

Roan shrugged. "Curly Wolf says we should post

extra watch on our picket lines tonight."

"We *always* picket and hobble our mounts, Mr. Kimball. It's a regular precaution of mine I hoped you had noticed. Now move out and start these Osages to earning their government pay."

It was late evening, the hanging light just a pallor. The wind freshening, the sounds of the bivouac softly muted. The voices of the women and children so alien out here, and the more blessed to hear.

Roan was conscious of a nameless need as he left the Osage camp and drifted toward the wagons. Beyond, in the center of the bivouac, stood the headquarters tent of Major Thayer, a conical Sibley shelter, shaped like an Indian tipi. Lanterns glowed there. Likely, the Major was poring over maps for the march tomorrow. Save for one here and there, the supper fires were out. Roan paused. Every evening, as on those evenings coming out from Fort Smith on the stage, Sara Thayer had taken her late stroll, a casual turn that took her around the circled wagons. It was time now. No sooner the thought than a figure materialized. He said, "Good evening."

The figure stopped. He could hear skirts rustling, and her voice reached him after a moment, "Good evening to you. I wondered when you'd find me."

"I knew you'd come by here."

"How did you know?" They stood well apart, two members of the command chancing to meet, thus passing the time of evening.

"It's your habit. Your release from the day."

"You didn't come before. Why?" If she was annoyed, her voice didn't reveal it. She sounded wholly relaxed.

"I thought it best not to."

"Then why tonight?"

"Changed my mind."

They had, he saw, drawn within an arm's length of each other. "There's so little to say, isn't there, Roan?"

"I have another reason for being here."

"Yes?"

"After tonight, you must not walk outside the wagons. We're in Indian country now."

"Any other reasons?"

"I wanted to see you."

"That's a great deal, Roan."

"And so little, in a way, as you say. Not enough."

"I can live on little things from day to day."

The pulsing cleanness of her raked across to him, though he moved no nearer, and he was glad for the darkness hiding his face.

"You're a very fine woman, Sara."

"I believe you've said that before," she answered, her tone listless.

"It's true."

"Why do you keep saying that?"

"I want you to believe it."

"You mean I don't?"

"I mean don't be afraid."

"I'll try not to be. Will you look for me tomorrow night?"

104

"No—and you must not walk outside the wagons. Hear?" He studied the hooded shapes of the wagons. Blurred figures moved in front of the headquarters tent. "They'll be posting the guard any minute now," he said. "Good night."

He was walking on when she spoke, her cultivated voice expressing the urgency of a late thought, "Jamie loves his Indian puppy. Plays with it all day, sleeps with it at night. We both thank you." (In the distance the Sergeant of the Guard was barking out orders.) Now hurriedly: "Good night, Roan."

The sky was growing much darker and the wind was rising. Unmoving, he stood listening to the brush of her light, even steps through the prairie grass. When he could hear them no longer, he made for the Osage camp, an absolute loneliness plunging through him.

No alarm shattered his sleep that night, nor the next. Neither did he see Sara Thayer strolling around the bivouac.

On the third night he came awake as if by instinct, disturbed more by sense than by sound. He sat up, hearing only the grass-croppings of the scouts' horses. Close about lay the dark shapes of the Osages, reins tied to wrists. At a moment's notice they could spring to their mounts.

Over there, outside the wagon corral, grazed the command's horses, neatly picketed in troop lines. A damn-fool way to handle horses in Indian country, inviting an adept Kiowa or Comanche to slip in, knife the single guard assigned to each troop line, cut leather

105

hobbles and picket ropes, and start the horses drifting, to be gone in moments. After discovery of the luckless white man's ear beside the trail, Roan had suggested bunching the horses inside the corral at night. He could hear Thayer's rebuttal yet:

"I prefer to reason that no Indian raiding party would be so foolhardy as to attack a command of this magnitude."

"True, Major, not in the open. Not anywhere unless the fight was on their terms. But anytime you dangle picketed horses at a Kiowa, he'll try for 'em."

"Even under guard?"

"Even under guard."

Inside the conical Sibley tent the buff lantern light behind the Major cast a marblelike shadow over his face. "I believe that's all, Mr. Kimball."

Roan lay down and closed his eyes; less than a minute later he opened them and flung back the blanket. It was wrong. Was that a choked cry? A movement? Whatever, it was too muffled to ferret out. At times like this it was safer to rely on your senses than logic and indecision.

His horse, loosely saddled, was picketed a few feet away. Rising, he slipped on the bridle, worked the curb bit home, tightened the cinch, and became still, listening. It was yet minutes before daylight.

It happened as he had feared it would, as it always happened, just before dawn, without warning. One high-screeching signal whoop, the cry of Plains Indians raiding for horses, followed by the thudding rush of hoofs.

A sentry's carbine banged.

Movement erupted around Roan as the Osages jumped up grabbing weapons and faced the bivouac. They loomed as giants in the murk. No one shouted or spoke. They were, Roan sensed, waiting as he was waiting before they rushed anywhere.

A wedge of horses swept past, bringing the distinct flapping of slashed leather hobbles. Roan bit his lip: Troop C's mounts, the nearest horses to the Osage camp, fleeing to escape the fiendish cries behind them.

Now. Roan hit the saddle, aware of the Osages doing likewise, their nervous horses dancing with eagerness. In mass, the scouts tore out, Roan in their midst. Even though he couldn't see the Troop C horses, the raiders' cries marked their eastward direction.

It seemed a long time that he rode headlong, and blindly, yet not so long until he made out a dark clump moving like a spearhead cleaving the night.

For another space it seemed that nothing changed. Still, when light cracked the eastern sky, Roan was startled to see how close the Osages were. And Troop C's mounts stringing out, the raiders behind them and on the flanks, riding like jockeys, the first light painting greasy rays across their bent bodies.

And then Roan saw the horse takers turning abruptly, a brave thing to do outnumbered, broad, stocky figures as the Osages were broad and tall—Kiowas turning to fight. In moments Roan was jerking his horse this way and that, in the eye of a swirling

107

fight, the Kiowas shrilling, the Osages gobbling.

A wraith on a bay horse suddenly bulged before Roan, war club swinging, face contorted, teeth bared. The man ducked just as Roan fired his revolver and missed. Roan, glimpsing the stone head of the club descending, swayed left and the club crashed the pommel of his saddle, the Kiowa so close Roan caught the reek of grease and sweat and wood smoke and saw the buff paint streaking the savage face. Earing back the hammer, Roan fired. The man cried out and, clutching the bay's mane, went veering off into the dissolving murk.

Seconds later the wolf-shrill cries ceased, and Roan realized the raiders had vanished.

The scouts were trailing back to the command, driving the still-nervous Troop C mounts, when Curly rode up beside him. "You missed first shot." And thrusting a stone-headed war club on Roan, "Take this, my friend. Use it when you fight in close."

As they neared the bivouac, Lieutenant Jernigan dashed up. "Report to headquarters. Both of you."

"What's up? We got the horses."

"I'm not at liberty to speak for the Major."

Roan and Curly rode directly to the headquarters tent. Thayer, pacing back and forth, brushed vigorously at his mustache, a gesture that Roan recognized by now as the one sure sign of annoyance or impatience.

"You are supposed to be the eyes of this command," said Thayer, clearing his throat. "You and your Osage friends." (He could never refer to the Osages without ridicule, Roan thought.) "You're responsible for security outside the bivouac at night."

"We brought back every Troop C mount, Major."

"That's not the issue, Mr. Kimball. A Troop C sentry's throat was slashed—he's dead."

"You can't picket horses beyond camp, with one sentry to a troop line, and expect to keep out Indians."

"That's exactly what I do expect."

"If you're gonna picket outside, Major," Roan said, fighting back feeling, "you—"

The Major's voice slammed across before Roan could finish. "I trust I make myself clear, Mr. Kimball."

"I reckon you do, Major."

"Then good day."

Roan was immersed in thought as he rode off. He could expect Thayer to perform like a martinet, always hewing to the book, when the book didn't fit out here. But there was something more, something deeper. Was it Sara?

CHAPTER 8

Yet that night no mounts were picketed outside the bivouac and none thereafter as the column traveled toward the site of the new cantonment on Cache Creek. There, Roan recalled, a daring trader named Abel Warren was said to have erected a stockade some twenty years earlier. Indians had burned it to the ground when he left.

Roan and the Osages rode over the location in the brightness of early morning. He liked it at once. A sweet-water spring hard by. Timber to draw on for the stockade and blockhouses. Abundant grazing in all directions. Southward a few hundred yards the shoaling creek formed a placid pool before slipping lazily into Red River. Far to the north rose the eroded humps of the Wichita Mountains, standing like broken battlements in their cloaks of blue haze.

One drawback of the site bothered Roan, however. That was the northward ridge, beyond rifle range, that overlooked the position. Had the ridge figured in the old post's end? He wondered.

Across the river where Texas began, the land seemed to flow away from the eye and reality as well, a limit-less dun-colored summer sea, the folds of prairie as undulating swells under an immense arch of sky. Coming back, Roan felt a sense of sanctuary. And he knew this was what he had actually wished for back in Missouri, simply because he belonged here. Perhaps Valerie was right as she had often accused, that his inclinations were closer to a Plains Indian's than those of an officer and gentleman.

By the time Roan and the Osages left on their first scout, hastened by a Fort Washita courier bearing word from Colonel Emory that "Texas authorities are demanding immediate action because of an increasing number of Indian raids in the vicinity of Fort Belknap and the settlement of Jacksboro," Major Thayer had the troopers cutting logs and digging holes for the stockade. Meanwhile, he named the site Cantonment Emory in honor of the Colonel.

Second Lieutenant Cass Povich and Troop C accompanied the scouts. Povich's orders called for "a careful reconnaissance upriver, searching for bands of hostile Indians invading the State of Texas for warlike purposes. Any Indians sighted shall be attacked at once and driven back."

"Gad," Povich groaned as the Osages fanned out ahead, "it would take a thousand troopers to plug this border. All an Indian has to do is get on a horse and cross the river."

"True enough," Roan agreed, "but they have their favorite crossings. Curly says our best bet is to locate the main places, and scout back and forth."

Before noon the Osages located a crossing, a hoof-pocked passageway worn into the reddish soil of the sloping river bluff, and bearing fresh unshod hoof-prints and droppings. Dismounting to gaze through the bluff's V-shaped gap down to the river and beyond, Roan had the instantaneous impression of sighting along the barrel of a rifle aimed straight at Texas.

"Just missed a bunch," he told Povich. "Maybe two hours. Maybe one."

They continued upriver. The afternoon, spawning heat and wind, became uneventful and monotonous. Around three o'clock Povich, who was busy studying the glittering landscape through binoculars, turned excitedly to Roan and Curly.

"See there! We're going to charge!"

Roan, seeing Curly's covert amusement, said nothing. Both had noticed the tan-colored shapes. Already Povich was shouting, "Left front into line. Gallop—harch!"

The bugle was sputtering Charge and the flying shod hoofs were flinging bits of prairie sod as the troop of fifty men spread out and racketed forward. Roan and the Osage dropped behind, following at a trot.

About a mile on Roan saw Povich throw up his arm and pull in his mount. The bugler blew Recall. Povich reformed his troop by fours and started back, riding slowly. When he came up, his ruddy face bore a strawberry flush. He shook his head and laughed at himself. "Let me say it. No antelopes were ever put to quicker flight."

After the near-miss at the crossing and Povich's diverting dash, a period of unrelieved boredom set in. Each day was the same, riding from one crossing to the next, scanning the burned distances through field glasses. Yet Roan was content, even after four days, when duty began to gnaw and he realized they were getting nowhere. It was frustrating to reflect that within a day or two's riding, possibly nearer, breathed Indians and white renegades, Army deserters and riffraff from the settlements, aware of Sanaco's whereabouts. And the child, Emily Dawkins? Fugitive figures as elusive as the mirages that flickered between earth and sky, distorting, flowing, constantly changing.

112

He gave a start. For out of the dancing heat waves he now discovered his first Indians, about fifteen, a horseback file stringing toward the river. Curly, in advance, was cutting his horse in tight circles, signaling: Enemy sighted.

Roan cased his field glasses. "Real Indians this time, Povich. Let's go straight at them just as we are, in column of fours, without any bugle calls."

Povich stood high in the saddle and swept his arm forward. "Trot, march!" And the troop quickened forward. "Gallop, march." Dust was smoking up from the prairie floor. A thundering jarred Roan's ears and he exulted as he always did to the pounding of the charge.

He saw the line of Indians halt, a cluster of bronze images there; for a second or so they stared at the charging troopers, seemingly puzzled, or was it utter disbelief at invasion of their domain? But no longer. They broke up and scattered northeast, racing away on small, fleet horses.

Povich spurred faster, drawing the troop into a dead run. For drawn-out moments they ran like that, and it seemed to Roan that they must be gaining, yet knowing they were not. The fleeing Indians appeared no closer. Their horses were out-running the heavier, equipment-laden cavalry mounts. Carbines began popping. The Indians raced on, nothing about them changed, and the futile firing slacked off. The Indians, out of range, were steadily drawing away.

At last, Povich pulled up. "Gad, Kimball—can't a man catch anything in this blasted country?"

"Not with all the gear our mounts tote."

"What do you make of that bunch?"

"Mostly young bucks. On a horse-stealing raid. A larger war party would have given us a fight."

They flushed no more Indians that day, nor for a week. The country presented a face of deceiving peacefulness. By now low on rations and tired of buffalo meat, the troopers grumbled as they went into camp midday at the first crossing Curly had found. It was a main ford across the Red, the Osages said, but no war parties had passed since that first day.

Within the hour Thunder Walk, hastening back from a two-day scout to the north, reported a large war party camped at the edge of the mountains.

"Another empty-handed chase?" Povich suggested, his face wry.

"Big war party," Curly said. "Not boys, like ones we chased."

"How many?" Roan asked.

Thunder Walk's thick-fingered hands flew, opening and closing time and again. Finished counting, he gave a sinuous motion of his wrist, the sign for snake, or Comanche, and, his hand at his right cheek, fingers touching and slightly curved, moved his hand in a rotary motion, a cutting sign, the sign for Crazy-Knives.

"Seventy-five," Roan told Povich. "Maybe a hundred. Comanches and Kiowas. Way they're headed, he expects them to cross the river here."

Piece by piece, the Osages and Roan and Povich laid

114

the ambush. No fires tonight (the smell of dead supper fires might linger through morning). No pickets. The war party must be allowed to enter the gap before a shot was fired, and on Curly's judgment fell the responsibility of when to fire that first shot. Hold the horses out of sight below the bluff on the narrow flat by the river. To avoid firing into one another, post men only on one side of the gap; station others back a way on both sides along the base of the bluff facing north. The Osages would fire the first volley, then the troopers, odd-numbered men first.

At dark, after grazing the troop mounts, horse holders took them below and the younger Indians drove down the scouts' horses. It was well after dark before Roan rested. As if by habit, he sealed the day's events from his mind and found his ease. Every evening about now, when the earth seemed to stand still, Sara and the little Dawkins girl haunted his thoughts, vivid but yet unreal. They were still there, unresolved, when he pulled his hat over his face and fell into instant sleep.

The timepiece of old patterns waked him, conscious of the cloying incense of the prairie, damp-sweet, and of the moist breath of the river rising through the gap. Dawn was close and the wind was still and there was no movement to the north. He thought: They're not coming. It was too much to expect to ambush a war party. The fawn light was strengthening, wave upon wave, stronger and stronger, routing the night. Beside him he heard Povich whisper, "What do you think?"

"There's still time," Roan said.

Minutes. A battle was taking place inside him. His impatience telling him no, you never trapped Plains Indians, his curbing, calmer voice tugging and saying wait and see. He strained to pierce the muddy light waves and saw nothing, just the formless murk. On the other side of him he heard the scrape of Curly's moccasins as he shifted.

At the same moment Roan detected a single patch of movement, darker than the half-light, top the low swell of prairie north of the gap and become still; saw another dark patch follow, another and another. He leaned toward Povich:

"They're coming."

Ever so slowly, the patches imparted the shapes of horsemen, and behind those, as the dingy light dissolved, rolled an unbroken mass of riders. Roan caught his breath. Not just seventy-five—but a horde.

Perhaps their very numbers lulled them into carelessness, he wondered, and being at ease in their own open land, where they had never been challenged before; perhaps they were visualizing the Tejano booty across the river.

In the lead rode a young man of splendid athletic physique, whose position in the cavalcade and whose proud manner indicated an established warrior. Stripped to the waist, he rode a racy-looking buckskin and carried on his high-horned Spanish saddle a blue shield decorated with yellow dots. No warriors painted; it was too early, because that ritual was

116

reserved for shortly before a raid.

As the Indians approached, the ruffling of horses jogging through the short grass became audible to Roan; and now that muffled cadence of unshod hoofs switched to a sharper, harder drumming. They were riding faster as they neared the crossing, eager to cross. Within Roan rose the fear that some last warning might whirl them away too soon, before enough came inside the jaws of the gap. They clattered along, however, some talking, the chopped-off, guttural Kiowa and the sonorous, flowing Comanche tones blending.

An oddness held his eyes—one rider wearing a broad-brimmed hat and white man's shirt.

Still, Curly didn't fire. Roan stiffened as the lead warrior rode farther into the gap, in advance some yards. Roan moved his eyes. Were the others going to hold up? But no, they were following, taking their time, their attention on the distant side of the river.

Roan's mind tightened. *Now, Curly, now.*

Curly's rifle slammed in Roan's ear, and that side of the gap flamed with a deafening roar. Through the blooms of powder smoke he saw riders dropping and horses rearing and pivoting, ramming into the horses behind them. They struggled in that confused tangle, a scattering of Indians returning the fire, when the second volley struck. Warriors' cries mingled with troopers' shouts. As the war party was hurled back again, the third volley caught them. Riders reeled and clung to floundering horses. Some riders broke free, horses running after jumping away, only to be hit again, first from one flank, then the other, as the troopers posted along the north base of the bluff opened up.

With gobbling cries, the Osages went rushing down the slope to scalp the survivors, looming like awesome giants taking seven-league strides. Roan didn't like it; he never had when the Tonks caught a luckless Kiowa or Comanche. But when you used Indian scouts, you often fought like an Indian and sometimes you had to look the other way.

On his feet, Roan saw the rider in white-man hat and shirt twist to rise and flop back, his left leg caught under his dead horse. He lost the hat. A vague recognition flicked Roan's mind as the man planted his right foot against the horse, heaved and tore his other foot free. He was scrambling up when Curly, scalping knife drawn, grabbed him by the neck like a wet dog and made a circular slash around his victim's head.

Roan, running and shouting at the Osage, saw Curly grasp the short, thick hair and jam his foot against the man's chest to rip off the scalp.

"No—Curly—no!" Roan grabbed the Osage's hard arm. "No—not him!"

Both startled and angry, Curly let go the mop of black hair and the Indian sprawled, blinded by the blood streaming from his scalp.

Roan had to shout above the din, "He's the Delaware—remember? He came to the fort—got away when we attacked the camp where the little girl was." The Osage jogged his head, full of disdain, and Roan took a horsehair rope from the Delaware's saddle and tied his hands behind him.

The primitive cries were fading and the fight was finished, Roan saw, over in these few savage moments, leaving the war party badly mauled at the cost of one trooper down and Thunder Walk hurt. Roan made no more attempts to prevent the Osages from scalping. Were these Osages and troopers ambushed here, instead, the Kiowas and Comanches would be taking their hair.

He turned away, to find Povich at his elbow, a sickish glaze paling his ruddy features. "Gad, Kimball, shall we give them a chase?"

"Couldn't catch 'em. If we did, we couldn't handle 'em."

"I see you took a prisoner."

"An important one. Let's put him under double guard."

They pulled away from the gap and made coffee and cooked breakfast. As they were eating, Curly said, "There was white man in that war party. He was way back."

"He would be," Roan said, his face clouding. "I missed him. Was it the Heavy Brow of the camp where the little girl was? The man we call Shell?"

Curly shrugged.

A little later, motioning Povich and Curly, Roan took a tin cup of coffee and sat it on the ground before the Delaware and untied him.

"Have some coffee," Roan invited.

The Delaware's watchful eyes rested longingly on the steaming brew. His wide nostrils quivered. Scornfully, he crossed his arms and a deliberate blankness curtained his high-boned face. He was short and muscular, his coal-black eyes intelligent and bold. The blood clotting his hair and forehead enhanced his defiant look.

"Drink," Roan commanded.

The Delaware moved not a muscle.

"I know you savvy English," Roan said. "I saw how you listened that day at the fort when Shell made his big spiel for the ransom. You savvied every word he said. Now talk—damn you! Why were you riding with a Kiowa-Comanche war party?"

The captive's blood-crusted face stayed mute.

"Where is Shell?" Roan, until now questioning him calmly, felt his deep-rooted feeling come pounding out. "Where is the little Dawkins girl—the other one with blue eyes and yellow hair? Where is she? Why didn't Shell bring her to the fort? Is she dead? Is she?"

Unshaken, the Delaware showed not the slightest change of expression.

"One-of-Us," Curly said, "I will make him talk, this trader-Delaware." Drawing his knife, Curly stroked it back and forth over a small stone, the strokes rasping across the stillness.

Suddenly, Roan roared, "Where is Sanaco? Where is his camp?"

The Delaware flinched. He batted his eyes. These

reactions and once again he presented his mask of indifference, and, with insolence, he kicked the tin cup and the contents sloshed across the instep of Roan's right boot.

"So you know about Sanaco?" Roan taunted. "You know where his camp is? Tell me." He got nothing back, just the stony blankness of the jet eyes. "Talk to him, Curly. Not with the knife. Ask him where Sanaco's camp is."

Curly, eagerly, spoke Osage, and nothing happened. He spoke Kiowa, gesturing to underscore his words, the last sign unmistakable, a darting slash across the throat. And, surprisingly, the captive answered. Curly said:

"Trader-Delaware says he never heard of this Sanaco man. Says he rode with warriors to take Tejano horses. Says he likes all Heavy Brows, except Tejanos."

"He's lying—they were hell-bent to take captives, else the Delaware wouldn't been along. Ask him where the little Dawkins girl is. The one Shell claimed he had."

This time Curly spoke ceremoniously, out of the deep well of his chest. The captive seemed to reply hesitantly, as if he had already said too much.

"Trader-Delaware," Curly continued, "says his eyes have not seen this Heavy Brow child. Says he loves children heap; never steal even one. Says Shell is like the wind, big talk. Says Shell makes him work hard. Hunt. Look after horses. Bring in wood. Cook. Says—"

Roan's motion of disgust silenced Curly. "He's

121

lying—that leaves us no choice," he concluded ominously.

"What do you mean?" Povich asked.

For reply, Roan picked up the horsehair rope and glanced toward the river, said, "There's a likely tree," and saw that meaning shuttle over the prisoner's face. "Get up."

The Delaware obeyed without protest, his eyes alone betraying his anxiety. When they reached an elm tree, Roan threw the end of the rope over a limb, fixed the loop around the captive's neck, drew the rope taut, and demanded, "Where is Sanaco's camp? Where is the little Dawkins girl?"

The captive's eyes and mouth formed scornful refusal.

Roan jerked tighter. The Indian suddenly sucked for wind; his eyes bulged a little. "Talk," Roan said, easing the rope. Gulping, the captive showed Roan unchanging insolence, no more.

Roan pulled until the captive stood on tiptoe, until his eyes rolled, until Roan saw Povich's revulsion. Of a sudden Roan let the rope go slack, dropping the Indian slumped to the ground, gasping. Before he could get his wind, Roan jerked him backward by the hair. "Where is Sanaco? Where is the little girl?"

The captive scrubbed at his throat and stared back, in his eyes a glinting triumph hardened by unyielding defiance, and the purest hate Roan had ever seen.

"Take him back," Roan told two troopers. "Stake him out on his back. Spread-eagle him. No food, no

122

water till we get to the post."

He and Povich trailed the others back. Near-reproach hardened the younger officer's voice. "For a bit there I thought you were going to hang him sure."

"I'd hang him dead if it meant finding the Dawkins girl, if it would lead us to Sanaco's hideout."

"I see. Makes sense. There's really very little dash and glory to this business."

"There's satisfaction sometimes. The Delaware is tough and he won't bluff. He'd die before he'd tell, and he's smart enough to know he's no good to us dead. Therefore, he knew I wouldn't hang him. Next time he might be wrong."

"I never saw a man killed in battle until this morning. It was horrible. That and the savage scalping." He stared at Roan, his eyes questioning. "Why didn't you stop the others—you stopped Curly?"

"It's a cruel game, Povich. Whenever you begin to get soft, just think of a little girl with big blue eyes and soft yellow hair, and God knows how many like her, and the poor women—many of them already used up and dead—and the ones we happen to find just human wrecks better off dead. Think of them. I've seen 'em."

CHAPTER 9

Halted on the vantage ridge north of the cantonment, Roan was struck by the transformation below—a high, rectangular-shaped stockade, a blockhouse buttressing each corner, the ends of the newly cut logs shining fresh-yellow, completed in these few days since the start of the upriver scout. He had to give Major Thayer credit. The man was efficient as hell around the post.

Roan and Povich went immediately to headquarters, where the junior officer made his verbal report to the post commander. Adjutant Jernigan was there, as usual at Thayer's elbow. Instead of appeasing his vanity, his new role as adjutant had multiplied his self-adulation. He was unsmiling as they came in, affectedly at attention, head up, back arched, as formal as a drill book, more unbearable than ever, Roan saw. It was impossible to believe that he had served "with distinction" in the Mexican War as he claimed, according to Povich.

Thayer exhibited rare animation as Povich finished. The Major pounded the desk. His pale eyes danced. "Very good, Lieutenant. Proves cavalry can handle undisciplined Indians in the field. I think we've long overrated these people. They're rabble when cornered, when met decisively. I want a report down to the very last detail, Mr. Povich. I want it at once. A courier will leave for Fort Washita when you're finished." A bare smile eased the inflexible mouth. "I can imagine Colonel Emory's pleasure. We're giving him results which will quiet the Texas authorities. Now about the prisoner."

Povich looked to Roan, who said, "He's the Delaware that was with Kirk Shell at Fort Washita. Won't tell us anything that helps. Claims the war party was on a horse-stealing raid. I'm convinced he knows

Sanaco's whereabouts, and where the little Dawkins girl is, if she's alive. He's flint hard—smart to boot."

Thayer's eyes discounted the last. "He struck me as a thickheaded sort, hardly capable of possessing vital information."

"Might miss something if we underestimate him, Major. He's Shell's right-hand man. Speaks English, though he refuses to talk it. I'm wondering if money might loosen his tongue."

"I am not authorized to offer bribes," Thayer said, a stiffness cooling his enthusiasm.

"In that case," Roan said, "I think we should let Curly and his scouts apply a little Osage persuasion on the prisoner."

"Just how much?"

"Whatever it takes. Imagine the Osages would whittle on him a notch or two. That failing, maybe build a little fire under him. Let him feel it good."

"Torture?" Thayer sat back abruptly.

There was a stir as Jernigan shuffled his boots and leaned in. "Major, such inhumane treatment only perpetuates the general Indian problem."

"As for inhumanity," Roan countered, "what about the traffic in captives—the women and children? The scar carved on that child's face at Fort Washita to make poor old Dawkins think she was his flesh and blood. You have to be just as unfeeling as the people we're dealing with. Maybe more so for effect."

Thayer held up both hands for silence. "Naturally, the Army doesn't condone torturing prisoners. These

125

are unusual circumstances, however. If the Osages could wring Sanaco's whereabouts out of him . . ." He left that choice stranded in thought. "Bring the prisoner in. Let's have another go at him."

The scuffing of moccasined feet and the tramp of a trooper's boots announced the prisoner. That morning Roan had relented and allowed him water and rations, and the Delaware had scrubbed the blood off his face. He faced them quite coolly, his black eyes measuring their intent, and indifferent to it. His hands were tied behind him. At Thayer's curt gesture he sat in a chair.

"Commence the questioning, Mr. Kimball."

It was futile, Roan knew, as he launched into the old questions. Where was Sanaco's camp? Where was Shell? Where was the Dawkins girl? Where in Texas was the war party headed? And who was the white man in the war party? Was it Shell? Was it another white man?

And, as before, Roan met the same thwarting blankness. English failing, Roan released the prisoner's hands and resorted to signs. Back, again, came the frustrating evasion, the vagueness. But Tejano horses, yes. He wanted heap horses. Everybody wanted heap horses. And yet the black, mocking eyes seemed to say, *I know. I know everything you want to know. But I'll tell you nothing, white man.*

"It's no use, Major," Roan said finally.

"I agree. Tie and remove the prisoner."

Afterward, Roan said, "We've got to let the Osages

126

work on him. It's that or bribe him."

"Should the Judge Advocate's Department get wind of any of this, look out," Jernigan interposed.

"There's more at stake than a little singed hide," Roan reminded him.

"Enough," said Thayer, rising. "Perhaps a few days in the guardhouse on bread and water will effect some co-operation. If not, I may permit the Osages to try their hand—within limits, of course. Good day, gentlemen."

Roan could hardly believe his ears. Thayer was actually bending, showing common sense. Good! Jernigan looked startled.

That afternoon Roan went to the hospital, stuck like a box adjacent to the southeast blockhouse, to visit the wounded C Troop man and Thunder Walk. The Osage seemed to relish the attention he was getting in the strange surroundings. Lying on a cot, he put Roan in mind of a huge brown bear hibernating for the winter. The instant Thunder Walk saw Roan, he dug into a hide bag and dangled a black-haired scalp, still rusty with blood. He displayed it proudly.

"He shows that dang thing to everybody that comes in here," the trooper complained. "Makes me sick to look at it."

"When he goes back to camp, he'll mount it on a willow stick," Roan bantered. "Makes a right pretty doodad."

As Roan was leaving, a woman entered from the porch. It was Sara Thayer. She was bringing a cloth-covered plate that smelled of fresh cookies. He stood aside for her to pass. Intent on her mound of dainties, she did not notice him at once.

She turned suddenly, her eyes straight into his. In that swiftness of recognition, he glimpsed her as through the window of herself as she really was: without pretense, a unique woman, warm and generous, lovely and fair, and also lonely. The large eyes softened and she started to touch him, at the last instant drawing back her hand. Roan froze, resisting the impulse to take her arm.

Then, as if aware of others, the orderly at his desk and the pair in the cell-like ward, she took command of herself and tendered him a civil nod. Roan touched his hatbrim and went out to the porch.

His chest was hammering as he stood there, half aware of the afternoon drowse hugging the stockade, the stillness so acute he could hear the distinct chock-chock of a wood-cutting detail northeast of the post. A dry, hot wind flung grit against the east wall. He was waiting in the porch's narrow shade when suddenly she came outside.

Her face was pale, softly turned at seeing him. "That Indian showed me a scalp," she said, shuddering. "How horrible."

"To him, it's a symbol of honor. Means he's brave. There's nothing more important to an Indian." And he thought: Valerie would have shrieked. There'd been a scene.

To a passer-by Sara Thayer was chatting casually, as

128

one would expect of the post commander's lady. She looked perfectly at ease. Now and then she brushed at a strand of hair that persisted in falling across her forehead. He could see the tint of gold. Her voice was not calm:

"I was terribly afraid for you, Roan."

He tried to sound matter-of-fact. "The Osages made a big difference. And we got lucky. We took a captive who may lead us to the Dawkins girl. How've you been?"

He saw the familiar expression emerge, baffling, obscure. Her silence gave her a mysterious reserve and strength. Yet he knew.

"And Jamie?" he asked.

Her mood lifted, as always when she spoke of her son. "He loves it here. I'm having a time keeping him inside."

"Just the place for a boy."

"You love children. That's one reason why you're so set on finding the Dawkins child."

"Any man would want to."

"No—not any man. A lot wouldn't bother unless they could profit. Oh, Roan, you need a family."

"Except I'm particular, and I know I can't have you."

Her careful calm fell away. "What can possibly be done?"

"We have no choice, Sara."

"There's always duty, isn't there?"

"You have a fine young son and I . . . well, I must not interfere in your life more than I have."

"You haven't. You've made it bearable. What would I do without you?"

"You'd have to go on living. You're brave."

"I wonder if I'm brave at all." She was watching him closely. "Are you trying to tell me something, Roan? Are you, without saying it? Is it—good-by?"

Before he could reply, before he could tell her she had misunderstood him, he heard the orderly's boots sounding toward the doorway. By the time the trooper reached the porch, she had collected herself and was saying, "We're so glad you're all back, Mr. Kimball," and stepping down off the porch.

"It's that big Indian," the orderly said. "He wants to see you, Lieutenant."

Roan went inside. Thunder Walk said he was hungry for buffalo meat and the Heavy Brow soldiers had none.

Returning to his picket quarters, a ten-by-ten room he shared with Povich, where the wind-driven dust, filtering through gaps in the chinked logs, coated the bunks as with rust-colored powder, Roan was thankful that Povich wasn't there. It was over. He knew it. It had to be. Yet how badly he had handled everything! How clumsy he was back there, while not meaning to be. Because he had meant to tell her he loved her. Why hadn't he got that said before the trooper came out? Just a word—the one thing she needed most? The constant reassurance, just that he cared? Worse yet, the one fear he was trying to avoid had happened: He had hurt her. He had seen it shadow her lovely eyes as she

130

turned to leave the porch, as the trooper appeared, and Roan was powerless to say a single mending word.

Distressed, he walked to the stables south of the cantonment where Thayer had constructed sheds and a large, rugged corral of saplings, saddled up and rode to the scouts' camp in the woods. The Osages had killed two deer and were busy cutting thin strips of jerky for drying. Thunder Walk was all right, he told Curly, and hungry for meat. The wounded Osage would be riding again soon. Roan ate with the Osages and stayed until after Retreat.

He strolled the interior of the stockade, hoping to catch sight of her, but did not. Having come full circle, he paid a call at the hospital and afterward angled across to the guardhouse. There he learned from the bored sentry that the Delaware was the only prisoner. By then it was coming dark and he returned to his quarters, unable to shed his depression.

Listening to the lift and fall of Povich's steady snoring, he heard the bugle blow tattoo, then taps. A long time afterward he strayed into sleep. He was dreaming, seeing flashes of blank faces and places that had no connection. He was walking the streets of a great city, in the current of a vast crowd. A woman turned and he saw Sara's face. He was shouldering a path through the throng, calling her name as he went; but when he reached the place where he had seen her, she had vanished, and though he kept turning and searching, he didn't see her again. Around him there was a mighty shouting and the faces changed unaccountably, becoming hard and high-boned and proud, the faces those of the war party and the place the gap leading to the river through lead-gray light.

A shout tore at his consciousness. He heard it again. A real shout. He sat up. Outside somebody was running and shouting:

"Sergeant of the Guard! Sergeant of the Guard!"

Roan pulled on pants and boots and ran outside, Povich's sleepy query trailing him, "What's the fuss?"

It wasn't yet dawn. The husking wind bore out of the southwest. Roan could see dim figures sprinting for the guardhouse. He ran across. "What is it?" he demanded of the first man he came to, an uneasy anticipation clawing through him before he got the trooper's gasped-out reply, "That Indian knifed the guard—got clean away."

CHAPTER 10

The shod hoofs of the Delaware's mount, taken from the main corral after knifing another trooper, tracked north by northwest. When the trail disappeared, as it often did, the Osages fanned out like prowling wolves and before long they would pick up the prints again, and the five of them, Roan and Curly and young Runs-Against-the-Sun and Iron Head and Yellow Horse, would go rushing over the short-grassed prairie.

Their man had a start of several hours, at least. His escape hadn't been discovered until the guard changed at four-thirty. Hence, Roan reasoned, the escape could have occurred soon after midnight, when the unlucky trooper came on duty. There followed more time-killing, temperish jawing at headquarters.

"I think we should go after him," Roan told Major Thayer.

"Catch an Indian?" The Major was a narrow man who disliked suggestions, especially from junior officers; now, as if possessing superior experience concerning Indians, he threw it back at Roan.

"We can sure try," Roan insisted, keeping his impatience down, wishing that Jernigan didn't have his nose stuck in here. He was like a bird dog, always sniffing, always here when Roan was, always throwing his opinion behind the Major's, always counter to Roan. "That Indian knows where Sanaco is," Roan said. "He's our only chance. We've got to run him down, Major."

"You're needed here, Mr. Kimball, as are all the scouts."

"I want just a few. But I want Curly. He'll leave Traveling Elk in charge. He's reliable. He knows what to do. He's a warrior of high standing."

"If I may express an opinion, it strikes me as a wild goose chase," Jernigan remarked, his smile patronizing. "By now the escapee is probably at some dirty Indian camp in the mountains, reciting his daring escape from the pony soldiers."

"A camp that could be Sanaco's headquarters," Roan said.

133

Jernigan assumed an incredulous air. "You have a constructive imagination, Lieutenant. This Sanaco, as you call him—you talk as if he were some sinister figure. Some hideous ogre who deals in captives as a business."

"That and more," Roan replied firmly. "Add murder as well."

Thayer, his fingers beating a staccato on the desk, said, "You might as well look for the proverbial needle in the haystack."

"He's the only lead we've had so far, Major. Our one chance."

"We have to chance nothing of the sort if I oppose it," Thayer responded, very clipped, brushing at his mustache, on his high horse of dignity. "Of far more immediate urgency is to continue turning back the wild bands from crossing the Red into Texas."

"Traveling Elk and the other Osages, with one troop, can patrol the crossings."

There was another side to the Major. He could, to score a point, stroke another man's vanity. "Although I am somewhat loath to say so, Mr. Kimball, you work well with Indian scouts. I can't afford to let you go off on a fool chase."

"With all due respect, Major, I don't see this as a fool chase. The Delaware holds the key right now."

"You're playing hunches, Mr. Kimball. No more."

"I regret to remind you, sir, but I must. In the field I act under verbal orders from Colonel Emory. Those orders were to get Sanaco at just about any cost."

134

Thayer's face flamed. He jerked up from his chair. "Within certain limits, Mr. Kimball, which means within the discretion of the commanding officer, who happens to be myself."

The room became completely still. Roan saw that he had gone too far, pricked the Major's most sensitive area of conceit, the extent of his command. Roan had the sensation of plunging ahead recklessly, his voice sounding terse and strained, remote and alien to his own:

"Sir, every minute we delay is costing us. That Indian might lead us straight to the wolf's den. I say again it's worth the gamble. Besides, he killed two troopers. He's fair meat."

"I see," Thayer said, ominously calm, "I must make myself clear for the final time. I shall call a special court-martial here, or request the department commander to authorize a general court-martial, if you persist in disobeying orders by roaming off half-cocked across the country. Is that clear?"

"It is, sir."

Roan was trembling inside, angry and frustrated. As casual as he could make it, he saluted and left, not missing Jernigan's glint of satisfaction, which stayed before his eyes as he went to his quarters.

He jammed his hands into his pockets, waiting for his feelings to subside, realizing that he was tangled in the one fix he had dreaded since Colonel Emory had instructed him to use his own judgment—and take the consequences. Sometimes verbal orders had a nasty

135

way of leaving a man high and dry. It wasn't just Sanaco alone—it was what he stood for and the breadth of his operations and the gut-felt misery he caused; it was the little Dawkins girl, if she still lived, and more like her and the dead-faced women like those Roan had seen in Texas. In his obsession with Sanaco, whom he now visioned as half white, half Indian—Kiowa or Comanche or Kiowa-Apache—Roan had failed to bring the captives into his argument. Not, he supposed, that it would have mattered much. Thinking of the captives gave him strength and clarity, and he set about collecting his needs.

Within minutes, he walked out of the post with his gear, saddled his horse, and galloped for the Osage camp. It was then, in motion, his indecision laid by, that his thoughts carried back with a delayed insight. Was he doing what the Major, secretly, wanted him to do, so he could be court-martialed?

The direction of the tracks puzzled Roan as they continued to slant away from the Wichita Mountains, rising as low humps clothed in blue haze to the east and northeast.

"Where do you figure he's headed?" he asked Curly.

The Osage, head down, scanning, rode to a swell in the prairie before he replied. "One-of-Us, this man rides good horse."

"I know. He took Stone Face's Kentucky sorrel. Think he's going to the Washita River? Kiowas and Comanches don't range that far north, unless it's for buffalo."

Curly was thoughtful. "Maybe the Spirit Place."

"What's that?"

With his hands, the Osage described low buttes, a series of them, and a winding river. He said it was two or three sleeps away.

"Why do you call it the Spirit Place?"

"If we go there, you will understand," and he said no more.

Whatever, this was all new country to Roan, boundless and open, free as the eye could see, rich with short grasses, speckled with buffalo; from time to time flashes of white betrayed bands of antelope, their bobbing rump patches giving them away.

It was growing late the second day when the Osages killed a fat buffalo cow and made camp by a cedar-lined spring that offered up its slim trickle of sweet water.

While everyone gorged, Curly said, "Trader-Delaware's horse, which is used to Stone Face's grain, is getting tired like old stud. He was foolish, this man, two times today. He hurries too much. He rode over soft ground when he could ride over red rocks long way and make us waste time hunting for his tracks. He did that because he is hungry, this man. He stopped to eat red plums." Although Curly had more to relate of the day, he let his liking for loquacious ceremony take over, and he paused, reflecting, then continued, "He is also wise like coyote, this man. Sometimes when he comes to high place, he ties horse below and lies on belly and looks back. At night he ties reins of Stone

137

Face's new bridle to his wrist while Stone Face's fine horse grazes, and he rolls up in Stone Face's new horse blanket and sleeps good, this man. If anybody comes close, horse will jerk his head and wake this man, this trader-Delaware who wears white-man clothes."

Roan nodded and Curly talked on. At times Iron Head and Yellow Horse said something. Runs-Against-the-Sun, because he was the youngest and unproven, said not a word out of respect for the older warriors.

When Roan saw that Curly had finished, he asked, "Whose hunting ground are we on now?"

"Walks-the-Prairie People," Curly explained, "and the Big-Nose People."

Roan understood. The former were Cheyennes, the latter Arapahoes. He reasoned on that and got nowhere. Since neither tribe raided into Texas, why would the fugitive flee so far, away from the Cut-Knives?

Unexpectedly the tracks evaporated next day not far from a creek that emptied into a shallow river winding below little round red hills like a curling ribbon; in fact, everywhere Roan looked the land was flame-colored. At the river, which Curly called "Tipi-Pole-Timber River," the white man's Washita, the five of them singled off to ride up and down the river's south bank for tracks.

They found nothing. Across, they scouted upriver and down and rode slowly through the round-topped hills, while before them grew a fledgling creek in indolent passage to the river.

Runs-Against-the-Sun dashed ahead to the creek. After a moment, he lifted a signaling arm. Hurrying with the others, Roan saw the crumbled bank and leading away, on firmer footing, the naked prints of shod hoofs.

"Ho," said Curly, soberly approving. "Trader-Delaware rode Stone Face's horse down creek on other side of river and came up creek here. One-of-Us, this man is wise."

Curly dismounted and followed the tracks some twenty yards and crouched. With a forefinger, he touched the indented earth; crouching lower, he blew on the loose grains of red dirt. Suddenly he rose and led his horse back, his mouth pursed in thought.

"Stone Face's horse is limping," he said, keeping his voice low. He pointed downward. "See how he favors one foot, not putting it down hard? Just little time ago he passed here." An extra watchfulness stood in his coffee-amber eyes. "He is close now. Everybody watch."

He signed for them to spread out. Quietly walking their horses, they moved on, the eager Runs-Against-the-Sun in advance. Ahead, Roan saw a clump of trees. Movement flashed there, going away. Runs-Against-the-Sun yelled and clapped heels to his horse, tearing ahead.

A rider in white man's clothes burst out of the trees, rein-lashing his horse. A cavalry mount, Roan saw, that was limping badly.

Runs-Against-the-Sun reached him first, knife out,

139

and hurled himself headlong, sweeping the rider clear. They struck and rolled in the short grass, a tangle of arms and legs. The young Osage was strong as an elk. He threw the man on his back and thrust repeatedly with his knife. His gobbling cry lifted. When Roan rushed there, the Osage was standing over the Delaware, who was writhing and gasping. Curly's shout stopped the young warrior.

The man was terribly hurt; great gouts of blood funneled down his chest. Slipping off his horse, Roan made his voice deliberately harsh. "Where is Sanaco's camp?"

Death glazed the dark eyes. The strong, wide mouth was drawn in a snarl.

"We will try to help you," Roan said, easing up. "You have nothing to gain by holding back. Sanaco would not protect you. Tell us where his camp is."

Bright red foam bubbled along the tortured, open mouth sucking for air. Straining, as if calling on the last of his intensity, his hate, the Delaware spat at Roan and sank back, strengthless. Bit by bit, he turned his face to the sky, eyes bulging wider. A cloud seemed to pass over his features. He appeared to grow smaller against the red earth. Roan could not but feel pity as his life left him then.

Roan got to his feet.

"Runs-Against-the-Sun," Curly said, reproving him, "you are brave, but you did bad thing. Now trader-Delaware can't lead us to Sanaco, the bad one." Curly was angry, truly angry, which was unusual for him; for a moment Roan thought he meant to quirt the younger warrior.

"Had the Delaware lived he would have told us nothing," Roan said, and turned to examine the dead man's horse while the chagrined Runs-Against-the-Sun took the scalp. The sorrel gelding had a loose left front shoe. Using his belt knife, Roan pried off the shoe, pulled the loose nails, and trimmed and cleaned the tender hoof. The horse would continue to limp for a time, for he had been used hard, but an extra mount might be useful.

"You have the honor of leading Stone Face's mount," Roan said, and handed the reins to the surprised young Osage.

A letdown of uncertainty gripped them; they stood around, gazing off, letting the tired horses graze.

"The Delaware was heading northwest from the time he escaped," Roan reflected after a while. "Which way is the Spirit Place you told me about?"

Curly pointed northwest, his eyes narrowing in thought.

"Let's go," said Roan.

Hours later they continued to ride northwest, gradually climbing, through a world of grass, over one rounded prairie swell after another, at the moment beginning to pass through endless masses of buffalo. It was the rutting season and the amorous young bulls were staging savage duels for the cows, pawing the red earth, stumpy tails high, hair bristling, bloodshot eyes rolling. An older animal stood alone, horned out of the herd, forlornly eying his tormentors.

"Look," said Curly, not without compassion, "they have thrown him away. He is no good, like old man without woman. The wolves will get him by winter."

Iron Head suggested they kill a buffalo. Curly said no, not yet. "Where there are many buffalo, there are Indians. Maybe so many Indians and we are few."

A strange-looking butte became visible, its rounded top emerging from the prairie floor like a crumbling battle tower of another age. They passed it and another much like it. And all at once, reaching the backbone of a rise, Roan saw a cluster of isolated buttes, aloof and mysterious, and past them the broad curve of a river and the eye-burning glitter of its sugar-white sands. Everything seemed glazy and awesome and vaporous, the buttes standing guard as sentinels overlooking the forbidding reaches of the river. Although the heat was stifling, Roan felt a chilly sense of being on queasy footing. He had stopped his horse. So had the Osages, who were strangely quiet.

"I don't like this place," Curly said. "Bad things happen here. I came here with hunting party when I was young man, younger than Runs-Against-the-Sun. Walks-the-Prairie People jumped us one morning. We lost five good warriors. Now, One-of-Us, you know why we call it the Spirit Place."

Runs-Against-the-Sun wanted to climb the nearest butte and scan the country across river. "Go," said Curly, "but don't stand up like young buffalo bull, ready to fight. Stay down."

142

Roan decided to go also, and they climbed the rocky slant. Flattened out, Roan uncased his field glasses and took a sweeping look. The sun glinted on broken rock and sand. Nothing moved along the river. Across, the land roughed up into reddish bluffs. Stubby timber scrawled the course of a creek. He showed the Osage how to use the glasses. Fascinated, the young man held them to his eyes for a long time. His interest seemed to fix on one place.

"See something?" Roan asked.

"I see no people, no horses, no buffalo. If camp is there, it is back near creek."

"See any smoke?"

"No smoke."

They descended and reported. Roan was agreeable to crossing the river. Curly, however, was uneasy. He pulled up a blade of grass and, studying it with the pre-occupation of one whose thoughts were elsewhere, said, "If Sanaco is there, he will have people watching from bluffs. We will rest here and cross just before dark. I don't like this place, One-of-Us."

They were no more than dimly moving blurs when they felt the soft crunch of sand under their mounts and watered the horses in the thin stream and filled the buffalo paunches the Osages preferred instead of canteens. Curly was moving across when he halted abruptly. Roan smelled it at the same moment, the faint yet distinct scent of wood smoke. Curly faded downstream, carefully walking his horse.

It seemed like such a long time before he crossed

143

into the broken line of low bluffs on the north side of the river. He seemed to be feeling his way; once he slid down and led his horse. At times he paused to listen. When finally he turned west toward the creek, the rising moon was a pale disc and the light on the short grass was like a veiled glow.

Curly entered timber. Here he dismounted, here they would camp. No one spoke. Roan unsaddled and picketed his horse in close and lay down, feeling the swift grip of sleep. The last sensation his drugged senses relayed to him was the wild incense of wood smoke carried on the wind.

Mere moments, it seemed, and he felt a touch on his forehead and he sat up in total darkness. There was a paleness behind the eastern sky. He rose stiffly, without a word; discerning Curly's intentions, he stepped alongside the Osage and left camp.

Roan thought of two wolves prowling the predawn darkness, sniffing the coolness, the sweet earth smells, ears cocked for hostile sounds. He heard only the light sounds of their feet brushing the short grass.

The smoke? He smelled none. Had a campfire died its last, left by hunters to smolder out? As Roan moved along in thought, a dog barked—or was that a coyote's yip?—and a bell tinkled musically, the sort of bell you would loop on the neck of a gentle mare whom the other horses followed. He froze, as did Curly. The tinkling was coming from over the low wedge of ground ahead of them. They crouched and reached the place, seeing no shift in the darkness, and got down. By now the bell sounded in the pooled blackness below the rise.

The light arrived gradually, dull gray streaks stabbing the east, the advance of a pinkish, approaching world, and behind that, suddenly, a flood of fire charging toward the west.

Below the murk was peeling away and Roan saw a band of loose horses and the prickly spires of tipis scattered on the flat of a creek. Not a large village, some twenty lodges, and just beyond the tipis the round, treeless knob of a lookout hill.

CHAPTER 11

They lay amid thick, redolent weavings of summer-dried grass on the rounded swell, bellies flat. As the light increased, they crawled to a thicket of plum bushes.

About then Roan noticed the first gray figures leaving the camp, bound for the creek, followed by quarrelsome camp dogs. Indian women, his glasses told him, though by now a white woman, sun-blackened, head down, a buffalo paunch for water over her shoulder, would look Indian from here. Indian women and young girls, the girls gathering wood.

When the first Indian man appeared around the lodges, Curly Wolf gripped his arm and hissed, "Look— a Cut-Knife! Why they come way north?" Other men were visible now; some boys came to see about the horses. Roan followed each man through his glasses.

More Cut-Knives, Curly said. Some Comanches. Others dressed like Heavy Brows. "Off-breeds." Curly snorted his contempt.

Roan set the glasses again, watching the children, and slowly brought his hands down. Not one was white that he could see, though the way they turned and stooped for wood, and in the early light, he couldn't tell with certainty. He began to feel a letdown.

Around noon Curly slipped back for water. Heat smothered the plum thicket. Below, the camp appeared to doze. Here and there men sat around the tipis. To occupy his time, Roan studied each lodge. One in the center of camp attracted his attention. Painted bright red, with the dark, flat figures of horses and warriors in battle. When Curly returned, Roan point out the lodge to him.

Curly, using the glasses, said, "A chief's lodge. Only important man paint his lodge like that."

Throughout the afternoon they watched. No hunters rode out, none came in. To Roan there was something amiss about the camp. Was it that, feeling secure from attack, they had become slack and neglectful, unmindful of danger? And why the unusual mixture of tribes?

Later the women and girls returned for wood and water. He was adjusting his glasses to bear on the children, when they scattered down-creek into thicker timber, and thus he lost his chance to catch a glimpse of their faces.

At evening Roan and Curly put back to camp. They

146

chewed on jerky, of which the Osages had an ample supply, and lay down. Sleep evaded Roan. He was troubled. Had they traveled this hard distance to learn nothing? To find just remnants of bands seeking refuge in a remote place, far from the pony soldiers and the war along Red River?

A realization gathered force, clear and strong. "Curly," he said, half calling, "we must ride into that camp tomorrow."

He could hear the Osage shifting on his blanket. "Ride there? Lose our hair?"

"Watching tells us nothing."

"What you tell these faraway people?"

"We will go to the red lodge and we will give the headman Stone Face's fine sorrel as a gift. They won't kill us if we come with an impressive gift."

"What you tell Red Lodge Chief?"

"Tell him we're looking for Army deserters."

The Osage expelled a throaty grunt of skepticism. "Ho. Why Cut-Knives help you, one soldier man? Their enemy?"

"But we come with gift. A fine horse."

"Ho. So you bring fine horse. Red Lodge Chief take fine horse. Ho. So we ride away. What you learn about Sanaco?"

"That's up to us. We'll talk, we'll look around camp. I want a good look at the Red Lodge Chief." As he spoke, Roan was thinking back: I keep remembering Sanaco's other name—Scar-Arm.

"One-of-Us"—Curly sounded weary—"tomorrow

147

may be bad day, because I know you are going into that camp, and I cannot let you go alone because we are friends. Let us sleep."

The sun was well up when they prepared to leave next morning. Curly put on his best leggings and moccasins and took out his small looking-glass; using bone tweezers with great care, he plucked his brows clean and attached his quivering roach of deer-tail hair and turkey-gobbler beard, and to the side of his head he fixed the tail feather of the golden eagle. When Curly had finished, Roan saw that he had grown appreciably taller. Appearing to draw power and confidence from his preparations, Curly also donned a buckskin shirt, under which at his belt he stuck a second knife.

"Never trust off-breeds," he swore, striking a superior air.

Roan could not resist bedeviling him. "You mean only Osages are trustworthy?"

"Today that is true, my friend."

With Roan leading the sorrel gelding, they clattered down-slope where Roan saw a willow-fringed spring flowing into the creek. It was here, he realized now, that the women had filled the buffalo paunches. As the two made for the red lodge, walking their horses, the lean camp dogs rushed forth barking and snarling. Nothing moved atop the lookout knob on the other side of the village.

An old woman in the first lodge peeked at them as they passed, eyes startled, and jerked back. Her high-pitched voice welled out in warning. Men became visible at once. Roan, except to see they meant no harm as yet, pretended to ignore them. Curly's expression was haughty. An Indian dressed like a white man stared, then strode across to a tipi on the far side.

Three Indians in like garb posted themselves before the entrance of the red lodge. There Curly halted, gazing down at them scornfully. Roan, closing in, noted that each man had a new Army Springfield rifle.

Curly cut signs meaning Chief and See and, pretending heap generosity, gestured grandly toward the sorrel. The Indians said no word; their stiff expressions did not change. Curly, unperturbed, switched to nasal, choking Kiowa; again they displayed their hard silence, their eyes saying: We will tell you nothing. Go.

Curly paused and glanced at Roan, who addressed them in English: "We want to see your chief. We bring him a gift."

He saw their high-boned faces quicken—they understood!—but before he could say more, one jogged his rifle violently at Roan: Go.

The Indian's left hand formed the pushing-away sign. He drove a single Kiowa word at them: Go.

"Friends—we are friends," Roan kept on, and saw the snout of the Springfield freeze level with his chest. The face behind the rifle looked rock hard. Something twisted in Roan's stomach, and he felt a sudden cold sweat. He was about to speak again when a voice spoke harshly within the lodge in Kiowa. Although he didn't understand all the words, he got enough and the tone, though not friendly, was even and controlled:

149

"Let them come in."

The rifle holder stepped back and Roan, breathing freer, dismounted and flung the guard the reins.

Ducking inside, Roan entered the temple dimness of a commodious lodge—its trappings rich, furs and robes and war shield and lance, a dozen scalps displayed upon the last, the skin covering of the lodge rolled up at the bottom for coolness—seeing at the rear a sitting figure. An Indian man. He waved a woman and small girl outside. They hastened past Roan before he could see their faces. His glimpse of the girl was momentary. A slim shape clad in a pretty buckskin dress of muted lemon color and intricate beadwork designs. The man motioned him and Curly to sit, and Roan sank into the soft luxury of tanned buffalo robes.

A pause ensued. The host had a lean face and body, his features smoothly formed, the dark eyes as sharp as flint points, his mouth firm, a severity that suggested the self-discipline and muscled hardness of an ascetic. His black, straight hair hung to his shoulders without ornamentation. He wore a red cloth shirt of uncommon quality, a string of blue beads around his neck. Silver rings on both hands accented long, sensitive fingers. The man's skin had a pallor, as if he were part white—half white, Roan decided.

"We come as friends," Roan said. When the host did not reply, Curly, in Kiowa, explained their mission. The man replied then, after which Curly said aside to Roan, "He says he has seen no Army deserters. If he had, he would have killed them."

"Tell him about the gift."

Following another exchange, Curly said, "He has many fine horses. All he wants and more."

"Tell him he hasn't seen the sorrel, which is a fine animal. Kentucky stock, if that means anything to him."

Without any warning, the host burst into sardonic laughter. "You white men amuse me. You think you can offer an Indian one lame horse and he will give you anything. I observed your coming. I saw the horse. I would give such an animal to a herd boy."

Roan, throttling his astonishment, said, "You speak very good English."

"A missionary taught me. A well-meaning Quaker. I was his prize student—for a while. I don't speak good English, white man. I speak *excellent* English." He reached under a robe and drew out a newspaper and rolled it up and waggled it like a club at Roan. "I'm Indian, but I'm not ignorant. I keep up. I know what is going on in your Texas settlements where the buffalo-killers live. Your newspapers tell me much. That is another thing I have learned about you whites. You are like crows. You tell everything you know. Caw, caw, caw." He flung the newspaper down, contempt burning his eyes.

"Who are you?"

There was a cold edge to the voice. "Red Shield. My mother was white—a captive. My father Comanche."

"You live a long way from your people."

151

"Comanches and Kiowas are going downhill, becoming reservation Indians, living off what the whites throw them. Feed a dog once and he will slink back for more scraps." He swept his hand about. "These are my people—free people of many tribes—come here to live in peace—away from the smell of you whites." A smile that was not a smile curled his straight mouth. "What is it you want, white man? Speak."

"We're looking for deserters."

"I told this Wa-sha-she Osage, I have seen no deserters." Suddenly he bent Roan a penetrating look. "What fort?"

Caution delayed Roan. He was going to say Fort Washita when Red Shield threw back his head in imitation of a hearty laugh. "Fort Richardson, Belknap, Washita? You didn't want to say the new soldier house on Red River, did you? I know about that fort. Every Indian does . . . Whites always lie. I know. Rangers raided our camp, killed my father. They took my mother and me as a boy to the Texas settlements. They promised her a home. It was a log prison where they kept her so she couldn't go back to the prairies. She was a captive of the whites. She died of a broken heart. After she died, they didn't care about me because I looked like the Indian I am, except for my pale skin, which I hate, and which I hide under this shirt. It was easy for me to escape."

Roan had an odd, uneasy feeling as Red Shield spoke. The man's powerful stare had a hypnotic quality, a driving force. He was strong.

"Not all whites are like that," Roan said.

"I need no white man's sympathy. Count yourself lucky. If you were a Ranger or a Tejano settler, you would be dead by now. I kill every Ranger and Tejano on sight, just as they kill every Indian."

Roan nodded. "What you say is true."

"I always tell the truth."

"The Tejanos do that because Indians raid across Red River."

"The Tejanos would kill us if we didn't raid. Now that you have found our camp, which we thought was safe from you whites, go—leave us alone." Red Shield rose abruptly, a clear signal for departure.

"I would like to make more talk with you tomorrow," Roan said.

"Our talk is finished."

They filed out past the guards. Roan swept a scouring look back and forth, but only the guards were in sight. One pushed the reins at him and Roan mounted. As he swung to saddle, his eyes were attracted to the lookout knob, bald when they had gone inside. Now a single rider there was watching them. At this distance, in his white man's clothes, he looked like any of Curly's "off-breed" Indians. Only his mount was distinctive. A big bay with an irregular blazed face. Roan saw Curly's eyes flick that way also, briefly. Then, leading the sorrel, they rode eastward out of camp.

Roan didn't speak until they watered the horses at

the creek below the spring. "Was that Sanaco? Was that Scar-Arm?"

Curly's gaze rested thoughtfully on his horse's flicking ears. "He had on shirt. I couldn't see his arm. He is very strong man. I could feel his power."

"So could I."

"He shoots every Ranger or Tejano on sight. So he raids Texas. No Rangers or Tejanos come this side of Red River. So he could be Sanaco."

"True. Did you get a good look at the little girl?"

"No. But she was dressed like favorite child."

"You didn't see her face?"

"One-of-Us," said Curly, wincing, "Red Shield's woman passed between us. I could not see."

Roan was discouraged. He had expected Curly's sharp eyes to note more than he had.

"You saw the Springfield rifles? Brand new. Later models than ours at the Soldier House."

"Only a rich man could own so many shiny rifles," Curly said enviously.

"Only a rich man could furnish them, I'd say."

Roan was engrossed as they filed past the spring. When they reached the plum thicket, which hid them from the camp, he said, "Go on with the horses. I want to watch awhile."

"Ho. You think Red Shield come damnbetcha quick?"

"Not yet. I don't think he wants any trouble."

"We found his faraway camp. Why not kill us now?"

"He can always try that later. He didn't believe our

154

story, Curly. He wants to find out why we came." Suddenly Roan turned back. "You saw the man on the blaze-faced horse on the hill. He wasn't there when we rode into the village."

"Ho."

"Was he Indian or white?"

"One-of-Us, brave as I am, strong as I see, long way off, like hawk, I no see everything. But maybe this man on hill was white."

Crawling through the low-growing plum bushes to the lip of the overlooking ridge, Roan wasn't certain why he chose to watch the strangely indolent, well-armed camp and its still stranger mixture of tribes, unless it was the unseen face of the child in Red Shield's lodge that bothered him.

He burrowed out a place to lie. The day dragged into afternoon, the smothering heat trapped in the bushes. His eyes became heavy and he nodded, hearing the endless hum of insects and now and then the bark of a dog in the village.

He woke with a wrench, realizing that he had dozed for a spell. The red eye of the sun had slipped several notches down its westward grade, and mottled shadows cloaked the creek. And children played there in the coolness, darting from tree to tree, while women filled the paunches at the spring. He took up the glasses to study the women. Their faces seemed close enough to touch as they talked and laughed. No white faces. He was positive. His discouragement pressed heavier, and he turned his attention to the children, first on the coltish boys, dashing about, imitating warriors in battle. He could see each face fairly well—every one an Indian.

There were seven girls, ranging in age, he judged, from about six to twelve. He was studying the fourth one when, as if by impulse, they swarmed to the creek to go wading. This one he studied was slim as a willow and brown-skinned, and her hair was wrapped in a red headcloth tied under her chin. At that moment, before he could see her face well, a taller girl slid between him and his subject but not before he noted the younger one's beaded dress.

Meaning charged through him. The dress—the fancy, intricate, geometric bead patterns—the little girl in Red Shield's lodge had worn it. He remembered it vividly now, just as Curly had. Curly's words returned: a favorite child. He still couldn't manage a clear view of her face. His mind seemed to knot, squeezed harder and harder. He could wait no longer. There might be no second time.

Leaving the binoculars, he snatched up his canteen, which was down to a few mouthfuls, and went unhurriedly downslope toward the spring, swinging the canteen by its strap.

The women ceased chattering when they saw him, and the children quit wading to stare at him. In as much as he was afoot and showed no weapon, he realized that to sharp Indian eyes he was an object of curiosity rather than a menace, the pony soldier who had entered their village and left without threat. Walking at a slouch, he pretended to have no interest in them.

Nobody ran when he tossed the canteen into the spring's oval pool to let it fill, kneeling laxly, holding the strap, feigning indifference to their gaping. Out of the edge of his eyes he could see the girls staring like young does. He must look in the next seconds if he was to find out now; it must be a careless glance. By this time the women were drifting away, wary of him, though he appeared not to notice.

Now, he thought, as the filled canteen sank and he drew it in and capped it and glanced across at the women, and past them, seeing the slight shape, the beaded-dress shape and the shawl-hooded head and the deeply tanned small face.

It was the eyes that shocked him, a startling clear blue, they were. He seemed to quit breathing. He wanted to shout and dash forward and scoop her up and run over the slope to camp. Instead, he took off his hat and washed his face, deliberate movements that took him nearer the creek. The women were calling the children. For a swaying moment the blue-eyed one didn't move. The women, laden with water paunches, were toiling up the other bank. Picking up his hat and hand-wiping his face, he looked once more at her and pitched his voice softly, almost soundlessly, "Emily . . . Emily."

He thought he saw a flash across the blue eyes, and the small mouth crimp a bit, puzzled, or possibly he imagined it because he wanted her to remember her name.

By then she was turning to follow the other children. Roan, slipping the canteen strap over one shoulder, went up the long slope without glancing back, as slow of step as he was coming down to the spring. Out of sight on the other side of the swell, he ran to the plum bushes, found his hole, crawled in, and grabbed the glasses and adjusted them quickly. He picked her out at once, walking alongside a slim young woman.

Presently, they entered Red Shield's lodge.

CHAPTER 12

Curly was posted on a knoll above the Osage camp, watching toward the village, when Roan found him and told him. The rich brown eyes became grave.

"One-of-Us, I know what you do now," he said, which was as near as Roan had ever seen him come to expressing weariness. "When women and children come to creek tomorrow morning, you will steal her. Only not many Osages to help this time."

"You're wise like the coyote."

"You forget Red Shield? Sanaco, the Bad One?"

"The little girl comes first."

"What about Soldier House Chief's orders?"

"We don't know Red Shield is Sanaco."

"But you think maybe he is." Curly flung up a hand. "Trader-Delaware was coming here. Red Shield won't stay here long. He's no fool, this man."

"We can find him again."

Riding to the lookout before dawn, Roan had his doubts. Last night the plan had seemed convincing. A short time ago, Runs-Against-the-Sun, with Yellow Horse and Iron Head, taking lariats, had eased into the village horse herd and, each leading a mount, drifted the horses to the river and scattered them downstream. Runs-Against-the-Sun, being the youngest, would hold the party's horses while Roan carried out his part of the scheme.

Much, Roan realized, hinged on chance, on timing: that the women and girls would arrive at the usual hour, before the herd boys discovered their loss; that when Roan took his canteen to the spring, he could position himself close to the girl without suspicion, grab her, and run up the slope to the Osages. There was yet another hazard he hadn't reckoned with: The girls, busy gathering wood, would not be wading early in the morning coolness, and likely he wouldn't find himself in the advantageous circumstance of yesterday.

He crouched, waiting for daylight. By and by, the grudging sky shed a dove grayness and the hills revealed their somber expression, and as the light came bolder, he picked out figures leaving the village. Right away he had his first inkling of wrongness—there were fewer women and children this time. He was too far away to distinguish the small, shawl-hooded head in the murk.

He waited until the women crossed the shallow creek to the spring. Rising, he stepped boldly down the slope, taking the careless, noisy strides of a sluggish man just risen from his blankets, hatless, hair unkempt, scratching at his stomach and ribs, yawning as he went.

159

The instant he tossed the canteen into the spring and turned his head, he knew something wasn't right. The languid, talkative women of yesterday were silent, intent on filling the unwieldy paunches, and although there was a plentiful supply of fallen branches on this side of the creek, within several feet of the spring, the children did not cross; they worked in a bunch, not scattered and carefree as usual. Their close grouping hindered his view; also some had their backs to him.

He forced himself to take time, scrubbing his stubbled face and neck, and arms and hands. The canteen had filled and sunk when he retrieved and capped it. He cut his eyes at the children, was alarmed to see them straying down-creek. Drying his face on his shirt sleeve, he fixed his gaze on them. His casualness vanished. He could see clearly by now. He kept scrutinizing them, a sustained look, and was suddenly at a loss, aghast. Emily wasn't among them.

In time he remembered the women. Looking down at the canteen to cover his shock, he gathered himself before he moved. Without haste, he took the canteen strap and rose, walking heavily back up the slant, feeling eyes following him.

"She wasn't there," he informed Curly upon reaching the off side of the plum thicket. "Something's wrong, I know. Let's go back to camp."

"Wait," Curly cautioned, and jerked.

Roan, shifting that way, saw a slight figure in a buckskin dress slipping along the brushy spine of the slope. Her hair, cut raggedly, Indian style, and down to her

160

shoulders, was as yellow as an ear of corn.

Roan's elation burst. By God, she was going with them. But when he moved toward her, she froze like a wild thing, lips working, trembling, as if groping for unfamiliar words.

"You go—go way," she said.

"Go away! You're coming with us—now!"

She seemed to shrink, to grow smaller. "No—you go."

He stepped across. Her blue eyes widened. Still, she didn't evade him and he touched her face, her cheeks, her left cheekbone, his mind closing, remembering Dawkins' words, his eyes narrowing. At last he saw it high on the cheekbone, pale beneath her deeply sun-browned skin, old and dim, having become more inconspicuous with her young years; but unmistakable, like a light waiting to be seen—the crescent-shaped scar that Samuel Dawkins had described.

"You *are* Emily," he said, his voice awed. "Emily Dawkins. Don't you remember your father? Your mother? Your brothers?"

A mixture of pain and bewilderment flew into her distraught face. She said, with difficulty, "Red Shield my father—you go. You stay—they kill you." Her right hand swept down and out, palm up, the sign for Knocked Over or Dead.

"You're going with us, Emily."

"No—my name—Little Star." A pleading turned her small voice more childlike. "You go—I go—" And she flung around, whipping back up the slope.

161

"Emily, come back!"

She was running like a frightened colt, all legs. There was movement upgrade in the thicket.

Curly yelled something in Osage and his rifle blazed. Roan spied a low-moving figure, appearing and disappearing. He snap-fired the revolver once, then again. The bushes shook violently, ebbed to a quivering, and were still. A shot cracked, followed by a puff of smoke. Iron Head doubled up, his rifle clattering.

Roan couldn't wait. He made a flying mount and kicked out after her, flushing from the bushy tangle upslope, at his horse's feet, the Indian who had shot Iron Head. Roan smashed into him, feeling the gelding's front quarters striking bones and flesh, hurling the Indian spinning, his broken body rolling, not rising. Farther on a third figure broke clear, sprinting for the village.

Roan let him go and tore ahead. She was dodging, fleet as a coyote. He had the gelding running full tilt, and he leaned low and swept her up, no heavier than a cornstalk, kicking and clawing. Pivoting his mount around, he galloped back where Curly and Yellow Horse were hoisting Iron Head to his nervous horse.

Once across the white-sand dismalness of the river and the snake of shallow water, Roan switched her to the sore-footed sorrel. They rode like that to the battlements of the Spirit Place. Of a sudden Iron Head pitched from his horse, and when he turned his slack face to them, his eyes had the glaze of a dying man.

They carried him to the shade of a butte, waiting, in silence, for him, to die. Afterward, they took him to a high niche and sat his body up, facing east, and piled rocks around, and the Osages sang the Death Song as they rode on.

Emily, hushed until now, kept looking back. "Red Shield will come," she said, and Roan saw the shriveling scorn of an Indian for him. "My father will come."

He spoke sharply. "He's not your father. Your father's living in Texas."

Her bluest of eyes, her child's sensitive mouth, the tilt of her head—all of her denied him. "Red Shield— my father." No dust tails of pursuit smoked up behind them, which meant the villagers hadn't yet caught their scattered horses, and it was yet light when Roan saw the welcome sheen of the Tipi-Pole-Timber River below the round red hills. They watered the horses, ate, and rested. Until now there had been no time to reason with her or question her. To Roan, sitting nearby, she looked small and forsaken, her large eyes solemn and appealing.

"Emily," he began, "listen to me."

"My name—Little Star."

"That's your Indian name. Your white name is Emily Dawkins. Your father's name is Samuel Dawkins."

"White men kill my white father. Red Shield find me on prairie. Give me food."

"Do you remember when Red Shield found you? Did you see white men kill your father?"

163

That seemed to unsettle her; for the first time Roan saw her doubt. "Red Shield tell me," she admitted.

Poor, lost child! Sympathy for her drenched him. She was too innocent to know evasion. Using his most patient voice, he said, "Your father is alive. I saw him at Fort Washita," and he pointed southeast. Then he described Shell and told her about Shell's trick of trying to substitute the other girl for Emily. "Do you remember a white girl like her? Did she come from your camp?"

Emily was unresponsive.

"Remember the man Shell? Maybe he has an Indian name? Did he come to Red Shield's camp? Did he try to buy you from Red Shield?"

Again, nothing. She sat still, hands clasped, drawing further within the silence of herself. She was defending Red Shield; that was plain to see. Finally, she said, "Red Shield no sell me." That was the truth, Roan saw, and explained why Shell had tried to substitute the other blond child. Encouraged, Roan said:

"Think back—try to remember your white father. He's a small, lean man. His eyes are much like yours, except yours have a deeper blue. Maybe you have eyes like your mother's?"

"I remember only Red Shield. He is good to me—all time." Animation glossed her eyes, made them beautiful and clear. "I am his favorite." Her face darkened. "But sometimes—sometimes his wives beat me."

"Why did they beat you?"

She touched her yellow hair. "They say I have white

people's hair. They make me cover it. They shame me."

"You needn't be ashamed of your hair—it's very pretty."

She almost smiled.

"Remember your mother?"

She froze at the words, her liveliness vanishing. He talked on, not pressing her, just chatting. Perhaps she remembered other things? The house where she lived with her mother and father and two brothers? The horses and cows and chickens? And didn't she have a fat puppy or a soft kitten?

Into her eyes crept that intense, faraway, unseeing expression he was beginning to recognize, that inwardness. He held back, hoping she was about to release her trapped thoughts. But she did not speak. The vitality left her eyes, and he saw that she was on guard again. He continued to chat. Several times he coaxed her back to when she said Red Shield had found her. But beyond that, any venturing into the dark pit of her memory, she shied away each time. It was, he thought, as if everything that had happened up to and through those terrible moments, her entire childhood up to then, had been rubbed out. Was it, he asked himself, that she willed herself not to recall the horror surrounding her mother's death? That by not recalling she made the horror nonexistent?

He had one last piece of evidence, one last, tangible, undeniable link with her past, and so he decided to use it now. He took the gold locket and unwrapped the

165

square of cloth protecting it, and extended it to her on his palm.

"Your father gave me this, Emily. He said if I ever found you to show it to you and that you would remember. It was your mother's. She let you play with it. You played with it often. Shell returned it to your father at the fort to prove he had you, though he didn't."

Little by little her head came up and her eyes fastened on the glistening object, her mind retracing, reliving, perhaps, and he had his hope. She stirred forward and caressed the locket lightly, and suddenly, very suddenly, she went rigid and jerked back as if she had touched fire.

Roan said gently, "You had it around your neck that day. And Shell took it, didn't he?"

"You lie," she snapped. "Red Shield says all whites lie. I hate you. I hate all whites."

He laid his hat on the ground between them and placed the locket on the crown, so she couldn't ignore it. "Emily," he said, as gently as he could, "listen to me now. If your white father was dead, how could he give me the locket?"

She turned her head, keeping her eyes steadfastly averted. Her voice had the drilled-in monotony of rote when she spoke. "You lie. Red Shield my father. I hate you."

"If you hate me, why did you come to warn me to go away?"

"Red Shield—my father—tell me. No trouble. He wants peace."

166

"If he wants peace, why did he send warriors to shoot us?"

"They afraid you steal me."

Her strength was taxed. He noted the weary sag of her slight shoulders, and her smudged face, which ought to be alight with a child's love of living, bore visible strain in the fading light.

"I will ask you one more thing," he said finally. "Is Red Shield called Sanaco or Scar-Arm?"

She sat perfectly still, lips closed, eyes unseeing again, revealing not the faintest response.

Acknowledging defeat for the time being, he pocketed the locket and reached for his hat. "You are tired," he said. "I will fix your bed."

During the night Roan woke to the wind chanting through the treetops; behind the red hills a wolf howled. Nearby, he heard the steadfast croppings of the grazing horses. These natural sounds hadn't stirred him, however. Seeing the outline of her blanket-rolled form, and thus assured, he lay back and returned to sleep.

Soon afterward, it seemed, Curly's voice sprang him up. "One-of-Us, she has run away, this child."

It was dim daylight, clear enough for Roan to see the empty blanket, shaped as before, rolled to resemble her sleeping form.

There were no tracks. Not even the adept Osages could be expected to trail the printless moccasin steps of a slight-bodied child over earth left dry by summer. Roan figured there was only one way for her to go, only one way that made any sense, and that was north for the village and the man she called father.

They were two hours beyond the river when something moved in the rolling, red-earth emptiness, movement so blended with the landscape that Roan doubted his eyes. Something rising and falling, like a wounded antelope.

He spurred ahead, the Osages a tight knot around him. They reached a series of undulating swells, dipping and climbing, as if borne on waves, unable to see beyond until they topped each crest. Off to the right some hundred yards, Roan made out a tiny figure. It was Emily, her buckskin dress blending with the swarth prairie, and she had fallen in a rough place; she couldn't go on, else she had stopped to watch her pursuers. To reach her, they had to ride straight ahead, then angle along a shallow draw. Roan lost sight of her as they galloped down the next slant. Rushing up the other side, he heard an unexpected rumbling and drumming crashing nearer.

That was the only warning he had as they tore to another crest, before he saw the riders, dead on, at the bottom of the draw, turning toward Emily as they were. Indians. Eight—ten. A half-naked rider on a paint horse leading them. Both parties so close neither could give ground.

But the Osages had downhill momentum, a brief advantage. Mouthing gobbling cries, they shook loose their war clubs and charged, Roan also, their suddenness hurling them upon the others before they could use their rifles.

The shock of colliding horseflesh smacked in Roan's ears, and he, bent low on the neck of his horse, gripping his gift war club, found himself part of a dusty whirlpool of wheeling horses and contorted faces shrilling cries. Curly, looming massively, gobbling, swinging a stone-headed club, knocked one rider to earth. A horse went down, throwing rider. Runs-Against-the-Sun, whooping, rode him down like a straw man. A rifle blasted and Runs-Against-the-Sun swayed and fell, and as the young Osage hit the ground, he threw up his hide shield protectively.

An Indian dressed like a white man was frantically struggling to rein his crazy-eyed horse under control, at the same time to bring his heavy rifle to bear on Roan. Roan cut inside and clubbed him from the saddle.

Jerking back, he flinched away from a rush of color shooting past—the paint, wheeling nimbly as only a trained war horse could, and pivoting around, the lance of the half-naked rider set to impale Roan. In that flashing moment, Roan recognized Red Shield. Curly was close, but not close enough. Leaning across, he took a mighty swipe at Red Shield, missing narrowly, but forcing him to give way and lift the lance.

By then the point of the lance was past Roan. He struck savagely, a glancing blow. Red Shield disappeared over the side of the paint horse.

At that, there was a shout, a slackening in the slashing circle. The snarl of riders broke up. Horses streaked north.

It was over, Roan realized, over in moments that had seemed to last forever. He hacked for wind; his chest burned. He stared in dull surprise at the war club he gripped. Glancing up, he saw that Yellow Horse had a new Springfield Army rifle and was taking the owner's hair. And Runs-Against-the-Sun was slumped on the short grass, head bowed, bloody from shoulder to waist. Red Shield's paint stood heaving, reins dragging.

Curly was staring at Red Shield, who was beginning to revive.

"Look!" Curly said, pointing.

Except for breechclout, leggings, and moccasins, Red Shield was naked. His light brown, smooth-muscled arms bore no scars. Not one.

"Not Sanaco—no scars like rope," Curly said, and Roan nodded. "I was certain he was."

Red Shield sat up, as if roused by their voices, just now seeing them. One side of his scalp was bloody. He put a hand to his head.

"Get on your horse," Roan ordered.

Red Shield staggered up, blinking. Seeing what had happened, he faced them defiantly, head up, hands at his sides. Contempt poured into his slim, ascetic face. He was, Roan saw, waiting to be killed.

"Go," Roan said. "I won't kill you."

Bewilderment creased the high forehead. The nostrils flared. He wedged his disdainful lips together. He still didn't understand.

"The little white girl says you were good to her—

170

that's why." Roan motioned roughly. "Go."

Not believing, not trusting, Red Shield took uncertain steps to his horse; for a moment he clutched mane, still puzzled. Then he flung himself up, the paint in motion before Red Shield was firmly seated, rushing northward at a dead run.

"One-of-Us," Curly said, "you should kill your enemies. Why you let him go?"

Roan turned his head, not quite certain himself. "Guess I was thinking of Emily. If I killed Red Shield, she would never accept her own people."

CHAPTER 13

Riding south to the river, they cut two cedar poles and fashioned a travois for Runs-Against-the-Sun, who had lost much blood, and found prickly pear and made a poultice for his wound. Other than exhaustion, Emily showed no ill effects from her flight. Traveling out of consideration for the wounded warrior, they found sweet water by afternoon and killed a young buffalo bull and dared make a fire and early camp.

Roan hadn't spoken to Emily unless necessary, and she had not protested her recapture or asked questions about the fight. Nonetheless, he often saw her watching him, her eyes following him.

She ate like an Indian, with her fingers, gorging like an Indian, feast one day, famine the next, relishing the half-cooked liver and other delicacies. Curly and

Yellow Horse nodded genial approval of her manners. Her supper finished, she began to wipe her hands on her dress.

"Stop," Roan said curtly, getting up, and he led her to the spring and signed for her to wash her hands.

She reared back like a balky colt, her small chin out-thrust. Whereupon, he wet a bandanna and vigorously scrubbed her hands and wrists and arms and cleaned her face, then her neck and ears, his motions awkward but gentle.

"In the morning," he said, half scolding, "you will wash your hands and face before you eat."

She threw him her sheer defiance, lurking behind it, however, the slight trace of a smile. "You make Osages wash, too?"

"They are men. You are a child, Emily."

"My name—Little Star."

"All right. Emily Little Star Dawkins."

"I hate you—white man pony soldier."

He shrugged.

Her clear blue eyes were busy gauging him. "What you do—I no wash?"

"I'll spank you," he said promptly.

"Spank?" she queried, her mouth forming a perfect "O." In explanation, he flattened his hand and made spanking motions.

"Indians no spank children."

"You said Red Shield's women beat you."

She was caught, only momentarily. "Red Shield—my father—never spanks me. I am his favorite."

172

He took her back. After the horses were watered again and picketed, and the sky was darkening, she said to Roan, "You did not kill Red Shield."

"How did you know?"

"I heard horses coming. I got up. I saw fight—big fight—I know his paint war horse. I saw him ride off, alone. He is very brave—my father."

"That is true."

"He will come—he will take me back."

"Maybe he'll try. Maybe not."

She grew angry. "I am his favorite."

"He won't get you."

"Where—you take me?" She sounded concerned.

"To your real father—Samuel Dawkins. In Texas. Remember Texas?"

"No—no bueno."

He felt sympathy for her and was at loss to comfort her, and he answered, "That will not be soon. It's a long way."

The sky was changing. Darkness fell. Not liking what he knew he must do, he took a picket rope and tied one end around her left wrist and the other around his right. As he went to his blanket, her Indian-sounding voice trailed after him, clear and loathing, "I hate you—white man pony soldier."

Come morning, before breakfast, he took her to the spring again. "Wash your hands and face," he said, sensing her refusal.

She stood very erect, head at a resisting angle, determined blue eyes straight ahead, mouth squeezed in anticipation of punishment.

"Emily," he said, somewhat sharply. "Wash your hands and face."

Her small shoulders rose and fell in refusal.

"Emily. Wash your hands and face."

She stamped her feet.

In a flash he had her over his knee and was spanking her, once, twice, and also in a flash he was ceasing, arrested by guilt. How could you rightfully punish a child turned into a savage? She flung to her feet, humiliated instead of hurt, and astonished most of all, which told him that Red Shield had spoiled her. They faced each other in total silence.

Not speaking, he doused the bandanna and took her left hand. She tried to break away at the first scrubbing touch. He continued to scrub. A moment, a longer moment, as he felt the tension go out of her.

Without comment, he finished her hands and cleaned her face, without haste, and let her be, free to walk alone to camp. She stared at his face, confused, then ran back to the Osages.

Throughout breakfast the locket bore on Roan's mind. They were saddled and ready when he held it out to her. "It belongs to you," he said.

She regarded it for the longest time, her lips opening and contracting, her breathing slowing, then quickening, while around them Curly and Yellow Horse waited with patience, understanding the struggle, and Runs-Against-the-Sun stirred in silent pain on the travois.

Just when he thought she might accept it, he saw her face settle and stiffen; saw her guardedness forming, and her withdrawal, as when he had first shown her the locket, after which her eyes moved upward to Roan's and he saw the brimming Indian hate.

And so he had lost her once more.

Passing through the gate at Cantonment Emory on the forenoon of the sixth day, Roan was surprised to find the garrison turned out to meet them, everyone's eyes on Emily and the wounded Osage on the travois.

He scanned the crowd and found Sara Thayer's upturned face. She was making her way toward him, her eyes flicking back and forth from him to Emily. He raised his voice. "She's the Dawkins girl. Will you look after her?" It had not occurred to him to ask anyone else.

"Of course. The poor child."

"Her name's Emily, and she has an Indian name— Little Star."

Sara Thayer smiled up at Emily. "Hello, Emily Little Star." Emily, her face a cameo of engraved suspicion and fear, pulled back and gripped the saddle.

"We're all your friends," Sara said, giving her another undeniable smile.

The stiff buckskin figure on the sorrel horse seemed to bend just a little.

"Emily," said Sara, reaching up and taking Emily's hand, "please come home with me. You're welcome to stay as long as you like. If you don't like it there, you don't have to stay. Please come with me."

175

As if contrary to her will, as if still uncertain, yet unable to deny the friendliness of this strange white woman, when she had expected hostility, Emily slipped from the saddle into Sara Thayer's arms. There was an outbreak of applause. The women dabbed at their eyes, and the crowd parted as Sara, holding fast to Emily's hand, led her away.

A kind of haste prodded Roan. At any moment he expected someone to challenge him. Leading off to the hospital, he halted and called for an orderly, and when one came out Roan and the Osages and the trooper carried Runs-Against-the-Sun inside.

Not long arriving, Captain Alvord, the surgeon, bent critical eyes on the cumbersome poultice that Curly had fashioned, and lifted it gingerly and peered at the wound. "What sorcery is this?" he asked wonderingly.

"Prickly pear," Roan explained. "An old Plains Indian remedy."

"Hmmnn. Rather remarkable. I think you can come after him in a few days."

Boots thudded in unison at the doorway behind them. Roan, turning slowly, knew without looking, and saw First Lieutenant Jernigan and Second Lieutenant Povich.

"You're under arrest," Jernigan told him, arching his back. "Need I state why?"

"Why, yes, I'd like to know."

Povich shifted uncomfortably at the exchange.

"Disobeying orders," Jernigan said. "As if you didn't know."

176

"Depends on the interpretation of orders. I suppose this means the usual confinement to the post?"

"To your quarters. Major doesn't want you taking off again."

Curly moved forward suddenly. "One-of-Us, they are taking you away. Why is this thing?"

"It's a long story," Roan said, motioning him back. "While I'm gone, Stone Face will pick a new officer to ride with you. I hope it's that man there. Lieutenant Povich."

Roan left the ward at once, walking in advance to the bachelor officers' quarters. "By the way," Jernigan said carelessly, "fill out a report. I trust you can do that properly."

The hackling Roan felt swelled higher. "It may interest you to know that the little girl we brought in is the daughter of Samuel Dawkins. Right down to the identifying scar."

"And where is the terrible Sanaco?"

"Didn't find him, though we thought we had for a while. Half Comanche, half white. Only no scars. No Scar-Arm."

"I see." The Lieutenant was teetering on his boot heels. "Failing in that, you thought that by bringing back some nameless waif, you could dodge the disobedience charge. It won't work. Furthermore, Lieutenant Povich and I were witnesses to your disparaging reference back there to the commanding officer."

He turned stiffly, gone before Roan could reply. Povich, staying, muttered, "Sorry," and shook hands.

177

"Thanks, Povich," Roan said, and half in apology: "If the Major calls a special court-martial here, will you represent me as counsel?"

Povich didn't hesitate. "If you want me to. But you need an experienced attorney."

"Right now I need a friend. I don't know the other officers. Just Jernigan—and he's on the other side. You can read up."

"There's one rub. As C.O., Thayer can appoint the defense counsel. He could appoint Jernigan."

"Hardly. Jernigan will head the prosecution. He wouldn't pass up that pleasure."

Afterward, washed and shaved, Roan flopped on his cot and faced up at the rough-barked log ceiling, exhaled a long groan, and fell into instant sleep.

The blaring of bugles woke him, bugles on the parade ground south of the post, he realized, and momentarily his mind took him to the drill field and Major Thayer calling out curt commands, sending his toy soldiers through precise wheelings and close-ranked columns they would seldom, if ever, use in an Indian fight. That meant afternoon; he had slept three hours or more. He sat up on the edge of the cot, listening sluggishly to the brassy sounds; forcing himself to stand, he slouched to the table, pawing through the clutter of old copies of *Harper's Weekly* and *Leslie's Illustrated Newspaper* until he found pen and ink and writing paper. His brows crinkled as he collected his thoughts and began writing:

Cantonment Emory, Indian Territory, August 17, 1860. Major Hamilton B. Thayer, Fifth Cavalry, Commanding. Sir: I have the honor to submit the following report . . .

He got no further, sensing a just audible movement at the doorway, and within the rim of his eyes the outline of an unmilitary figure.

He drew around and felt shock whip through him, startled to see Sara Thayer, alone. "You can't come here," he said, getting to his feet, but even as he spoke she entered and said, "It's drill—everyone's gone."

"Not the women—if you're seen . . ."

"I come and go a lot. I'm head of the Hospital Visitation Committee."

"This isn't the hospital, Sara."

"I had to come."

Each hesitated, and then suddenly Roan threw his arms around her and held her close, his lips tight against her mass of lavender-scented hair. Continuing to hold her, he knew that nothing had changed. Nothing. It was the same. True. Good. He kissed her and felt the wonder of her flowing through him.

"You were gone so long," she said at last. "Hamilton said you were all likely dead."

He wasn't used to concern; it unsettled him. "It was close enough. We lost Iron Head. A good man."

"Now you face court-martial."

"We'll see. We'll see." He didn't want to talk about it. "Tell me about Emily. Did we find her too late?"

"She seems so lost. Just sits and stares at nothing with that faraway look. Oh, Roan, she's Indian—not white. I'm not at all hopeful she'll ever be happy among her own people again. I'm not."

"It will take time. A week with you will make a big difference."

"I've started making her a dress."

He was elated. "You're making progress already. Here's something to give her when you think the time is right. Not today. Not yet." Fumbling, he found the locket and passed it to her and told her the story that Samuel Dawkins had related to him, and Emily's later refusal to accept it.

"Why do you suppose she wouldn't take it?"

"Maybe it reminds her of something she wants to forget. Meanwhile, by staying an Indian, she can keep it at a distance. You have to go now, Sara, before someone comes in here." Guiding her gently by the shoulders, he started her toward the door. There she stopped and looked at him. "I also came to tell you something. All women and children are being evacuated back to Fort Washita. Colonel Emory's orders."

"I agree. It was a mistake bringing families out here."

"It's more than just that. There's war in the air. The newspapers say Governor Sam Houston wants to keep Texas in the Union, but that Texas will pass an ordinance of secession."

"No doubt. I'm a Texan. I know how they feel. It's coming, Sara." He could see his own depression and

180

dread filling her eyes.

"How do you feel, Roan?"

"I don't want to see the country split."

"And the raids—the Indians," she went on. "The Osages report more war parties have slipped across the river since you left. It's getting worse. We're exposed here. Colonel Emory's afraid we might be attacked in force, cut off."

"That means he'll abandon the Cantonment, too."

"Not immediately. No time's been set. Two troops will stay here."

"When are you leaving?"

"In three days. I hate going." She regarded him tragically, her green eyes deepening. "Hamilton will win. He has before when a junior officer crossed him. That's one reason why he's not liked. Why many men hate him . . . I must tell you these things so you can defend yourself—I must, Roan . . . He knows his ground, every prescribed jurisdiction as laid down by the Articles of War. You'll be broken—you'll be placed in prison—your life ruined."

"Colonel Emory will have something to say about that."

"But you were on the post when you disobeyed Hamilton's orders. Not in the field."

He looked at her, impressed. "I see you know the particulars."

"I've listened. Jernigan comes to our quarters. How I detest that man! He reminds me of an eel—so unctuous. And Hamilton relishes a fine point. He knows

181

where he stands. I'm afraid for you, Roan, and I'm afraid for myself. I'm afraid I'll never see you again."

He went quickly to his pack, and when he came back he held a tiny buckskin sack with a drawstring. Opening it, he removed a brooch of delicate pink carving that always reminded him of a perpetual flower.

"I want you to have this," he said, and started to press it into her hand.

She drew back. "I can't," she said, and in her eyes he saw another truth: She thought it had belonged to Valerie.

"It was my mother's," he said. "Now it's yours." He folded her fingers about it.

"I ought not," she said, while loving it with her eyes, caressing it with her fingers. "It's so lovely."

"You can keep it somewhere."

The parade-ground bugles were blowing Recall. He glanced beyond the anteroom and, seeing no one outside, drew her back into the room. Tilting her downcast chin so that she had to look up into his eyes, he laid his lips over hers, holding her, his movements extra gentle, and afterward he said, "Is there something you haven't told me? Something about yourself? How you might feel?"

As he searched her face, there was an instant as the somber green eyes seemed to elude his, as he thought she tried to look away. Before he could think about it, she was smiling up at him and saying, "Nothing that hasn't been said," her voice composed. Moving away from him to the anteroom, she picked up a basket. During that he saw her face alter, somber again, and she went out, bound for the hospital.

Sick at heart, he watched her enter the hospital. What in the name of God could he possibly do for her? And felt the heaviness of resignation. There was nothing, no choice, for he was virtually out of her life, powerless to act now.

He lived a caged existence the next two days by order, taking his meals in his quarters. Major Thayer and Jernigan sent no word. Povich, there in the morning and evening, had heard nothing. A discouraged Curly Wolf came to see him. His scouts reported many Indians north in the Wichitas, and many lodgepole tracks leading into the mountains. When would One-of-Us rejoin his friends, the Osages? Why did Stone Face keep One-of-Us penned up like a mule?

Roan pondered the delay. Thayer was probably letting him sweat. Roan considered his chances. A special court-martial here, limited in size and jurisdiction, should move faster. It also might damage his case, if Jernigan was a member of the Court or presenting the prosecution's case as Judge Advocate. The other possibility, a general court-martial, would mean traveling to where the headquarters department ordered the court to convene—Fort Gibson, Fort Leavenworth, Jefferson Barracks—which posed a prolonged trial slowed by tedious protocol and charges and specifications.

Early the third morning he noticed the changing tempo of the post, the telltale hum of final preparations

183

for departure: the incessant voices of women, the rushing back and forth, the steady poundings, and finally, standing in the doorway of his quarters, he saw the stout wagons rolling in, and enlisted men carrying out boxes and crates, and, last, the embraces and good-bys.

He saw Sara and Jamie and Emily take seats in an ambulance whose side curtains were rolled up against the incredibly hot day. The boy played with his spotted pup. Emily still wore the buckskin dress, which conveyed a good deal to Roan. She had not given in. Had she, she would be wearing the dress Sara would have finished for her by now. The ambulance driver shook out the reins and the mules stepped away.

Everyone was waving at everyone. For a moment Roan saw Sara's wave meant for him; he waved back. Only Emily did not wave. The ambulance was nearing the gate when Roan saw her turn her head and look back at him. He waved. Across the lengthening distance her eyes seemed to bore into his, holding that unwavering Indian expression. That was all. Turning front, she did not look back as the ambulance lumbered through the gateway. And he thought, the whole of his new life, impossible from the start, begun by coincidence, complicated by events beyond his control, was passing with the wagon train, and he was helpless to change it.

Early that afternoon in his quarters Roan became aware of a voice. A voice that, although muffled by the log walls, sounded familiar, yet not enough that he

184

could place it at once. He sat up on the cot, head cocked. As the voice rose to a hoarse peak, he swung his booted feet to the floor and went expectantly to the outer door and looked out, not quite believing his eyes.

A knot of off-duty troopers loafed in the shade of the commissary shed, grinning at a scarecrow man dressed in dusty black, his left hand holding a Bible while he rebuked them with his right. A bundle tied to a stick was propped against the shed.

The Reverend Noah Loftus looked leaner than ever, more haggard, more hard times, but his powerful voice was charged with reproach:

"I peer at it this way, boys. It's never too late to side in with the Lord. That's why I aim to talk to you about your immortal souls and repentin' your sins."

"Man can't be nothin' but an angel out here," a trooper said and nudged a companion. "No booze, no women."

At Hatsboro the troopers would have ignored him. Here on the frontier an itinerant preacher provided rare entertainment, a break in the monotony of post routine.

Unruffled, Loftus said, "Never was an Army post that didn't have booze around, an' where there's booze there's painted women." Aware that he had his audience in hand, he raised his craggy face and, for effect, took great sniffs. "There's whiskey here. I can smell it."

The troopers burst into laughter. One, pretending dire thirst by raking fingers at his throat, let out a strangled, "Lead us to it," and they all laughed again, and the performer executed a capering little dance.

185

"Sin's ever'where," Loftus roared, an old-time hell-fire grimness replacing his moment of jollity. "I say to you, repent 'fore it's too late to come back down the wrong trail. Put a halter on sin, boys. Sin's even out here in the wilderness. The old devil he tempted Jesus, remember? That was in the wilderness. You betcha. The devil he took Him high up on a mountain and showed Him all the kingdoms of the world an' said, 'It's all yours, if you'll jest throw in with me.'"

The bugle sounding drill broke up the guffawing, and in a twinkling the Reverend Loftus whipped off his slouch hat and held it out just so, just right, his unkempt face beaming tolerance. A trooper pitched him a coin and Loftus trapped it with practiced skill and called them "boys" again and promised to "visit" with them tomorrow about mending their sinful ways. As he watched them hurry away, the vitality drained out of his bony face and the dark-rimmed eyes seemed to sink deeper and the brooding, enduring mask that Roan recalled was his habitual expression returned.

"Reverend!"

At Roan's call, Loftus swung about, his features lighting up once more. He long-strided across and pumped Roan's hand.

"What held you up?" Roan asked. "I was afraid Indians had you."

"My fool mule wandered off one night. Found me a family of Chickasaws an' preached the good news there for a spell. That Indian lady was a right nice cook, too."

186

It was refreshing to see Loftus again, to rediscover his earnestness, his disdain for abject poverty.

"Get any converts?" Roan chided him.

"Let's jest say I did better than at Hatsboro."

Seeing Jernigan's stiff-backed figure leaving head-quarters and the Lieutenant staring at Loftus, Roan said, "The Osages are camped northeast of the post. Go there. Tell them One-of-Us sent you. You'll be wel-come. Better go now."

Jernigan intercepted Loftus before he could pick up his pack. "Civilians aren't allowed inside the post. How'd you get in?"

"Sorta walked in an' started preachin'. Guard told me I'd have to have a permit if I stayed long."

"You're leaving immediately," said Jernigan, obvi-ously annoyed.

"Lieutenant," Roan spoke up, "this is the Reverend Loftus. He was at Fort Washita. I can vouch for him."

"Out," Jernigan ordered, as if Roan hadn't spoken.

Loftus shrugged, his resignation that of one accus-tomed to ouster from various premises, and picked up his pack and slung it over his shoulder. Taking a step, he looked fully at Jernigan for the first time, and stopped, his attention becoming a close thing. It was an odd look, cut short as he nodded at Roan and went his way.

Jernigan kept his eyes on Loftus until he cleared the gate.

"That man is all right," Roan said. "I know him."

"Does that give him clearance?"

187

"You could issue him a permit. He's just preaching around."

"I'm quite aware of post procedure, Mr. Kimball."

On the instant Roan realized that their voices were rising, on the edge of heated argument. He said, more slowly, "By the way, when is the big show?" and heard his voice strike even higher.

"Show?"

"My court-martial. That's what it is, isn't it—a show? A circus?"

"You'll see soon enough."

"When?"

"Day after tomorrow."

Roan went stiff. "I request Lieutenant Povich as counsel."

Jernigan inclined his head slightly, feigning a bow of courtesy. "Your request has been granted already, thanks to Povich himself, who asked it. Major Thayer just told me. I was on my way to tell you."

"That's neighborly of you, Jernigan. On top of that, you've generously allowed us less than two days to prepare our case. Too, I'll bet I can guess who the prosecutor is."

"Now could you?" the other replied, looking pleased.

"Yourself. Who else? You will enjoy it."

"You have an uncanny sense of prediction, Mr. Kimball." He stood back, the fever of dislike burning his eyes, and Roan had the quick, racy feeling that they were as two antagonists, and suddenly he demanded, "What is it you have against me?"

"For one thing, you're always reaching out beyond the extension of your orders, and meddling."

"Everything goes back to Kirk Shell and poor Sam Dawkins and the traffic in captives, doesn't it?"

"You ruined the only reliable go-between source we had."

"Reliable, hell. Shell plays both ends against the middle, and you know it. Now I'll tell you what I think of you. You're sour over lack of promotion. You resent any man who shows a pinch of initiative and gets results. Furthermore, you're a pompous ass."

Jernigan's carefully barbered face shed crimson. For a little Roan thought the man was going to strike him. Roan didn't move, waiting, struggling to curb his own wild longing to smash him.

"I see that we understand each other completely, Mr. Kimball," Jernigan replied, finding an icy calm. "Day after tomorrow will tell, though I warn you that your chances are equivalent to a snowball in hell. For the word is out, mister. The Old Man wants you sacked."

"Over an interpretation of a verbal order?"

"You're more dense than I thought. Perhaps the company of your gut-eating Osage friends has dulled your perceptions."

"Leave them out of it. Come out from behind the bush, Jernigan."

"You'll wish I hadn't. At the moment I'm merely trying to spare a fellow officer's honor."

"Your concern touches me to the heart." However, something behind Jernigan's cocksureness warned

Roan, clarifying slowly but surely as he saw it first reach Jernigan's exulting eyes and then Jernigan's mouth, his lower lip curving downward, hurling the attendant ugliness and insinuation:

"It's Mrs. Thayer. The Old Man *knows*. He's had her followed since the first day she went riding. You're through."

CHAPTER 14

"Before you start asking questions, there's something I want to say."

It was early evening. The single lamp cast a dull glow like yellow dust over the cramped room. Povich, standing, was gazing down at a copy of the Articles of War and a large tablet of blank paper, and pencils and inkwell and pen, which he had just laid on the table. He did not respond. When he did look around, his round, ruddy features appeared adrift in thought. He took an absent-minded swipe at his sweeping blond mustache.

"What was that, Lieutenant?"

"I've placed you in jeopardy," Roan said. "By acting as defense counsel, you're killing your chances for promotion as long as you serve under Thayer. I want you to back out."

Povich, as if suddenly waking, clapped a hand to his forehead. "Gad, I couldn't do that."

"The verdict's already cut and dried. It's a kangaroo

court. Jernigan told me that with great delight this afternoon. The C.O. has told the Board what he expects, and he'll get it or else. So why waste yourself?"

"Why the sudden change?" Povich sounded disappointed.

"I was thinking solely of myself. Now that I've had time to reconsider . . . Well, why fight a losing cause?"

"It's not lost yet. We can delay. We can call every witness to the stand we can think of, including that big buck Osage friend of yours—even the C.O. himself."

"You'll only ruin yourself. I've seen this happen before. Once at Fort McKavett. A noble young officer, loyal to his friends, offers his services for the defense—and is a gray-haired second lieutenant years later, serving under the same commander. No, I won't let you do it. It's all off. I'll tell Jernigan tonight. I'll represent myself."

"You'll do no such thing," said Povich, a combative gleam flecking his eyes as he came around the table. "You're the one who's being noble—and blind. You make me a little sore, too. Who are you, sir, to spurn the coveted services of Cassius J. Povich, Defender of the Doomed?" He struck a high-headed pose, hand inside his jacket, a stance that forced Roan to grin. "What you don't realize," said Povich, serious again, "is that appointing me makes the C.O. look fair-minded. It's a gesture on his part, see? Didn't he appoint the counsel you wanted? What he doesn't know is that I read law in my grandfather's office for a

191

year before my appointment to the Academy went through. I bird-dogged a lot of trials for the old gent. As a matter of fact, he told me I had the makings of a first-rate jackleg lawyer. I'm no Henry Clay, but neither am I the raw junior numskull the C.O. thinks."

"I tell you the verdict's already sealed."

"I don't seem to hear well today, perhaps it's the dust," Povich grunted, pulling at an earlobe. "Now, sir, as your counsel, I trust you'll see fit to confide in me as to the events leading up to this unfounded charge."

Major Hamilton B. Thayer, being a punctual officer, convened the special court-martial precisely at 9 A.M. in his office. Roan, flanked by an armed trooper, entered the courtroom, halted and saluted, and crossed to his place at the defense counsel's desk beside Lieutenant Povich.

Roan saw that everything was quite proper, quite proper, indeed, when he observed the three-man Board of Court, and he felt no lift of spirit. Each member of higher rank than himself, each man in full dress from spurs to silk sashes, and each sitting at the long table in the order of his rank and length of service. First, Major Thayer, then Captain Randolph Cruce, Troop D commander; then Captain Augustine Vaughan, Troop C commander. Cruce and Vaughan, Roan realized, had little likelihood of promotion through the usual pace of Army advancement, and even less should they act counter to the commanding officer's wishes for a guilty verdict. In a way, they were as hemmed in and helpless as Roan himself.

Captain Cruce, florid, loose-jowled and bulging to tallow in a tight-fitting uniform, was tired of eye and had the stamped dullness of a man who had spent twenty uneventful years in the Army, mostly at Eastern posts.

Roan knew him only by hearsay, and less of Captain Vaughan. At the moment Vaughan was surveying the courtroom as one might a barracks during Sunday morning inspection, as his ferret's eyes searched for wrinkled blankets and dust behind foot lockers. Roan's judgment was of an officer gone to seed long ago, humorless, bored, his dyspepsia constantly griped by Army chow, a slightly built man confined in a matrix shaped by regulations, orders, and endless reports.

Thayer was the presiding officer. As such, he would pass on motions and arbitrate points of law, and also could vote, which left even less doubt as to the case's outcome. If stumped by some technicality, there was the Major's legal adviser, Lieutenant Jernigan, today's Judge Advocate and prosecutor, a connivance from which there was no recourse for the defense. And for this morning Major Thayer had acquired an extra correctness, an extreme formality, an inordinate coldness.

These imprints raced through Roan's mind as he settled himself. Already he could feel the close heat. Captain Cruce dug at the vise of his collar. His chair squealed as he cupped his hands against the melon of his stomach. Captain Vaughan's narrow face acquired a foxlike alertness. At last the room fell still. Thayer banged the gavel three times. "This Court is in session," he announced.

Before Jernigan could stand, Povich was on his feet. "Sir, we respectfully request a continuance of one month." He spoke directly at the Major.

"On what grounds?"

"One day and two evenings hardly constitute enough time in which to prepare an adequate defense, sir."

"By the same token, Mr. Povich, the exigencies of border warfare hardly allow us the indulgence of the civil courts, noted for their irresolution and procrastination. Your request is overruled." Thayer turned away, a motion of impatience, the signal for Jernigan to commence.

Povich, still standing, continued coolly, "Sir, at this time the defense would like to present another motion before the Court."

Jernigan, halfway up from his chair, sank back. Thayer, flustered, glanced at Jernigan, who nodded that such was proper, and the Major said, "Tell the Court."

"We request a change of venue to Fort Washita," Povich said.

"Your premise?"

"Well, sir, in order to subpoena Colonel W. H. Emory as a witness," Povich replied, clearing his throat, "in so far as the defendant was acting under Colonel Emory's verbal instructions."

"Motion overruled," Thayer snapped, his mouth set to speak before Povich had finished. "The Judge Advocate will read the charges and specifications." That, and the Major sat back and folded his arms.

Povich bowed and sat down, and Roan saw how it was going to be: swift and to the point, no ramblings, no maneuverings allowed, a perception that broadened when Thayer, turning to the clerk, busy scribbling, ordered, "Strike that from the record. It has no place here. Also strike the previous motion."

A surprised look quivered in the clerk's face. He recovered at once, hastily crossing out what he had recorded.

Roan, catching Povich's eyes, understood further. If the case were ever reviewed, which was doubtful, these motions so vital to the outcome would be missing from the record.

Vaughan, apparently, had caught the meaning as well, for he surprisingly leaned over to whisper to Cruce. The Major pounded for order and said, "The Court will now hear the opening statement of the prosecution."

Jernigan rose and arched his back. "First, we're going to prove that Second Lieutenant Roan Kimball did willfully and openly disobey his commanding officer's orders not to leave the vicinity of Cantonment Emory on August the fifth, Eighteen Hundred and Sixty; that said defendant was gone from the Cantonment in disregard of his duties with the Osage scouts until August seventeenth."

"Objection," Povich called, snapping up. "The prosecution is implying a personal intent on the part of the defendant, whereas he was merely following higher orders. We request a rephrasing of the charge."

Thayer jutted forward in his chair. "Overruled. Sit down, Mr. Povich. You are beginning to annoy me with your needless interruptions."

The busy clerk finished a page and started another, dabbing paste from a pot at his elbow on the new sheet. As the trial moved along, the record would grow into a voluminous snake, writhing on the floor.

"Continue, Mr. Jernigan," Thayer instructed.

Roan noticed that Povich had fixed his attention on the three-man jury. Without warning, before Jernigan could speak anew, Povich got up and politely inclined his head toward the Major. "If the Court please . . ."

"What is it this time?"

"The defense is quite appreciative of the fact that the trial is being conducted in the most proper manner, sir, to give the defendant the fullest opportunity to prove his innocence."

"Come to the point, Mr. Povich. Connect what you're driving at."

"Yes, sir. I'll do that. Specifically, I am referring to the proper official dress of the court-martial as laid down by the provisions of military law and—"

"Mr. Povich," Thayer roared, "find the point or I'll hold you in contempt."

"I was just coming to that, sir."

"Then do so, damn it."

"It's Captain Cruce, sir. His collar's unhooked."

Roan stared, aware that Vaughan and Thayer and

Jernigan were doing likewise.

"Captain Cruce," said the Major, "hook your collar."

Croce, grimacing, teeth bared, went to work on the collar. He fumbled and pawed and pulled, then dropped his hands, the collar still askew. "Sir," he said, his fleshy face aflame, "the hook is broken."

Thayer slapped his boot leg and jackknifed to his feet. "Retire at once to your quarters and repair it. Meanwhile, this Court is in recess for thirty minutes." He whipped out of the courtroom, followed by Jernigan.

As Roan and Povich entered their quarters, Curly sprang up from the floor. He shook hands ceremoniously, pumping first Roan's, then Povich's. The Osage was frowning. His long-fingered right hand plucked at his buckskin shirt, a sign of anxiety.

"What's wrong?" Roan asked.

"Bad. If we had our women with us, they would be keening in fear. Many Cut-Knives in mountains. Many Snakes. Some Walks-the-Prairie People. Their scouts come closer each day. All day they watch the Soldier House." By Snakes, Roan knew, Curly meant Comanches.

"You think they'll attack the Soldier House?"

"They are strong enough."

"Meanwhile," Roan said, aside to Povich, "the Major merrily conducts his kangaroo court."

"One-of-Us," the Osage went on anxiously, "the Heavy Brow with the Jesus book, your friend, came to see you this morning. Soldiers made him go away."

"Loftus," Roan nodded.

"Says he must talk with you. No other man."

"What about?"

"Medicine talk—big medicine."

"Bring him here when the sun goes down. Tell him to take off his hat. Throw a blanket around him like an Osage. I will talk to him here."

When Court resumed, Povich stood and faced Major Thayer. "Sir, the defendant has important information that has just come to his attention."

"Is it relative to the case?"

"No, sir. But it is relative to the security of this post. Very much so."

Jernigan, with a thin smile, broke in. "Major, this is just a ruse on the part of the defense to incur favor with the Board. I suggest it be denied."

"Denied," said Thayer, the cold recesses of his gray eyes seeming to grow colder. "Court will resume."

Roan was standing and the words were hurtling out of his mouth before it occurred to him that he was speaking. "Curly—the Osage—says there are many Indians in the mountains, including Comanches and Cheyennes. Their scouts are getting bolder. He thinks they may attack the post. I think we should—"

"You are in contempt, Mr. Kimball. Take your chair or I'll have you placed in irons."

"Sir—the situation is worsening—I'm simply reporting what my chief scout—"

"Guard!"

The guard at the door froze to rigidity, and Roan

198

eased down in his chair, thinking that at least he'd got it said for everyone to hear.

Waving the guard across, Thayer stood and his voice crashed upward. "Station yourself behind the defendant. If he rises or speaks without the Court's permission, use whatever force necessary to control him to maintain order. Even to using your pistol barrel."

The guard, a Troop C veteran who had ridden on the successful upriver scout with Povich and Roan and the Osages, obeyed at once. But his eyes dropped when Roan looked at him.

Thayer drew his gold-cased watch and checked the time, a kind of hurry to his movements. Snapping the case shut, he said, "No more interruptions will be tolerated. Do I make myself clear, Mr. Povich, Mr. Kimball? The Judge Advocate will now read the second charge."

Second charge? There wasn't time for Roan to puzzle it out.

A dry voice, cynical and matter-of-fact, interrupted. "One moment, Major. For the safety of the Board members, who are directly across from the defendant, I hasten to point out that should the guard see fit to use his pistol, and it be discharged, that we are in the line of fire." It was Captain Vaughan, who until now had said no word.

Color pinked the Major's neck and face. "Your observation is well taken, Captain. The guard will not employ firearms in the courtroom to maintain order, only physical force. Proceed, Mr. Jernigan."

With a rustle of papers, Jernigan nodded to the Board and began. "In addition to the first charge, the prosecution is going to prove that on August seventeenth, Eighteen Hundred and Sixty, that said defendant did on that date refer to his commanding officer, Major Hamilton B. Thayer, in a manner unbecoming an officer and gentleman. To wit: did refer to his commanding officer as Stone Face in the presence of First Lieutenant Charles S. Jernigan, and Second Lieutenant Cassius J. Povich, and several Osage Indian scouts, including the one known as Curly Wolf. Said derogatory remark being made within the environs of the hospital at Cantonment Emory." Finished, Jernigan shot Povich a savoring look. "Any objections?"

"Why, yes," replied Povich, all smiles. "We consider the charge as mere supposition and lacking in direct connection or reference to Major Thayer. We move it be stricken."

"Overruled," Thayer rejected curtly. "The defendant may answer to the charges."

Roan stood. "I plead not guilty to each and every charge."

"Is the defense ready with its rebuttal statement?"

On that cue Povich appeared to stretch up from his chair, a languid movement of self-confidence. Nodding first to the Major, and then to each member of the Board, and, finally, to Jernigan, he moved around the desk and addressed the Board:

"Gentlemen, you realize without my reminding you that this entire case—and I am not referring to the frivolous second charge of insubordinate name-calling the Judge Advocate has contrived—hinges on one point: interpretation of orders—verbal orders. The defendant was acting within the jurisdiction of verbal orders from Colonel Emory at Fort Washita. We shall prove that. And all of you know from experience where verbal orders can lead you. Often hanging on the end of a limb and nothing under you. I daresay that you, Captain Cruce, and you, Captain Vaughan, as senior officers accustomed to command, have experienced such a quandary during your long and honorable service in the Army of the United States of America."

The legs of the Major's chair scraped on the plank floor as he interrupted, his voice charged with exasperation. "We have no time for Fourth-of-July oratory, Mr. Povich. State your case."

"We are only laying the groundwork, sir," said Povich, a courteous smile lighting his ruddy features. And, facing the other Board members, for it was to them that he was really speaking: "Specifically, what was behind this order of Colonel Emory's? What caused the defendant to risk his career, which, believe me, is above reproach and will stand the stiffest official scrutiny . . . ? So let's go back a bit. Why was Lieutenant Kimball called from his comfortable station at Jefferson Barracks to take a mission on the bloody Texas frontier?" He leaned toward the two captains, his air confidential, his voice low-pitched. "Well, sirs, I can tell you exactly why. Lieutenant Kimball was ordered to the frontier to bring in, dead or alive, the principal figure behind the despicable traffic in captives. A sinister figure known as Sanaco or Scar-Arm."

He paused dramatically. "Let me picture for you briefly Sanaco's victims. Fair-faced Texas women, eyes averted from the burning sun, trudging along, barefoot, innocent babes in their weary arms. Older children, fear haunting their eyes, tagging at their mothers' ragged skirts. Each human being worth from five hundred or less to fifteen hundred dollars on the 'slave market' at Fort Washita, depending on the means of the distraught father or other relatives. If unable to raise a few hundred dollars, what then? Gone, gone—never seen again. Those fair faces and gentle voices just seared-in memories. Gentlemen, I—"

Roan saw it massing like a thunderstorm on Thayer's hardening face. Then the Major said, "Enough, Povich. Enough. Complete your opening statement and sit down, else I'll have the guard put you down."

"Sir," said Povich, imperturbably calm, his voice a polite purr, "I must state certain facts. The background is essential to our case."

"I'll give you three more minutes." Thayer's tone was metallic. He dragged out his watch.

"Very good, Major. Signal me if I go over my limit."

Roan smiled to himself. Delay. Delay. Povich was accomplishing that. But what good would it do with the verdict already sealed? The room was stifling. The Board captains were digging at their high collars and discreetly mopping their sweatrunneled faces. Povich swept on, citing Roan's record at Fort Belknap with the

Tonkawa scouts, the number of captives he was instrumental in rescuing, his field promotion to a junior officer. He was still talking when the Major's voice struck like a thunderclap:

"Time's up, Mr. Povich."

"Thank you, sir." Roan saw the strain on his counsel's face as he sat, a tautness that relaxed when Thayer, making a helpless gesture, announced, "It's noon. We recess until one-thirty." He was up and gone from the room in a flash of movement.

Roan and Povich lunched in their quarters. "I'll call up a string of witnesses to keep this going for days," the attorney swore. "I've never seen a judge as dead set against a defendant. I'd almost say there's something more behind it than Thayer's touchy ego to command, though he's got plenty of that." He studied Roan curiously. "You're not holding out on me, are you, my good friend? Is there something else in the Major's craw?"

Roan shrugged. "There's no other god but Thayer, is there?" No matter what happened, he would keep Sara's name out of it.

"It's almost as if he bears an old grudge."

"I haven't known him long enough for a grudge to develop."

"You amaze me. Here your career's at stake and you hardly seem worried. I hope you understand that even a two-to-one verdict against us will be fatal? It doesn't have to be unanimous."

"I do. I'm worried, despite all your good efforts. And

I'm worried about what could happen to two troops of cavalry. We're in very grave danger, Povich. Curly wouldn't be concerned without cause. Yet Thayer ignores it. He's underestimating the fighting qualities of Plains Indians. Out here that's the mark of a damned fool. It could get us all killed."

"I agree. Now let's go back and beard the lion."

Entering the courtroom, Roan had the tight sensation of time running out. As he took his chair, Major Thayer told the Judge Advocate to call his first witness. Jernigan had a sly look as he said, "The prosecution calls Major Hamilton B. Thayer, if you please," and eagerly took up a Bible for the swearing in.

"I believe it's the clerk who does that, Mr. Judge Advocate." Roan turned. The speaker was the stickler for detail, Captain Vaughan.

Jernigan was momentarily ruffled. "So it is. Thank you, Captain. The clerk will swear in the witness."

That done, the Major went to the witness stand and folded his arms, face grimly set.

"Describe for us, Major, the conversation that took place between you and the defendant just prior to his sudden departure from the post last August fifth to the north."

"I'll make it brief and to the point. It happened the morning after the captured Delaware broke jail. Mr. Kimball wanted to go after him. He said the Indian might lead him to Sanaco's headquarters, if such exists."

"To your knowledge does such a person as this Sanaco exist?"

Thayer let a rare smile show. "Absolutely not. It's a myth. A figment of Mr. Kimball's fertile imagination. I reminded the defendant that he was needed here, to work with the Osage scouts, that our purpose was to turn back Indian raiding parties crossing the Red River. That the political implications were—and still are—of the direst importance. By stopping the raiding, the federal government hopes to keep Texas in the Union." He turned to the captains. "You gentlemen understand the importance of that."

"What was the defendant's response?"

"He persisted in his views."

"Did you order him not to leave the post? Did you warn him that he faced a court-martial if he did?"

"I did."

"Were you outside the environs of the fort when the conversation took place? Specifically, Major, were you *in the field?*"

Thayer was amused. "We were in my office—in this very room."

"Did the defendant leave the post in defiance of your orders?"

"He did on or about the morning of August fifth."

"Relate to the Court what else he did in connection with leaving the post in defiance of your orders."

"He took off at once, taking with him Curly, the Osage headman, and three other Osages."

"In your expert opinion, sir, did that leave the post without proper command for the Osages?"

"It did."

"That's all, Major. Thank you."

Thayer was half off the stand when Povich shot to his feet. "The defense would like to ask some questions, Major."

Jernigan whirled. "I object."

"Surely, sir," reasoned Povich, "we have the right to pursue this from our standpoint?"

"Never mind," said Thayer, waving off the prosecutor. "I shall be glad to repeat my testimony for the Board."

Jernigan stepped clear and Povich moved in. "Sir, were you not apprised of Colonel Emory's orders regarding Mr. Kimball before you left Fort Washita?"

"In a general way, yes. But—and I repeat—we were not conducting a field operation when Mr. Kimball rushed off."

"Just what were Colonel Emory's orders as you understood them?"

"Quite vague, as I recall. To the effect that Mr. Kimball could act as he saw fit under field conditions, and yet also within certain limits."

"And what were those limits, Major? Please specify."

"Limitations that I saw fit to impose to ensure the safety of this cantonment. By rambling off, God knows where, Mr. Kimball was endangering our security."

"Yet Mr. Kimball returned and brought with him a white captive he and the Osages rescued."

"That is correct."

"And the main body of the Osage scouts continued to function, did they not, at your command?"

"Except Curly Wolf, their headman, went with Kimball."

Povich paused to scan his notes. His head snapped up. "It is my understanding that the Osages were left in charge of Traveling Elk, a noted warrior."

"I'm not aware that this Traveling Elk is a noted warrior."

"However, the Osages performed well, did they not, even turning back two raiding parties?"

Thayer glared at Povich. "That is correct."

"The defense thus takes the stand that the post was not left without adequate scouts or command thereof. We have no further questions, Major," purred Povich, bowing a little. "Thank you, sir."

Thayer, returning to his chair at the table, then asked, "Does the prosecution wish to call other witnesses?"

Jernigan, at stiff-backed attention, nodded at once. "The prosecution calls Mr. Povich."

Povich, with alacrity, was sworn in and ready, waiting, as Jernigan began. "Were you in the hospital on or about the afternoon of August seventeenth when the defendant was there?"

"I was."

"With whom?"

"Yourself, sir."

"Tell the Court our purpose there."

"To place Mr. Kimball under arrest."

"Ah. Concisely told. Did you hear the defendant,

when he spoke to Curly Wolf, the Osage, refer to Major Thayer with an expletive?"

"Beg pardon, sir, I heard no expletive."

"Just how did you hear him refer to the Major?"

"The defendant used a figure of speech—*Stone Face*. An Indian way of speaking. You know, they have a colorful way of referring to us whites. It was not an oath."

"But the defendant did say *Stone Face?*"

"He did—but his tone was not disrespectful."

Jernigan smiled. "You are impeaching yourself, Lieutenant. Earlier, the record will show, you said the remark had no direct connection or reference to Major Thayer."

"It was merely a figure of speech—meant for the understanding of the Osages."

"Thank you, Lieutenant, for your co-operation. That will do. The prosecution now calls First Lieutenant Charles S. Jernigan."

Jernigan, upon being sworn in, addressed himself in a legal-sounding voice. "On or about the afternoon of August seventeenth did you hear the defendant refer to Major Thayer in an uncomplimentary manner?"

"I did."

"Where?"

"In the cantonment hospital."

It was ridiculous, Roan saw. A mockery.

"What term did the defendant use?"

"Stone Face."

"What was the defendant's tone?"

"Disrespectful."

Jernigan rose and swept the defense a triumphant look and faced the Board. "The prosecution rests, gentlemen."

"The defense," countered Povich, just as quick, "moves for dismissal of each and every charge on the grounds that the prosecution has failed to prove a prima facie case."

"Overruled."

Povich swallowed, his combative eyes disavowing the stiff correctness of his manner. "Very well, sir. The defense will present its case. I call Mr. Kimball to the stand."

Even though he hadn't expected to testify yet, Roan wasn't startled. He seemed to move through a false haze as he was sworn in and seated himself and faced the Board. Their faces, set stiffly above high-necked collars, appeared as wax figures while his mind, far away, dwelled on the mountains and the war parties concentrating there.

"Mr. Kimball."

Suddenly Roan realized that Povich, sharply, had spoken his name a second time. With effort, Roan keyed his senses to respond as Povich finished the question. ". . . . how long have you been in the Army?"

"Since Forty-nine."

"Where did you enlist?"

"At Fort McKavett, Texas."

"Tell the Court where you have seen service."

"Seven years along the Mexican border, stationed at Fort Clark most of that time. About three years at Fort Belknap, and this past year at Jefferson Barracks, Missouri."

"In what capacity at Fort Belknap?"

"In charge of the Tonkawa scouts."

"Objection!" Jernigan was leaping up, shouting. "The defense is deliberately leading the witness through a circuitous and time-delaying narration of irrelevant facts."

Povich faced him, feet balanced like a fencer. "We are merely establishing that Mr. Kimball has an outstanding service record. That he's an officer of unquestioned reliability."

"Go on," grumbled Thayer, resting his chin on the palm of his left hand. "Keep it brief."

"Where did you receive your commission?"

"At Fort Belknap."

"Under what circumstances?"

"We were fortunate in rescuing a number of women and children held captive by the Indians and some white renegades."

"How many captives?"

"Objection!" Jernigan shouted. "All this has been introduced in the defense's opening statement."

"We're proving it through direct testimony now!" Povich shouted back.

And Thayer, predictably: "Objection sustained. Proceed. Step up the rate of march, Mr. Povich."

Povich, left arm across his middle, right hand tugging at his chin, head bowed, paced out a small circle before the witness stand, stopped, and said, "Mr. Kimball, relate to the Court where you first heard of Sanaco."

"At Fort Washita from Colonel Emory."

"And who else told you that Sanaco is a real person?"

"Curly Wolf, the Osage headman."

"What is Sanaco—white, Indian, Mexican?"

"I don't know. He could be some of all. He could be all of one."

"Is he known by another name?"

"Yes. He's also called Scar-Arm. His left arm is said to be badly scarred."

Povich, Roan saw, was consuming time, carefully and slowly phrasing each question, pausing between each. Moving to the defense table, he scanned his notes, turned one page and scanned it, and another page, and drifted back, his polished boots squeaking at each slow step. The Board, except the Major, leaned in to catch Povich's next line of questioning.

"Sanaco, Sanaco," Povich mused, his tone wondering. "A name to reckon with. Where is he believed to keep his headquarters?"

"Apparently he shifts around a good deal. However, Colonel Emory, based on information from Texas informants, believes Sanaco stays this side of Red River, away from the Texans. It's safer."

As Povich paused again, delaying, there came the warning snap of Thayer's watch case closing, and

211

Thayer's prodding voice. "Move along, Mr. Povich. We're not out on maneuvers."

"Yes, sir. Thank you for the reminder." And quickening: "Mr. Kimball, what was the gist of your orders from Colonel Emory?"

"Bring in Sanaco, dead or alive."

"That in a nutshell?"

"Yes."

"Were the orders written?"

"No—verbal."

"Did you and the Colonel discuss the possibility that your verbal instructions might conflict with Major Thayer's?"

"We did."

"And what did the Colonel say to that?"

"He told me, when in the field, to use my own judgment and to take the consequences."

"Was this made known to Major Thayer?"

"Colonel Emory said he would so inform Major Thayer. I have no reason to think he did not."

Ever so gradually, Povich faced Thayer and said, "Your honor, at this juncture the defense has no alternative but to request that a rider on the fleetest horse be dispatched to Fort Washita and a deposition be taken from Colonel Emory and hurried back here."

The two captains exchanged looks. Captain Vaughan leaned across to whisper to Captain Cruce; their voices rose. The Major pounded for order.

"Request overruled. The Court knows the limitations of the Colonel's orders."

"Sir," said Povich, "can't the Court talk this over? We need the deposition to show the intent of the original verbal instructions. If Lieutenant Kimball was to get Sanaco, he had to act as the situation demanded—whether he was on the post or not."

Vaughan grabbed a pencil and scribbled rapidly on a pad. Tearing out the sheet, he hurried it to Thayer. The Major read it, his mouth a rind of irritation. "Do you insist, sir?" he asked.

"I do, Major," replied the little man. His inquiring eyes were twinkling.

Thayer, visibly aggravated, called to the guard, "Escort the witness from the courtroom while we deliberate."

Standing, Roan met Povich's determined eyes. For the first time Thayer had encountered disagreement from his hand-picked Board. Although only a minor skirmish, it had its lift of satisfaction.

Outside, Roan dropped on a bench to wait, grateful for the respite. The jangle of disagreeing voices reached him, Thayer's metallic tones discernible above the others; now and then Jernigan's, high and pompous, and Povich's, deeper and calmer, and Vaughan's sharp, alert tones.

Half an hour went by. The voices trailed off to silence, after which Jernigan came to the door and motioned Roan in. Povich had a dogged cast to his roundish face as Roan sat beside him. "We lost the deposition," the attorney whispered. "But we had to try. Thayer and Jernigan, between them, rode Vaughan down. The Board had to go along. That's the way the game is played. Now Jernigan wants to cross-examine you. I can't prevent that."

"Good," Roan said.

Jernigan swept to the attack, his high voice crackling. "Describe to the Court what happened between the time you and the Osages, flaunting Major Thayer's orders, took off up north and returned."

Povich vaulted up before Roan could reply. "Objection. We request that that part of the question, 'flaunting Major Thayer's orders,' be stricken from the record, in as much as it reflects prejudice and has not been proved."

"Rephrase the question, Mr. Judge Advocate." Thayer was growing more and more petulant.

After Jernigan struck the phrase, Roan began to sketch the events briefly, until, catching Povich's coaching look, he adopted a slower, detailed account, and little by little related what had occurred.

"About this Red Shield?" Jernigan questioned, a cat's grin stealing over his face. "Did you at any time suspect that he was this . . . ah . . . shadowy Sanaco?"

"Yes. I figured he was our man."

"Why?"

"By the presence of the captive white child. Also the new Army rifles we saw. And the well-kept village. The fact that nobody went out to hunt. That they were well supplied."

Jernigan nodded agreeably. He was leading up to something, but what? "What caused you to change your mind, Mr. Kimball?"

"After the fight, when I saw him without a shirt. There wasn't a scar on his arms."

"So you still believe the story—that myth—if I may use that word without ruffling Mr. Povich's composure—about the scars identifying this so-called Sanaco?"

"I do."

"Tell the Court why."

"Because the Osages believe it."

"But you came back without a Sanaco. It was a fool's errand.

"Not at all. We eliminated Red Shield as a suspect, and we brought back the little Dawkins girl."

"If the Court please," Povich intervened, "this type of questioning is leading nowhere. I suggest it be stopped. He's trying to browbeat the witness."

"Overruled."

Jernigan, with a mocking bow, continued, "Just one more question. You did not find Sanaco?"

"We did not," said Roan.

"Which proves, sir, that you are an irresponsible officer. One who kites off across country chasing whatever mirage some superstitious Osage conjures up for you. That's all." He strode back to his desk, back arched.

Povich strolled across. "Mr. Kimball, in addition to being commissioned at Fort Belknap for your work in rescuing the captive women and children, did you receive a commendation outside the Army?"

"I did."

"From whom?"

"The State of Texas."

"I believe that is all, Mr. Kimball." And, turning to the Board, Povich asked, "Was not the life of one helpless child, since cared for with all the gentleness of a mother by Mrs. Thayer, worth that dangerous ride the defendant and the Osages took?"

Thayer's gavel-pounding halted him. "Cut the bleeding-heart histrionics, Mr. Povich. It's getting late. Any more witnesses?"

"Yes, sir."

"Oh? I thought you were about ready to rest your case. How many?"

"I haven't decided, sir."

"There will be no more pussyfooting, Mr. Povich. Understand? Court resumes at eight o'clock sharp in the morning." His implication was plain: The trial had better end tomorrow.

Leaving the courtroom with Povich, Roan felt worn and resigned. At best they had gained just a little more time.

At his quarters Roan saw, at first glance, Curly and another figure, ludicrous and gaunt, lost in overlapping buckskin leggings and shirt and wearing moccasins. A buffalo robe and a pack lay on Roan's cot. The odd figure turned and Roan felt his face crinkling in a pleased grin.

"Reverend," he said, "you make quite an Osage, though on the lean side. Any trouble getting in?"

"Got right by the guard. Thanks to Brother Curly Wolf and this here getup and that buffalo robe. Brought

216

my own stuff in a bundle."

"Good. What's on your mind?"

Loftus scratched his head, and his sunken eyes deepened, thoughtful and baffled. "Somethin' odd," he said. "Mighty odd. Maybe it'll help you. Maybe not. Brother Curly Wolf tells me you're in a peck of trouble."

"I'm being court-martialed." Roan introduced him and Povich. "Sit down and tell us."

"Remember the day you came to Hatsboro lookin' for a man, an' I said I saw a soldier ride in an' go to the cabin where them two came out—the fleshy white man an' the Indian?" Roan nodded. "Well," Loftus said flatly, "I saw that soldier here."

"Here?" Roan snapped out of his depression. "You're certain?"

"Sure as Satan. Right here. He was the one that ordered me outa the fort."

"Jernigan," Roan said.

"Don't know his name. Reckon he's some kinda officer. I know he was mighty uppity an' high on himself."

"Jernigan," Roan said again, absolutely still. He had the sensation of a vast ball of light exploding through his head and clearing away the smoke and doubt that had fogged his mind so long. His excitement burst like a dam. "Povich, do you see what this means? Jernigan went to see Shell after Shell failed to close the deal for the Dawkins girl. This whole dirty business is beginning to hook up. Maybe it explains why so many cap-

217

tives have been ransomed at Fort Washita. Reverend, will you testify in court what you just told me? Will you point Jernigan out?"

"You betcha, brother."

"Hold on," Povich said. "You realize what you're doing? You're accusing an officer of malfeasance of duty, of possibly sharing in the ransom. What if Jernigan can explain why he went to see Shell? Maybe he had an official reason."

"Official, hell. Emory had already told Shell to high-tail it back to the Kiowas Shell claimed had the little girl. And, remember, there were no Kiowas there when we hit the camp."

"It gives us a chance," Povich agreed.

"That's more than we've got right now."

CHAPTER 15

"Mr. Povich, call your first witness"

"The defense calls Mr. Curly Wolf, the Osage headman."

"Guard, escort the witness in."

Even Roan wasn't expecting the fearsome figure filling the doorway, naked to the waist, deer-tail-turkey-gobbler roach quivering, the high-boned face, broad and proud, painted the colors of danger, hideous streaks of orange and black, applied to frighten the enemy. At Povich's gesture to the witness chair, Curly Wolf took stately strides and, when seated, pulled the folds of his blanket around his loins.

"You'll have to explain the swearing-in to him," Jernigan scoffed.

"I daresay he knows what it is to give his word," Povich said.

When the clerk approached and spoke, the Osage rose and raised his right hand, his left on the Bible, and as the clerk finished speaking, Curly said, "I tell truth as my father taught me."

Povich, sweeping Jernigan a told-you-so look, turned to the witness. "Is it true there is a man called Sanaco?"

"True as Grandfather the Sun."

"Have you ever seen Sanaco?"

Curly moved his head once, in negation. "Only Cut-Knives and Snake People and bad Heavy Brows see Sanaco."

"Heavy Brows? Who are the Heavy Brows?"

"White men."

"Is Sanaco bad?"

"Bad—heap bad."

"Why is he bad?"

"He steals little children and women and sells them. I don't like this thing."

"Did you and other Osages go with Lieutenant Kimball to find Sanaco?"

"Yes. We ride hard. Long time."

"Were there some hard fights?"

"Two—for little white girl captive. First time Red Shield's men at camp near Spirit Place. Next time Red

Shield he came after us. We drove them away."

"How did the Lieutenant fight?"

"Hard, quick—like us."

"Tell the pony soldier chiefs in this room what kind of man the Lieutenant is."

"Good friend. He understands us. We gave him new name. We call him One-of-Us."

"Is it a custom of the Osages to give names to pony soldiers?"

Curly nodded, his abruptness setting his roach to trembling.

"Do you have a name for me?"

Curly, displaying a face-splitting grin, said, "Yes—we call you Laugh-a-Lot."

"I am honored," Povich said, smiling. "Now—"

"Objection!" Jernigan stormed. "What is this, a stage play, William Penn Among the Friendlies?"

"Move along, Mr. Povich," Thayer cautioned. "At once."

"Now," said Povich, "tell us another thing. Is it true that the Osages have a name for Major Thayer."

"Yes." Curly was no longer smiling, and Roan went taut.

"What is it?"

"Stone Face."

"What does it mean, this Stone Face name?"

Roan, dreading the Osage's literal translation, watched Curly flick the Major a look, then turn his eyes on Povich, smiling broadly once again. "Stone Face means hard like rock in fight. Face hard—show

220

no fear—but heart"—Curly patted his deep chest—"big for friends—for all Osages."

Roan felt his tension drop away. The Osage couldn't have carried it off more convincingly had he rehearsed, which he had not.

Povich, as if sensing a peak point, stepped back. "Thank you, Mr. Curly Wolf. I have no more talk."

"I have more talk," Curly said, rising suddenly, towering. "Talk for you—for everybody—for Stone Face here," and he leveled a forefinger like a gun barrel at Major Thayer, who reared back, flushing. "I tell you this thing, this bad thing." All the while Curly's hands, thick but expressive, were forming terse word pictures. He pointed north. "Heap enemies in mountains. Come here damn quick. Stone Face, you must get your men ready. Tie up your ponies' tails. Get ready for fight. Be brave. Dodge bullets. Dodge arrows. Like this." Suddenly crouching, he began jumping from side to side, ducking, pivoting, weaving, agile for a man his bulk. He lunged as if at an enemy, his right arm striking downward, then both hands grabbing, the right one making a circular slash, simulating a scalping. Finished, lofting the imaginary scalp high, he let out a gobbling cry and thrust himself to the door and out, past the astonished guard.

"A superb performance," mocked Jernigan, lightly patting his hands. "A savage's clever act to arouse sympathy for the accused, plus much scare oratory to distract us from the business at hand." He glanced at Thayer for approval, but the Major was staring uneasily at the door. When he turned after a moment, however, his face was smooth. "I take it that Curly Wolf is your last witness, Mr. Povich?"

"Not yet, sir. We call the Judge Advocate."

Jernigan's eyes widened. His jaw muscles knotted. Briskly, he marched to the stand and was sworn in, clipping out his reply.

"I believe," Povich opened, "you are familiar with the series of negotiations that have taken place at Fort Washita toward securing the release of Indian captives?"

"Indeed. If I may say so, I have performed a major role as Colonel Emory's official representative arranging the many details." His restless fingers brushed at the sleeve of his immaculate jacket. "My legal background, you know."

"And what did these details require?"

"Full reports in each case, for one thing, when Texas people came to the post inquiring for members of their families believed captured by Indians. I then sent word through some trusted Indian to the hostile camps."

"You mean, with word that a ransom was offered?"

"What else? That's the only way the Indians will release captives. Too, sometimes a Mr. Shell, Kirk Shell, would come to the post with news of a white child or woman. In that case, we tried to locate the family in the settlements. Sometimes we advertised in the Texas newspapers."

"You worked closely with Shell?"

"As much as I could. He's a strange man. Not very communicative at times."

"Do you recall how many captives were negotiated for and released at Fort Washita this past year?"

"I have to think on that for a moment." Jernigan cocked his head and gazed up at the ceiling. "About twelve, I recall."

"What was the lowest ransom figure?"

"About twelve hundred dollars."

"And the highest?"

"Two thousand."

"Do you consider Shell an honest go-between?"

"Absolutely. He brought in the people."

Povich cleared his throat and twice stroked his mustache. "You are, of course, familiar with the recent Dawkins case, and you were at the post the day Shell and a Delaware companion came there to parley and asked fifteen hundred dollars for the little Dawkins girl?"

"Yes, yes," said Jernigan, waving a discounting hand. "Everyone knows that."

"I remind you that when Shell's camp was raided there were no Kiowas there as he claimed, and the rescued white child turned out not to be the Dawkins child, but a poor waif he was going to substitute in her place."

Jernigan's expression changed slightly. "In my opinion, Dawkins just didn't recognize his own child after all those years—that's all."

"A father wouldn't know his own flesh and blood?"

Povich demanded incredulously. "We'll leave it there for the moment. You heard Colonel Emory reject the offer and you heard him tell Shell to return to the so-called Kiowa camp and negotiate for less money, did you not?"

"I did."

"Very well. The scene is set. Didn't you that same day, only minutes after the ransom parley broke up, hurry to Hatsboro and tell Shell the game was up—that he'd better clear out?"

"Sir," replied Jernigan, arching up, "you impugn my honor."

"Check your memory, Mr. Judge Advocate. Did you or not?"

"I did not," Jernigan replied, his voice unshaken.

"No more questions," Povich said, about-facing.

Thayer wore an inquiring frown. His uneasiness was back. He kept drumming the desk. "I surmise you have no more witnesses, Mr. Povich?"

"One more, sir."

"One more?"

"Yes, sir."

"Get him in here."

"The defense calls the Reverend Noah Loftus."

"Guard, bring him in on the double."

Battered hat in hand, worn Bible tucked under his left arm like a part of him, Noah Loftus paused in the doorway. He had changed to his seedy black suit and once more was the traveling evangelist on the lookout for lost souls, his genial scarecrow's eyes roving, as if ready to bring a new convert into the fold.

One look and Jernigan sprang to his feet. "What's this man doing back on the post? He's illegally on military property."

"He has information pertinent to our case," Povich replied evenly.

"He cannot testify without a permit to be on the post. To my knowledge no such permit has been issued."

"If you must know, he came back at our request. Major, sir, the Judge Advocate is employing delaying tactics. There's nothing in the Articles of War that says the defense cannot call any witness it chooses."

Thayer drummed the desk again. "For once, I concur, Mr. Povich. But I warn you his testimony had better tie in. This case must move along. Swear the witness in," Thayer ordered, stabbing his disapproval on Jernigan.

To Roan, Loftus appeared to be enjoying the unusual experience as the center of attention in so high a company. When the clerk held out a Bible, saying, "Raise your right hand," Loftus, the benefactor, said, "Like to use mine, if you don't mind. It's took me over many a rough place on the road to righteousness."

When the clerk pulled back, confused, Thayer, unleashing his impatience, bellowed, "A Bible's a Bible! Go ahead. Let's speed this up."

"Do you swear to tell the whole truth and nothing but the truth, so help you God?" the clerk intoned.

"Amen, brother. Amen."

Nettled, the clerk shoved the worn Bible at Loftus

225

and retreated to his station and took up his pen.

Povich, as if sensing the Major's hurry, yet not hurrying, asked, "Mr. Loftus, as a minister of the gospel your calling takes you many places, does it not?"

"Wherever the Lord calls me."

"You came here from Fort Washita?"

"That I did—spreadin' the Good News ever' step of the way. Stopped off a spell with a Chickasaw family. Had a right nice little visit there. Mighty generous folks, them Indians. Right smart sense, too. By the time I left they'd seen the light for certain."

Thayer's voice was a wedge driving between the witness and Povich: "Mr. Loftus will confine his comments to answering the question, else be removed from the courtroom."

Loftus crossed his rail-fence legs and leaned back for comfort. "Yer honor, I jest threw that in so you'd know Noah Loftus was never one to back off from the Lord's work. Next thing I'm gonna do is organize a temperance society right here amongst yer soldier boys. I can tell Old Demon Rum's hangin' round here. I know the signs. I—"

"Reverend," Povich implored, "just answer the question."

"You bet. Let's get down to taw. I came here from Fort Washita or thereabouts. Lost my mule on the way, though. Fool critter wandered off one night. That's how I happened to stop off with the Indian family."

"You've told us about the Indians. Now tell the Court what you did at Fort Washita, first."

226

"You're off the track there. I wasn't right at Fort Washita," Loftus responded, earnestly trying to oblige. "I got off the stage there."

"Where did you go from there?"

"Hotfooted it right smack to Hatsboro. That den of iniquity—that Sodom and Gomorrah." His voice was climbing, charged with damnation. His zealot's eyes glittered. "That devil's hangout where there's painted women an' banjo music an' innocent soldier boys go astray."

"Were you there in late June when a white man and an Indian dressed like a white man rode in from the west?"

"That I was," said Loftus. "I was an eyeball witness."

"Did you learn the white man's name?"

"Heard the saloonkeeper call him by name. Let's see. Had it right on the tip of my tongue." The long, eroded face had a strained expression. Suddenly he slapped a leg. "Amen. Remember now. The saloonkeeper called him Shell. That was it."

Jernigan's objecting voice sounded. "The witness is repeating hearsay. It has no relation to the charges here."

"Link the testimony, Mr. Povich," Thayer warned. Yet, somehow, Roan thought, the Major seemed more curious than impatient.

Lowering his voice to a near undertone, Povich asked the witness, "Did you see Shell and the Indian take the road to the fort?"

"That I did."

"Did you see them come back?"

"That I did."

"What did they do then?"

"Tied up an' went into a cabin."

"Sir," shouted Jernigan, flinging up a contemptuous hand, "this is no more than a delaying tactic. I object to such a line of roundabout questioning."

Surprisingly, Major Thayer motioned him down and leaned on his elbow, intently observing Loftus.

"Shortly after they returned," Povich continued in the same unhurried manner, as if Jernigan had not interrupted, "did you see a man in uniform ride up from the direction of the fort?"

"Amen to that—an' he was raisin' dust."

"Where did he go?"

"Straight to their cabin."

In a loud voice Povich then asked, "Is that man in this courtroom?"

"Right there he is," said Loftus, pointing out Jernigan. "It's the same soldier."

"I can explain everything," shouted Jernigan, bounding up. His face was pale.

Major Thayer gasped and sat back. The captains sat stunned, like the Major, staring at Jernigan. "You'll get your chance to refute the witness," Thayer said. "Sit down. Continue, Mr. Povich."

Povich's sharp question seemed to split the stillness. "How long was Mr. Jernigan at the cabin?"

"Ten minutes or so," Loftus said.

"Did he take the main trail back to the fort?"

228

"Come to think of it, he didn't. He rode into the woods."

"That's all, Reverend. Thank you for testifying."

"Mighty welcome you are." Jogging his head to the Court and the others, Loftus covered the distance to the door in half a dozen long strides and slackened, craning around to give Roan an encouraging look and went out.

"Mr. Povich," said Thayer, his voice grave, "you have cast aspersions on the integrity of a fellow officer. Therefore, I call the Judge Advocate in rebuttal to refute the previous testimony. I shall ask the questions."

"No objection, sir. The defense is only too pleased for Mr. Jernigan to take the stand."

Jernigan had retrieved his self-control, but his face was still pale. Major Thayer began:

"Did you go to Hatsboro on the day in question?"

"I did."

"Why did you say you did not?"

"Because I was there unofficially, without Colonel Emory's knowledge."

"Explain."

"I went there to try to persuade Shell to talk the Kiowas down to five hundred dollars; if failing, to sneak the child out of camp and bring her to the post."

"What did Shell say?"

"Said he would try."

"Which route did you take riding back to the post?"

Jernigan wet his lips. "I cut through the woods."

"Why?"

229

"To save time. I was on duty at the post you remember, sir, and I didn't want to be seen."

"Very well. Step down."

Povich, strolling back and forth, addressed the Court. "The defense points out that Colonel Emory had already told Shell to try for a lower ransom; therefore, it was hardly necessary for Mr. Jernigan to see Shell again about that. We also point out that, if the Judge Advocate was in such an all-fired hurry, he would have taken the road to get back to the post. The woods are quite thick. What matter if he was seen? Who would know his mission by then? And now I recall the defendant."

Roan sighed and stood, sensing that he could add no evidence that would sway the inevitable course of the trial. Throwing doubt on a fellow officer's honor was one thing, still another to prove it beyond question, even with the testimony of Loftus. At another time in another Court, perhaps yes; here, however, where evidence had little if any weight, that wasn't possible. He and Povich had managed to delay the outcome and no more. Within minutes everything would be over. He was preparing himself to accept that as he moved to the witness chair. Facing Povich, he swept his face clear of all feeling, and he seemed to hear Povich's voice as from a distance:

"Soon after Shell and the Indian left the post, did you take the road to Hatsboro?"

"I did, yes."

"What happened on the way?"

230

"I was shot at."

"Did you catch sight of the ambusher?"

"I couldn't because of the woods. However, I could hear his horse going away."

"In what direction."

"Toward the post."

"That concludes my questions and the defense now rests," Povich stated, head high, in confidence, facing the Board.

Major Thayer appeared pleased. Nodding, he said, "The Court will now hear the closing arguments. You are first, Mr. Jernigan, representing the prosecution."

Jernigan, his self-assurance restored, moved swiftly to the attack. "Gentlemen, we have proved beyond any doubt that the defendant did leave the post without his commanding officer's permission, that he was not in the field when he started his wild goose chase after the mirage of Sanaco . . . That, sirs, is the one point upon which this case rests. As for the parade of witnesses here today attesting to the defendant's character, I remind you that one is a primitive Indian, reared in savagery, and easily swayed by any white man who will squat down and dine on a pot of stinking, half-cooked cow's insides.

"As for the self-styled minister of the gospel, one Noah Loftus, he is no more than a drifting bum, a deadbeat hanging around frontier posts looking for handouts from the military. His word is nothing.

"Furthermore, as for the vicious insinuations against my own character, I stand on my unblemished record of service of fifteen years as a soldier and Christian gentleman, who, without fanfare, did all he could to bring back the young and the old from the darkness of Indian captivity . . . In turn, gentlemen, I ask you to return a verdict of guilty. Thank you."

"Mr. Povich—and make it brief."

Brief, Roan thought bitterly, so the verdict can be rushed to its absolute end.

There was a sharp edge to Povich's voice. "Gentlemen, the Judge Advocate makes this case appear simple when, instead, it is quite complex. Mr. Kimball acted on his own judgment pursuant to Colonel Emory's orders. Mr. Kimball took that chance as a man of duty and now he stands accused. But he got results. He brought back one pathetic child, just as he saved those many in Texas and was honored for it by the honorable State of Texas.

"As for the two witnesses whom the Judge Advocate so unjustly attacked, they spoke from their hearts. Curly Wolf is a man of high honor among the Osages. He testified for the defendant because they have fought and shared together. Since when is the word of an honorable man of copper skin less than a white man's? Civilization doesn't necessarily make a man honorable; by the same token, so-called savagery doesn't make an untutored man dishonorable.

"The prosecution would have you believe there is no Sanaco—that he's a ghost, a myth. On the contrary, gentlemen, to say that Sanaco doesn't exist is to say that Colonel Emory, our distinguished commander at

Fort Washita, is a liar. And why didn't the prosecution let us take a deposition from the Colonel, or grant us a change of venue? I'll tell you why. The prosecution is fearful of the truth!"

Povich wheeled, his eyes cutting from Jernigan to Thayer. "All along I have sensed personal motives behind these false charges, motives that dare not be revealed here." At once turning to the Court: "I leave you with that deepest of perceptions, gentlemen, and the defendant's proven innocence." He started to retire, then advanced closer to the Board's desk. "Also, two unanswered questions. Why did the Judge Advocate ride to Hatsboro that day to see Shell? And who shot at Lieutenant Kimball? In short, who tried to kill him and why?"

Major Thayer was speaking before Povich could reach his chair. "The clerk will strike the testimony of Noah Loftus as hearsay and unreliable. Also the Court will disregard any implication that the Judge Advocate rode to Hatsboro to see a man called Shell, or that the defendant was fired at on the Hatsboro road."

"We object," Povich flared back. "Loftus testified to what he saw. It was not hearsay. He *saw* Lieutenant Jernigan."

"You're on the brink of contempt, young sir," said Thayer, standing and ignoring him to look at the captains, a curtness that brushed aside Povich's argument. "Gentlemen, have you reached a verdict? Are we in agreement? Fill out your ballots and pass them to me." He then wrote out his own ballot.

Roan's protest was hammering. He saw Captain

Cruce fill out his ballot and, as if relieved, pass it to Major Thayer. He saw the Major, very quickly, and expectantly, scan the ballot and, raising his gaze to Cruce, nod approval. The Major sat down, drumming the table.

Captain Vaughan, immobile, sat with pen in hand, the small square of paper before him untouched, a far expression in his eyes.

A commotion at the door broke through Roan's concentration. A noncom burst in. "Major, sir, you'd better come at once to the northwest blockhouse. We can see horsemen massing on the ridge."

Thayer's jaw fell. Another moment and he shouted, "You're interrupting Court—get out!"

"But, Major—"

Thayer gripped the edge of the table and flung around. "Captain Vaughan—complete your ballot." It was an order.

Still, Vaughan hesitated, his crimped mouth and eyes mirroring his inner quandary.

"Captain Vaughan, you're holding up the verdict."

Almost in concert, Roan heard a nearby crashing roar and a distant, sonorous, single boom. He felt the room shake.

Everyone froze. Vaughan moved first, suddenly scribbling on his ballot and rising like an old tomcat shaken from his nap. His voice crackled. "We're under fire, Major. That, sir, was an artillery round." Grabbing his hat and plopping the ballot in front of Thayer, he made for the door.

"Vaughan—Captain Vaughan—come back here, sir. We have not adjourned."

The Captain kept going, past the noncom, past the guard, and out.

Major Thayer continued to face the empty doorway, his summoning right hand lifted in an attitude of peremptory command, of silence, unmindful of shouts outside the building. He looked down at Vaughan's ballot and a tiny sliver of angry surprise rippled along the firm lines of his lips. And then, as if smiling to himself, he said, "A two-to-one vote—that's enough. We have a verdict of guilty, gentlemen." The shouting seemed to penetrate his consciousness at last. "Court is adjourned."

CHAPTER 16

Rushing outside with Povich, Roan saw a jagged hole as large as a washtub on the stockade's north wall. Troopers gawked and ran headlong here and there.

Major Thayer, as erect and formal were he conducting post inspection, disappeared at a leisurely walk into the lower section of the northwest blockhouse, trailed by Jernigan and Cruce. Roan and Povich followed on the double, there to curb their impatience while first the Major, then the Adjutant and then the Captain climbed the ladder to the lookout.

A sentry and Captain Vaughan stood at loopholes. Vaughan was peering through field glasses.

Roan was startled when he looked. Swirls of Indian riders, so many the ridge appeared to move, sunlight picking up glints on metal, feathered headdresses fluttering in the wind.

Something walloped the stockade a splintering-sounding blow about the same time that Roan, flinching, heard the heavy *pum* of a fieldpiece and saw a bloom of dirty smoke west of the Indians, and hard on those sounds the post-script of Major Thayer's astonished outrage:

"How dare them! It's inconceivable. Where in God's name did they get it?"

Roan's mind throbbed, as if piecing together the raveled ends of a rope. Above the babble of excited voices he heard himself saying, "That's the twelve-pounder Napoleon lost on last spring's Red River campaign. Colonel Emory said they also got the caisson."

"Heathens!" Thayer raged, beside himself. "Savages!"

Vaughan lowered his glasses and said ominously, "Not savages, Major—but white men serving it—deserters, no doubt. They have to be. They're swabbing the gun now."

Captain Cruce, his cheeks like flabby red cushions, stepped to Thayer's side. "I suggest we abandon the post at once to prevent unnecessary effusion of blood."

Major Thayer jerked. He flung up a hand. There was a light, quick splat as his palm struck. Cruce recoiled, mouth ajar, right hand touching his flaming cheek.

"How dare you suggest such irresponsible action,

236

Captain." Thayer's austere face had the characteristic marbled coldness; his prominent eyes looked cavernous under the ledge of his forehead. "We shall defend the post as long as there's a log left standing. Captain Cruce, you will return to your quarters until further orders. Lieutenant Jernigan will remain here to relay my orders. Captain Vaughan, you will post sharpshooters on the walls. I want that gun crew picked off."

"No chance of that, Major. They're out of carbine range."

"Did you hear the order, Captain?"

Vaughan's eyes flung dissent, as bright as a terrier's. But he said, "We'll try, sir."

"I repeat, gentlemen," said Thayer, ramming his gaze over the group, "there will be no surrender of this post to a pack of heathen Indians and a handful of Army deserters and white renegades."

After a stiff pause, the officers stirred toward the ladder. As Roan started down after Povich, the Major suddenly screamed at Roan, "You are still under arrest. Meanwhile, see if you can be of some small service. Tell your gut-eating Osage friends to ascertain the strength of the enemy." His voice had a near-incoherent tone. He looked dazed, in extreme agitation. His hands shook. Roan had seen the same emotional state come over troopers under fire the first time.

"We know that, Major. Curly's reported several hundred warriors."

Another crash and bellow, and when the Major sprang to a loophole to look, Roan took his leave, feeling the ladder shaking under his hands.

He ran to his quarters for carbine and side arm and field glasses. Rushing out, he saw Vaughan busy posting the sharp-shooters. They began a steady popping. Aware that he was doing nothing, Roan ran to the gate, where a knot of C troopers crouched on the catwalk overhead, and climbed the steps to them.

The ridge, he saw, still boiled with riders. There was a dull screeching toward the fort and another *pum* and a new puff of smoke as the punished north side took another splintering blast. It came to him that the gun crew was spacing the rounds, not firing fast to conserve the piece.

By the time the Napoleon was swabbed and loaded and ready again, most of the smoke had drifted on. Into the range of Roan's glasses, some fifty yards behind the gun, moved the high shape of a horseman. A moment more and a man yanked the lanyard and the cannon boomed and the smoke blossomed upward again and Roan heard the round strike along the northeast end of the stockade. But in that short interval of clarity he saw the crooked white blaze on the bay horse's face; when the smoke cleared the horseman wasn't there. Roan tried to recall the rider. A hat—he'd caught that much, no more. White or Indian? And he came to the old nondescript, frustrating dress and its anonymity. An Indian in white man's clothes?

The gun crew started firing faster. With each shock, the fort shuddered and logs crashed, flinging dust and hunks of wood. These rounds were solid shot. A new sound came, a rattling of canister balls. A round exploded inside the stockade; cries racked up through the bedlam.

Roan saw two sharpshooters fall from the wall. Troopers ran out to lend aid. Taking the steep steps two at a time, Roan helped carry one man to the hospital; the other was past care.

By now there was a gap wide enough to drive a wagon through on the north side. Vaughan was there, yelling his men down off the wall.

"We can't take much more of this," Vaughan yelled.

Roan pointed through the gap, feeling a cold shock as riders streamed down the ridge in bunches. A bobbing wave of many colors, bronze bodies painted, war bonnets fluttering, scalps dangling from the bridles of fractious war horses, feathers on manes. They rode slowly, as if certain of their strength. Without a visible signal, they raced into a large circle, and quickly it became a revolving wheel several riders deep, moving toward the fort as it rotated, causing Vaughan to shout his men to the gap and start firing again.

When the carbines cracked, the wheel of figures stopped and the warriors, out of carbine range, bent away, yelling taunts. They disappeared over the ridge, trailing a pall of dust.

"What the hell?" Vaughan cried in surprise.

"Trying to draw us out," Roan answered, and shook his head.

"We could make a dash for the gun."

"It's bait, Captain. Before we got there, Indians

would swarm over that ridge like a wolf pack."

Roan heard a shout behind him. He saw Vaughan look around, he heard Vaughan curse.

Jernigan ran up. "An order for you, Kimball. Take the Osage scouts. Go after that artillery piece. Spike it."

"Spike it?" Roan echoed. "Indians are just on the other side of that ridge—hoping we'll try to."

"He's right," Vaughan joined in. "It's obvious they're trying to draw us out. They wouldn't leave the gun unprotected."

"That's the order," Jernigan snapped nervously. "Execute it." He hastened back to the blockhouse.

Roan was staring at the ground when Vaughan spoke. "What do you propose to do?"

"There's no choice, is there?"

"You could try to talk some sense into Thayer."

"Me? I'm the last man he'd listen to."

"By God, I'll try."

"No—it's a personal thing," Roan said, and saw that Vaughan didn't understand. Roan was walking away when Vaughan said after him, "Kimball, I want you to know I marked my ballot not guilty."

"I know. My thanks to you."

Curly and the Osages were grouped about the main corral south of the cantonment, in their primitive faces, Roan saw, the uncertainty caused by the smoke and thunder of the white man's big gun. Roan said, "Stone Face has ordered us to kill the white men firing the big gun. You know and I know Cut-Knives and

240

Snakes and Walks-the-Prairie People are on the other side of the ridge where the gun is."

Curly nodded gravely.

"You don't have to go. You Osages were hired as scouts. Not to fight like pony soldiers. You can stay here."

"We gave our word to Big Soldier House Chief," Curly said, gesturing to the east.

"As scouts, yes. Stone Face is ordering you to do a thing he won't order the pony soldiers to do. That is wrong."

"Ho. We are brave. One-of-Us, you treat us like herd boys."

"No—like friends. Most of you will be killed if you go. I'll tell Stone Face you won't make the charge."

Roan was turning to go when Curly's voice checked him. "Friends ride together," Curly said, and strode back to the Osages, both talking and making signs for Fight and Friend. Traveling Elk was having his say. And other older warriors. They talked a little more. When Roan saw them starting to paint their faces and fix their quivering roaches, he felt guilt fall upon him. They were going, going because of him.

He saddled up and waited, ready before they were. At that moment he heard the crashing impact of a shell against the fort and the bellow of the Napoleon, the sounds ramming close together. He could see smoke fuming up above the northwest corner of the post. He could hear quick-rising cries. It grew upon him that the commotion inside the stockade was mounting, higher than before after a hit. Everyone seemed to be shouting.

The last Osage put away his medicine bag and mounted. Everyone was ready, and they were brave, he thought, braver than they knew.

Roan seemed to reach for a deep breath as a sensation wound through him. A resignation. A recklessness. Catching Curly's eye, he led out. They were jogging around the southwest blockhouse when a trooper ran out the gate, waving his arms and shouting:

"Cap'n Vaughan says don't charge. Major Thayer's hurt—so's Lieutenant Jernigan. Cap'n Vaughan's taking over. He says for you to come quick."

Roan looked up, startled to see that the upper section of the northwest blockhouse no longer existed; black smoke was rising out of the wreckage. Roan hurried down and ran inside.

The first person he saw was Povich, near the tumbled-down entrance of the blockhouse. Inside men were shouting. "Just got Jernigan out," Povich panted. "Major's still in there—under a pile of timbers."

Roan ducked in, smelling the acrid stink of powder. Just ahead troopers strained at a jumble of logs. Moving up beside a man, Roan got his shoulder under a timber. Together they inched it upward. "Not too fast," a voice warned. "Whole shebang'll come down on us." Dimly, Roan glimpsed the marbled paleness of Thayer's face beneath the tangle. "Easy now," the voice cautioned. "Little more . . . little more."

Roan, straining, got so far and nothing gave. He

hacked for air and braced his legs and tried again, aware of an enormous weight against the log. There came an ominous creaking and shifting overhead. The man beside him swore and shifted his feet.

"Little more now."

Roan and the trooper strained upward again. The creaking sounded. Bit by bit the log yielded.

"Now," said the voice. "Quick!"

Hands reached in and under. For a terrible moment the forms seemed not to move; then a voice said, "Got 'im—pull now," and Roan heard the scuffing of a body being dragged out. There was movement at the blockhouse entrance as they took Thayer outside.

"I'm gonna let go," Roan's partner said.

"Come ahead."

As the man released his hold and eased by Roan, the mass overhead shifted, suddenly laying unbearable pressure on Roan. He shoved on the log with all his strength and jumped back, clear, the timbers rattling and crashing as he sprang to the doorway. Slumped, he saw four troopers carrying Major Thayer to the hospital.

A minute later he trailed across. Captain Vaughan stepped out on the porch, head down. "Major's in a bad way," he said. "We'll put him in a wagon."

"Wagon?"

"We're getting out of here at dark. I want an Osage guide, the rest to form the rear guard."

"All right."

A scream inside threw both men rigid. It tore higher

and higher. "Ah . . . ahhh . . . ahhh." It reached a crest of pain; suddenly it subsided.

Roan, of a sudden, had a sense of something vital slipping away before he could grasp it, lost because of propriety if he didn't go in there; something he must do against his wishes. He said, "Captain, I've got to talk to Jernigan."

"The man's dying."

"Maybe he'll tell me what he denied at the special court."

Vaughan's eyes were extra bright, also comprehending. "Go on in," he said. "I'll be a witness."

Roan, entering the ward ahead of Vaughan, was unable to feel much sympathy for Jernigan. The Lieutenant's face was ashen and he was breathing in labored gulps while Surgeon Alvord finished scissoring off the bloody, torn jacket. Alvord started on the bloodier shirt. He cut away the right sleeve. The short, steady strokes of the snipping blades exposed the chest and the dark red hole gaping there. Alvord cut upward from the left wrist to the shoulder. As he peeled back the sleeve, Roan leaned in to look. There were no marks, no scars, and he felt a dull surprise.

Jernigan's eyes moved. He spoke in a drained voice. "Still looking for the sinister Sanaco?" and he forced a crooked grin.

"Who is Sanaco, Jernigan? I think you know."

"I know nothing."

Roan couched his voice purposely hard. "You've been sharing in the ransom money, haven't you?"

244

Jernigan's lips moved, but he said no word. Mouth open, he struggled for breath.

"You shot at me in the woods, didn't you?"

A feeble grin curled one corner of the mouth, with a hint of the old mockery. "Come to crow over a dying man?"

"Be fair enough. Might make you think back to the women and children you bargained for like livestock, and the others you didn't bargain for because their kin was too poor. Not that I expect you to be sorry—I don't."

"Damn you, sir."

"You're not the only man passed over for promotion. Army's full of 'em, Jernigan."

"I wish . . . I wish now—"

"It's not too late. You can make up for it. Tell us who Sanaco is. Where we can find him."

Jernigan appeared to try. Roan saw the struggle taking place inside him. Jernigan's eyes bulged and his pupils got big. His lips stirred briefly. Just when Roan thought Jernigan might speak, he slumped and that was all. It was ended.

Thoughtfully, Roan stood up and moved outside, thinking as he watched Povich post troopers at breaks in the wall that with Jernigan went the last and best bet to unravel the whole cruel game. Walking out the gate, Roan studied the ridge, empty except for the Napoleon and its crew. And he thought: They're waiting for us on the other side. When we don't show up, they'll make another cut at us before dark. Maybe they'll come all the way. Dusk seemed a long time off.

CHAPTER 17

Not long before dark the twelve-pounder ceased its bellowing, reduced now to sporadic rounds. Hardly had the thankful hush settled over the post when a sentry on the north side fired. That one shot seemed to set off a terrific din.

Roan, near the gate with the Osages, heard a rolling rumble coming fast. The racket of horses running pell-mell and whooping riders. Gun flashes split the murk. Carbines rattled back. Like a roll of passing thunder, the mass of horsemen swept by, west to east, and faded northward.

Shortly, Roan heard Vaughan's intense voice. It produced an audible stir within the stockade. Troopers came forth carrying wounded to the wagons, parked hard against the south side of the post, axles freshly greased, wheel rims blanket-wrapped for silence. At the first solid onrush of early dark, the column formed and started for the river, Traveling Elk leading. When the last trooper passed, Roan and the other Osages followed.

As night came on, Roan felt the damp presence of the river, a heaviness that stayed for an hour or more as the column wound around, as the cavalrymen tugged and wrestled the wagons through sandy stretches and up slants; and then the command was changing direction, climbing a gentle grade, and Roan knew they had cut a half circle and were making northeast.

246

Povich drifted out of the gloom. "Captain wants to know how far you think he should go tonight?"

"Far as he can."

"He's thinking of the wounded. Major Thayer's no better."

"I'm thinking of the wounded too. Look back there."

Povich looked and groaned. "That glow."

"We didn't fool them very long. They're burning the post."

"Now what?"

"Long way to Fort Washita. Easier to jump a strung-out column than men inside a fort."

"Why attack us now? They have the fort."

"Nobody but a lawyer would ask that, Povich," Roan chided him gently. "More guns, more horses. Think what a hundred good carbines are worth, or will be, with the war coming on. The white renegades back there live on plunder. We left them nothing but an empty fort. But there's a stronger reason why they'll try to hamstring us."

"What could that be?"

"Red Shield. As far as he knows his favorite child, his white daughter, Little Star, is in the column."

The rising moon, veiled by drifting clouds, cast a sickly glow that etched the bobbing column like charcoal figures. To Roan the dark line of the command, following the well-defined trail made when the garrison had come out from Fort Washita, seemed to be stretching into nothingness. Much later Vaughan halted and rested an hour.

That was when Roan missed Curly. The Osage had vanished without a word.

The command was stopped for breakfast at daybreak when Roan saw him dragging in on a tired horse. He came up to Roan and said, "I heard many horses back there, many horses," and got down for coffee and hardtack.

Looking for Major Thayer, Roan saw him propped up in a wagon. Occasionally he coughed. Even now, even here, the Major retained his air of autocratic aloofness and formality. His feverish eyes bored into Roan. There was no charity in him and he asked none.

Roan uncapped his canteen. "Take a drink."

"Why waste it?" Thayer clipped.

"We've enough water."

"Anything's wasted on a dying man."

"Every man's tougher than he thinks, Major. You can make it."

"Strange, hearing encouragement from you."

"Better take a drink."

Thayer rolled his head from side to side and rubbed his hands up and down his rib cage, grimacing. "I don't seem to feel anything below. I have no breath. It's as if half of me has gone." Suddenly a fit of coughing racked him. When he hawked in his throat and spat, Roan saw bloody phlegm. Lying back, Thayer murmured, "I'll take no water from you." He lay very still. As Roan capped the canteen, the Major looked at him and said, "You gave Sara something I never could, though don't think me unfeeling toward my family. I

248

tried in my way. I'm just not a giving man. To me, it's a sign of weakness."

"You lost Sara long ago. Long before I came to Fort Washita."

Surgeon Alvord came to the wagon and looked in, giving Thayer a close study. "Get some rest, Major."

"What good would that do?"

Roan left them. The morning was too still, too bright, too peaceful, too perfect, and the realization that had persisted since Jernigan's death returned anew: His mission was a failure. He had reached a dead end. And so the traffic in captives would continue, if not at Fort Washita, somewhere else; and with the war a certainty, federal garrisons would be pulled out of Texas and the Territory and the settlements would be rolled back. And was the scoffing Jernigan right after all? Was there no Sanaco? Was Sanaco just a false face behind which many figures thrived, both red and white? A fictitious scapegoat, maybe, made into a legend of dread?

At seven o'clock the column moved on, a short, sluggish snake, the wounded in the center, raising spigots of dust that drifted back and laid a gray patina on the faces of the troopers. Flankers rode off, left and right. The Osages fanned out behind, forming a half-moon screen.

At midmorning the advance began passing through scattered bunches of buffalo. The huge, indolent beasts showed little, if any, suspicion as they parted like a dark brown wave to let the column through. At noon, when Vaughan called a halt after covering some fifteen miles, the shaggy creatures were still about, grazing steadily toward the southwest.

Vaughan was jubilant. "We've shaken loose—I think," he amended.

"Curly heard horses behind us last night," Roan said. "Many horses."

"Why should they follow us now?"

Roan cited the arguments he had given Povich, including Red Shield's possible reason, and said again in conclusion, "A hundred good Army carbines. Think what they're worth. He could make use of them in many ways."

"*He*?" Vaughan's voice projected an odd emphasis.

"I mean Sanaco."

"You don't give up easily, do you? You still think he exists? Why?"

"The Osages. They have no reason to lie. They're not in the business of selling captives. They're not protecting anyone. They're at war with the Kiowas and Comanches."

"So you expect an attack?"

"Not the way you've got us moving today. Both troops in tight. Flankers out. Advance points well ahead. A rear guard of Osages."

"Then," Vaughan laughed thinly, "we have nothing to fear."

Roan spread his hands and his tone was sober. "I like that fine—except Sanaco isn't one to take chances. He didn't at the cantonment. I doubt he'll jump us as we are."

"You're giving him credit for the bombardment?" Vaughan's manner was skeptical.

"It wasn't the Indians. You yourself saw white men serving the twelve-pounder. You saw how they spaced their rounds to save the gun."

"How could I forget it?" The Captain dropped his hands. His eyes hardened. "Do I understand you correctly? Are you suggesting that I deliberately place us in a risky position in order to draw Sanaco out? Jeopardize the entire command? I have the responsibility of seeing that two troops with the wounded return safely to Fort Washita. I intend to do just that."

"No argument there, Captain," said Roan. He rubbed a fist back and forth across his forehead. He caught his lower lip between his teeth. "What I mean is I think we need to put out some bait."

"Bait?" Vaughan's brows arched together in dislike.

"Meaning myself. With some troopers—all volunteers—and some Osages."

"Just where would you position them?"

"At the rear. Like stragglers."

"I don't like it." Vaughan crossed his arms. "If you are attacked, what then?"

"You will double back on us, hoping we catch them in between."

"In the event I couldn't reach you in time?"

"We'd just have to make out."

"It's foolhardy."

"If you were Sanaco or Red Shield, wouldn't you rather take us piecemeal?"

251

"Preferably. I'd also wonder why, of a sudden, there were stragglers, where before there had been none." His movements quickened. His eyes flashed. He beat his fist into his palm. "It has to make sense, Kimball. It has to look convincing. Why? Why the stragglers? You can't look like bait."

Both men, fretting, pondering, turned away. In the distance, on both sides of the trail, buffalo were grazing. Roan eyed them a moment. He swung around at the same time Vaughan did, seeing the same thought in Vaughan's eyes.

"You will go hunting," Vaughan said, warming to the idea. "That makes solid sense. Obviously, we are short of supplies. You will drop out of the column later in the afternoon. You will kill a few buffalo, load the meat on pack mules and straggle after us—provided we find more buffalo."

"The Osages say there should be game all along the trail."

Vaughan gave him a keen look. "If the bait isn't taken?"

"We eat buffalo either way."

It was around three o'clock as the hunting party formed: fifteen volunteer troopers, including Lieutenant Povich, plus eight Osages, counting Curly and Yellow Horse. As the command clattered on, Roan had his first misgivings. In limiting the number of Osages, he had explained the others were needed with the column, when actually his thinking was that the presence of all the Osages on the hunt might discourage attack.

He turned his attention to the buffalo. The wind was wrong at the moment, being from the hunters; the shaggies would spook at the first shot or the first rush of the Osages, who would hunt with lances. They would work around to come in against the wind, make their kills, and the troopers would bring up the pack animals. If the attack came, they were to form a circle with the mules and horses and make a stand.

Povich grew restless as the Osages rode off. "I've yet to shoot a buffalo," he said boyishly.

"Go on," Roan agreed. "Ride alongside. Aim behind the shoulder."

Waiting with the troopers, Roan saw the Osages, Povich an incongruous figure bobbing among them, circle to the southwest and approach a bunch of buffalo, riding slowly, then suddenly rushing. Before the buffalo could take flight, the Osages were upon them. Roan heard Povich fire twice. The buffalo lumbered off, leaving four dark brown shapes scattered behind, and the Osages turned back.

"Got one!" Povich yelled as Roan and the others reached the hunting ground.

The Osages made quick work of the butchering, slitting the undersides and peeling the hides back and laying the meat thereon, and then bagging it in the hides on the mules.

Roan saw no stir on the plain or in the hills. By this time the column was a thin line of dust to the northeast. Swinging in on the trail, Roan continued for a mile or more before he halted the hunting party, ostensibly to tighten packs. There was no movement anywhere. No dust. Nothing that hadn't been there before to the naked eye.

The afternoon wore away under the hot barrel of the sun. At times he lost sight of the struggling column. By five o'clock he decided the day's game was over. Buffalo-chip fires formed an orderly pattern of light when the hunters reached the bivouac. Vaughan was waiting:

"See anything?"

"Not a feather."

"What do you propose?"

"Try again tomorrow. Something. Maybe we stayed too close today. We'll hang back more."

"I'll talk to you later."

Thayer lay under a tree, apart from the other wounded, as if, the thought crossed Roan's mind, he must yet maintain proper distance between himself and the enlisted men. Roan went over and looked down at him impersonally. In the dimness the Major's face was a pale, cold-looking disc. He roused and his voice, though weaker tonight, carried the familiar abrasive quality:

"Is it your conscience that brings you back?"

"I was hoping to find you improved."

"Want me to think you noble, I suppose? Captain Vaughan told me about your little ruse. It had no subtlety. It couldn't succeed."

"It may tomorrow."

"I doubt that. Whatever you attempt will be too

254

crudely conceived. Your lack of proper field training is quite evident, Kimball. You're not qualified for a commission."

"In view of the fact that I'm not a West Pointer, you could wish us luck—extra luck," Roan said, matching Thayer's mockery.

"I wish you in hell." At once Thayer was struggling for self-control, for coherence. He raised up. Into his eyes burned a dreadful fixation. "I won't pass without telling you. It's getting dark and I want to see the expression on your face. I want that satisfaction." He had to pause. Roan could hear him breathing. He spoke, coldly malicious. "I followed you that day on the Hatsboro road."

"You?"

"You suspected Jernigan, didn't you?"

"He was the obvious one. I was spoiling his game."

"Well, I followed you, and it was I who shot at you. Regretfully, I missed. Even so, I've ruined your career. You are broken. I have that lasting satisfaction." He sank back.

"Good night, Major."

He walked to the darkening edge of the bivouac, thinking that, finally, all the pieces but one had slipped into place. Assessing himself at that moment, he discovered that he retained neither rancor toward Hamilton Thayer nor felt a stricken conscience. He walked to the Osages' fire and cooked his meat. There Captain Vaughan sought him out after supper.

"It won't make sense to hunt again tomorrow, after

you killed plenty of meat today."

Roan nodded. It was encouraging to hear the voice of command speak with clearheadedness. Vaughan had a new briskness, a contagious enthusiasm, as if after many years he had pushed out from under the stagnation of post inactivity and regulations followed to the letter.

"Instead, we will do this. You will have two wagons at the rear of the column. The first will stop for repairs. Meanwhile, the command will proceed uptrail. Inside both wagons will be sharpshooters; they will not show themselves unless you are attacked. How does that sound?"

"I like it."

Next morning as the column prepared to move out, there was a stir where the wounded lay in the center wagons, and an orderly ran back to Captain Vaughan, busy giving last-minute instructions to Roan and the noncoms among the sharpshooters.

"Major Thayer just died," the man reported.

Vaughan slumped, nodding a little. "A blessing for him," he said, and walked up front and spoke orders. A detail took shovels and chose a place beside the trail. Another detail wrapped Thayer's body in a blanket. In a short time the hoarse voice of Noah Loftus sounded through the stillness. There was no volley. The red-fresh earth was shoveled back, a headboard was driven, the troopers returned to their places, and Vaughan told Roan:

"I'm going to drop some Osages back to keep you in

sight at all times. We'll come as fast as we can. Good luck."

As the early morning passed, the long day began to assume the sameness of yesterday. Red-tailed hawks soared and dipped and climbed, undisturbed. At the base of the next rough hill a doe and her fawn watched, as serene as sculptured figures, the surest sign of all that no riders lurked nearby.

"Where are they, Curly?" and the Osage, his attention yonder, said no word.

The monotony continued unbroken, made more oppressive as the shimmering heat took rough hold and the column plodded on through generally open country. Little bunches of buffalo gave placid passage.

It was around eleven o'clock when Roan saw the series of humping hills, jutting up southwest to northeast, and, nearest the trail, a landmark hill, high and oak-studded, long-spined and shaggy, brooding over the trail.

He called a halt. A noncom and a private got down from the first wagon and inspected the front wheels. Crouching, they tinkered with the running gear. A trooper galloped back, appeared to confer with Roan, and returned to Captain Vaughan.

The column rolled on, leaving the two wagons in its dusty wake. The noncom started hammering on the iron rim of the left front wheel, while Roan and Povich watched idly. By now the rear-guard Osages had arrived. As agreed, half of them jogged ahead to catch the command.

Half an hour passed. The column was well ahead, stringing up the trail. As Roan looked, the tail end of the command disappeared around a low hill. He dismounted and tied his horse to the lead wagon's tail gate.

It was still all around, very still. Inside the wagons Roan caught the low bantering of the sharpshooters as they complained of the heat under the canvas. Other troopers loafed around the wagons. The Osages dismounted and sat in the grass, holding reins while their mounts grazed. Two troopers worked on the hub of the left front wheel. Now and then a banging sounded underneath the lead wagon.

"Shall we go on, Curly?" Roan mused, impatient.

Meantime, Povich, nervously, kept going to the first wagon and peering under, and after some moments coming back to Roan and Curly.

"Wait," answered Curly.

"You have patience."

"Be like Laugh-a-Lot there," Curly said, grinning. "Wait."

Watching the timbered landmark hill some hundred yards away, Roan wished now that he had halted farther back. He was looking there, scanning back and forth, when a hawk soaring over it abruptly wheeled and flapped away.

As he followed it with his eyes, questioning, it happened. A splatter of musketry. Smoke puffs flowered among the trees at the hill's base. A dismounted trooper lurched. A mule hitched to the lead wagon broke down, kicking and tangling the traces.

"Cut that mule free—bring the wagon broadside!"

As Roan yelled, he saw the driver of the second wagon whipping the teams and wheeling out to present a front, and the troopers and the Osages rushing mounts forward to form a rough circle anchored on the wagons.

Horsemen erupted out of the tree line, firing as they charged, motley white men and painted Indians. *Now—sharpshooters—now.* As the thought flashed, Roan saw the canvas jerking up on the wagons and the barrels of carbines leveling. He heard a volley crash. The center of the onrushing riders seemed to cave in, but there was no letup. When the men in the second wagon fired, he saw the riders waver and split, Indian fashion, peeling off to each side, and, Indian fashion, hugging the off sides of their horses. Inside the circle and in the wagons ramrods clattered. Smoke hung in dirty clouds.

Roan flung around, eyes jumping from first one bunch rushing past to another—too many. Was that Red Shield? He cut a hopeful look northeast, and saw no dust, no Vaughan.

"I can't see nothin' but legs an' arms," a trooper raged.

"Pick a horse," the man beside him yelled back.

Roan's carbine was empty. He was loading, digging a cartridge from his pouch, biting the crimped paper and pouring the black powder down the barrel, setting the bullet, ramming it down with the clattering rod, which he jerked free and jammed into its groove under the short barrel. He cocked the hammer, flicked off the dead primer, and thumbed a bright copper cap on the nipple.

When he looked up, they were already forming hurriedly for another charge, reloading in moments and coming again, a solid, galloping mass, bringing a drum roll that beat over Roan and turned his mouth dry and squeezed his belly. The Osages raised gobbling taunts.

Were they going to smash straight into the circle?

Roan fired at the lead riders. One toppled from saddle, clad half Indian, half white man, bouncing on the prairie and ridden under by the horsemen behind. The circle of troopers and Osages parted, lapping back to give the sharpshooters a clear field of fire.

Before the first volley ripped out, the horde split and blurred past. Roan swung with the bunch on his right, squeezing off revolver shots at the horse-clinging shapes. Powder smoke and dust mingled, acrid to his lips and nostrils. A big gray cavalry gelding seemed to go crazy. It jerked a trooper down, kicking viciously and scattering other horses.

Roan yelled, "Shoot that horse—" and when the trooper couldn't get his carbine up, Roan head-shot the gray. Rushing here and there, he joined the tugging and cursing to manhandle the horses back into the semblance of a circle. Bodies littered the prairie. And, here, underfoot, his roach still quivering, Yellow Horse lay face down.

Roan's revolver was empty. He bit, poured, set, rammed, thumbed on copper caps, and squinted northeast again. Nothing there. Nothing. Vaughan? Where th' hell was Vaughan? Where? Should be in sight by now. Time seemed to stand still. At the base of the landmark hill the other people were milling and making ready again.

His eyes dug at a blaze-faced bay horse and nondescript rider; he left them to shout the circle in tighter. Northeast again he looked, still seeing the damning emptiness, and he called out to the sharpshooters in the wagons, "When they reach that little rise—shoot the lead horses."

They were coming now. Just before they reached the rise, they spread out and checked up. Then, all at once, they drove straight ahead. As they topped the rise, the sharpshooters let fly. Horses floundered. Without pause, the rest rushed on, yet changing, splitting off, angling out into a pincers whose jaws would flank the wagons. A nerve-biting chant rose around Roan. The Osages were singing, singing death songs.

A new rumbling jarred across the oncoming horse clatter. It pounded against Roan's ears, insistent, growing louder, before he tore his gaze away, northeast. Something twisted in his stomach. There was nothing. The rumbling clung, stronger and stronger, rolling in from the southeast.

He had time for one brief glimpse, to catch sight of a column of fours rounding the hill. Vaughan, coming at a dust-powdering run. Instead of taking the obvious route back down-trail, he was rushing around from behind.

That sight stuck in Roan's vision as he braced to

meet the flanking charges. Quite rapidly, he saw the heads of horses take clarity, and then riders, bulging at the ragged circle's edge. And suddenly, like a high wave, he saw Indian horses, flashing all the wild colors of the Plains, slamming against the circle. He heard the cruel smash of colliding horseflesh. A paint horse broke through. Povich spun and shot the rider point-blank. A long-haired white man dropped like stone, his spade-shaped beard alien against his vermilion-streaked face. The Osages, at best in close where they could use their war clubs, tore in gobbling. But the circle was broken.

Roan's revolver snapped on empty. He laid about with his carbine, smashing at the weaving shapes. He slugged and dodged his way to where the circle had been, his arms leaden, the empty sacks of his lungs hacking, aware of the lessening pressure before him, unable to understand why until, dimly, he became conscious again of the steady rattle of carbine fire that came not from around the wagons.

Unbelievably, he saw the riders breaking off, scattering and melting away.

It was done. Done, his senses told him. Piece by piece, he understood that the troopers and the Osages still held the shrunken circle; in his after-battle stupor, he could see the riders dissolving across the prairie, their cries falling away, and also the firing, save where Vaughan's eager arrivals still pursued.

A horse rushed up. Vaughan loomed above Roan, looking ten years younger, his eyes glittering excitement. He was shouting hoarsely, as though the battle still raged:

"By God, Kimball—it was close."

Roan returned him an acknowledging nod. He wondered where his strength had fled.

"Let's take a look around. This is a strange outfit."

"Curly," Roan called, and left the circle.

Walking the littered prairie, he was shaken at the toll, seeing a familiar mixture of border types, whites partly dressed as Indians, Indians partly dressed as whites. The feathered prairie warriors so prominent at Cantonment Emory were missing.

"One-of-Us," Curly called to him, "see this man, this red one."

His legs were as posts which he planted before him, like a man on stilts. He looked down at the mane of reddish hair reaching to the thick-set shoulders, at the face yet as bold as sin, at the fringed buckskins. It was Kirk Shell, as dead as stone, his left hand still entwined in reins that led to a floundering horse. Roan stared dully, for it was a handsome bay as red as blood, a blazed face as white as snow, the markings irregular and distinctive and unforgettable. Roan continued to eye the bay horse, his mind closing and clearing.

Bending down, Roan knifed away Shell's left sleeve, tearing the buckskin naked to the shoulder, laying bare a maze of scars coiling from wrist to forearm.

"Sanaco—" Curly backed away, clutching the silver cross at his neck.

Roan said, "Sanaco—Scar-Arm—or Shell. One and

the same. We were close all the time and didn't know it, Curly. Remember the man on the blaze-faced horse at Red Shield's camp? That was Shell. He had Red Shield talk for him. He'd sold the little Dawkins girl to Red Shield, who wouldn't give her up to sell back to the whites. Shell was in the camp. That's why the Delaware was trying to get back to the village. He worked for Shell."

"Shell trailed the last charge," Vaughan said rememberingly. "When he saw us, he made a run for it. He didn't make it."

Those were the last words Roan heard. A close shape suddenly stirred to life and rolled toward him. Too late to move aside, Roan saw a reddish-blue flash and heard the blast as he felt the stabbing pain. The bullet knocked him back, head up. The sky was twisting, no longer bright and clear, and he heard Curly's cry as he dropped into a dark hole that had no bottom.

CHAPTER 18

He was dead—drifting on the dark horror of a sunless, endless sea, forever drifting, forever lost, forever alone, forever doomed to shadow and loneliness and pain. At times he thought he spied a distant glow, and each time when he struggled toward it, and each time when he failed to reach it, he saw, strangely, that its position stayed constant, no nearer, no farther, like a star, perhaps, and his efforts left him still weaker and he sank deeper into the swamp of darkness and he lost sight of it altogether.

Gradually, though he had no consciousness of measuring time, his solitary existence began to change. For the first time, he heard sounds in the distance, whispers and muffled passings, ghostly to his senses, and once, very real, he saw Curly's broad face and once he saw Loftus and, dimly, heard Loftus praying. Yet how could they be real when he was dead? And he called after them loudly, as he would shout when drilling recruits, continuing to shout when no one answered, hoping help would come. None did; even so, his voice was growing stronger, as were his eyes, for he could mark the glow, which was rectangular-shaped now, though it was no nearer.

About then, without warning, without reason, he came upon Valerie, very near, beautiful as always. Shining fair hair parted and drawn back over her shell-like ears and knotted on her pretty neck. Great gray eyes laughing and a glittering, low-necked dress baring her smooth white shoulders as she fluttered a silk fan. Around her milled a covey of faceless suitors. She singled one out with her eyes, and when the man stepped eagerly to her, she took his arm. She vanished in a moment, but Roan could hear her laughter in the darkness. She was gone, but he had no feeling, no sense of loss. Strange, because once he had loved her.

There came an interval when he was no longer drifting, when he no longer felt the sea gliding under him. Opening his eyes, he discovered light; real light this time. It slanted through a window. Beyond it stood a tree. A beautiful tree. He could see the leaves dancing in the wind, shaking little green spangles. Yet, he thought, they couldn't be real because he was dead. Just looking tired him. As he slipped back into sleep, he detected voices, different voices, as real as the light and the tree and the leaves, not the toneless voices of his off-and-on world of the dead.

When he opened his eyes again, his mind was unusually clear. He lay in a room of many foreign smells. A man stood beside his bed. Roan recognized Colonel Emory. He was smiling broadly and hopefully and he said:

"You've been gone on a long ride. Now you're back to stay."

"Not long. You know what happened at the cantonment. I was court-martialed and found guilty."

"Captain Vaughan told me the circumstances. You have nothing to fear. All charges are being dismissed by me, and appropriate entries are being made in your service record. I have that authority, you know."

Roan tried to speak and could not.

"There'll be a commendation," Emory said. "You got Sanaco."

"We all did. It was a long shot."

"Captain Vaughan tells me his stratagem of coming around from behind the hill, which took longer, almost lost the day. Yet, had he come straight to you, back down the trail, Sanaco would have seen him and scattered out of there."

266

Roan was becoming weary. His eyelids dropped.

When he woke again, Sara Thayer stood at the foot of his cot. He saw her familiar restraint, the old holding back, her steadfast sense of propriety, all the while the green pools of her eyes, fixed upon him, becoming larger and more intent. Her composure crumbled suddenly and she came swiftly around and bent down and kissed him on the mouth, a warm, tender kiss, and he drew in the lavender scent of her again and felt the lightness of her fingers smoothing back the hair from his forehead. He wondered if some fool orderly was watching, and cared not.

She rose and stepped back, and as he followed her with his eyes, he saw a child. A slender, pretty, ladylike little girl, blue-eyed and the ribbon in her flaxen hair also blue. Emily—so changed in appearance he hardly recognized her, her once raggedly cut hair neat and clean and braided; Emily, in a light blue dress. He stared as through a haze.

She favored him a shy smile. He smiled back.

"Emily has something to show you that I don't believe you noticed," Sara Thayer said.

Emily moved to the cot, her fingers busy with an object at her throat. She held it out for him to see and he saw the gold locket and chain that Samuel Dawkins had left in his care to give to Emily, if he found her, if he ever found her, which he had, and which she had refused.

"Emily Little Star," he said. "It's a good name." He lay back, feeling the weariness welling up and stealing

267

over him again, and the room swam and her small face lost distinctness.

Sara Thayer seemed to hurry. "Emily's going home to her folks in Texas. Jamie and I shall miss her dreadfully."

Roan nodded weakly in approval.

"We're tiring you," he heard Sara Thayer say earnestly. "I'll come again tomorrow."

Roan tried to protest their leaving. But his throat filled and before he could find his voice they were dimly gone, and he was drifting once more, afraid, powerless to stop.

When Sara Thayer came again, she was alone.

"You know everything?" he asked, his mind free at last of nightmare forebodings and frustrations.

She nodded. Though pale and drawn, she had never looked more appealing to him, as if her ordeal had left an imprint of lasting delicacy upon her features.

"The Major was a brave man, Sara."

"Yes—and also cruel. I know what happened at the special court-martial, how it was rigged. Rather a foregone conclusion, wasn't it? You didn't have a chance."

He let that pass. He said, "Your name was the last word he spoke."

He fully expected her to start weeping, perhaps to rush from the room. To his surprise she remained composed and sat on the edge of the cot beside him and leaned toward him, and he saw her most curious concentration.

"Why did you say that?" she asked softly. "Why, Roan?"

"I wanted you to hear it."

"You wanted me to hear a lie?"

"I don't understand."

"You wanted to make me feel better, didn't you? Oh, Roan, you're such a poor liar."

"Wouldn't any woman want to hear that?"

"If true, yes. Only you weren't even near Hamilton when he died. The column was preparing to move out. You were at the rear. Lieutenant Povich told me."

He held his face expressionless.

She went on, more softly, more earnestly. "Hamilton hated you, Roan. You represented something he never was, never could be. You're a free man. You will be, always. That's why, just then, you tried to give me something I never really had. Why you would even deny yourself." She paused and into her eyes came a searching. "I'd meant very little to Hamilton for a long time. He was too tied up in himself, his boundless ambitions. He didn't love me—he couldn't, though I guess he tried. We were never close. Yet he wouldn't let me go." She slipped forward until her hand lightly brushed his cheek. "Roan, I'm sad for Hamilton. I'm sad for my Jamie, sad for all those fine men who didn't come back. I'm sad for what could have been but never was. I know that now—but I'm also happy."

"Happy?"

"For another reason."

"Tell me."

Her face was radiant. He'd never seen a face of such beauty. "Roan," she said, "I'm going to have your child. I've known for some time."

He said, "You knew it at the cantonment, but you wouldn't tell me. I remember now. Come closer." He reached for her roughly and the sudden movement caused pain; not caring, he pulled her to him and said, "I thought I would never see you again. Even now, you don't seem real."

"I'm very real and I'll be here when you wake up again, and I'll be here when you're well." She touched a finger to his lips. "Hush now. Rest."

Center Point Publishing
600 Brooks Road • PO Box 1
Thorndike ME 04986-0001 USA

(207) 568-3717

US & Canada:
1 800 929-9108